ALL YOUR LITTLE LIES

MARIANNE HOLMES

AGORA BOOKS

ABOUT THE AUTHOR

Marianne Holmes is the author of *A Little Bird Told Me*, published by Agora Books in 2018. She was born in Cyprus and bounced around the UK, Germany, Kuwait and Belgium with her RAF parents as a child but is now firmly based in London with her own family. She has degrees in Classics (RHUL) and Linguistics (UCL), neither of which got much use while she worked in marketing.

facebook.com/MarianneHAuthor
twitter.com/MarianneHAuthor
instagram.com/MarianneHAuthor

First published in Great Britain in 2020 by Agora Books

Agora Books is a division of Peters Fraser + Dunlop Ltd

55 New Oxford Street, London WC1A 1BS

ISBN 978-1-913099-69-5

Printed and bound in Great Britain by Clays Ltd, Elcograf S.p.A.

For James, with love

THURSDAY EVENING

Annie squatted down behind Paul's car and reached into the exhaust pipe, her fingers patting gently until they closed around his spare keys. An owl called out near the railway lines and she hesitated, teetering between safety and danger, and then withdrew her hand. The keys dug into her palm.

She struggled with the external door to Paul's apartment block, while gusts of wind whispered and tugged at the hem of her coat. In the sudden stillness of the lobby, her breath rasped loudly. She paused, gathering herself, and listened for other footsteps before climbing the stairs. There was always a tang of transience in the building that at once absorbed and disturbed Annie. It was almost her perfect environment, but for the chance of coming upon another resident at the turn of a corridor or a bend in the stairs.

Paul's flat was the nearest door on the second floor. Annie had never seen anyone enter or leave the other two apartments. If anyone did live in them, they were leading quiet lives, out of the light. Annie knew all about life in the shadows.

A strand of hair fell into her eyes, and she pushed it off her face, noticing the sooty residue clinging to her hand. She kept her fingers away from the doorplate as the key slid into the Yale lock, gently feeling for the moment the mechanism engaged to push the door into the dark of his hallway. The smell of Paul's cologne lingered in the air and triggered fresh tears. Annie closed the door softly behind her. As the urgent sound of her heartbeats ebbed away, she became aware of the ticking of a clock somewhere in the darkness.

The light switch clicked when she pressed it, and the sudden glare stung her eyes like an explosion of fireworks. She blinked. A shot of guilt flattened her against the wall. She had no right to be here. Paul would be furious. But then, he had no right to shrug her off so casually, as if she were nothing. She just wanted to be seen.

She stepped out of her shoes and walked to the small bathroom to wash the dirt from her hands. The make-up she'd applied so carefully earlier stained her face like bruises, and her hair had come unpinned where she'd tugged and twisted at it on the train. Had she looked like this when Paul had pushed her firmly out of the bar on to the street? The team had stood behind him, surprise heating their faces, but not one of them had stepped forward to help her. Her skin reddened in the mirror as she stared.

Annie pulled off her name badge from the conference and put it down on the counter while she scrubbed the make-up from her face with the hand soap. She unpinned her hair and tugged his comb through the tangles, erasing her public self. Feeling fresher, she searched the cabinet for his cologne and sprayed a great mist of it onto her wrists. The droplets sunk into her dry skin, and Annie brought her hands up to her clean face, drawing in the scent. She snapped a photo of the cologne bottle and filed it away in the folder named 'Paul' in her phone. Then she replaced the bottle where she found it.

The lounge was stuffy and the bitter smell of the coffee dregs left in a mug on the mantlepiece made Annie feel sick. The wine she'd drunk earlier roiled and burned in her stomach. She crossed to the drawn curtains and forced a window open, and the wind shook the fabric around her. It brought the musty smell of damp leaves and sodden earth, and was that the faintest tang of brine and the insistent cawing of seagulls? Among the noise, the querulous voice of a young girl rose from below. Pools of light from the car park blackened the shadows, and whoever was speaking remained out of sight. Annie pulled her head in quickly, conscious that she would be silhouetted in the window.

She returned to the mantlepiece. Annie imagined Paul checking his tie there, the blue one embroidered with the tiny green birds that he was wearing today, and adjusting the knot carefully. He must have been in a great hurry that morning, to leave his dirty mug there. She took it to the kitchenette and made herself fresh coffee, sipping it while it was scalding, and checked her phone. Jenna was still live tweeting from the bar, image after image of smiling people enjoying themselves. Paul was in almost every picture — his face flushed with the effort of working the room. There was an hour, at the very least, before he could possibly get home.

Annie studied the photos. Did she detect a hint of loneliness in his expression? His dark hair, that he habitually pushed back with an easy sweep of his hands, fell untended across his eyes. It surely concealed the real Paul, the one Annie was convinced was in there, from the world. She wanted to reach out and take his sadness away.

She drained the last of the coffee and replaced the dirty cup on the mantlepiece exactly where she'd found it. Beside the cup was an invitation to a wedding all but hidden behind an old carriage clock. It was addressed to 'Paul and Partner'. Annie rolled the word 'partner' around her mouth. It felt too business-like, too matter-of-fact. She picked it up and turned it over, the card solid and confident in her hands. On the reverse was a lovebird printed in gilt that glinted as she moved it under the light. She propped it up carefully beside the clock and then saw the sandstone figure of a child that she'd given Paul in the Secret Santa. It lay on its side next to a paper-weight engraved with the firm's logo and a dusty tennis trophy.

Annie set the little figure upright. The smooth texture of it was warm on her skin, and she picked it up, cradling its soothing weight in the palm of her hand. She'd watched Paul unwrap it at the Christmas lunch and place it on the table among the jokey baubles and festive chocolates and, just for a second, he'd caught her eye. In that moment, she'd felt an understanding pass between them.

Annie held the little figurine in her fist as she climbed under Paul's duvet, enjoying the way his smell mingled with the slightly floral scent of laundry powder. She placed the little stone figure on the pillow next to her and stared at its round features, the knees drawn up to its wide face and the arms circled around them, until the whole thing swam out of focus. She'd found it in a charity shop, a foundling, and it tugged at some long-buried part of her that was hopeful and expectant.

The caffeine bubbled through her veins now, and she pulled open the drawer in his bedside cabinet. It was a whole treasure trove of Paul: old letters, certificates, and photographs. Annie found it charming and devastating. Such whimsical collections are not for people who need to pack up and move on quickly.

She flipped through until she found a picture of the team at that summer's sales conference. She'd been seated beside Paul at the dinner, and, though they'd hardly spoken, Annie had felt close to him. Paul had his arm along the back of Annie's chair and was raising a glass towards the photographer. His fingers had skimmed the skin on the back of her neck when he lent forward to put his glass down, and when he sat back Annie held herself upright in the chair, afraid that he would move his arm if she touched it.

She sunk into Paul's pillow and closed her eyes, exhaustion overwhelming her.

A crash broke the silence and Annie leapt from the bed. The front door to the apartment block had banged shut downstairs. How long had she been asleep? She peered at the screen of her phone, the numbers swimming frustratingly. It couldn't possibly be Paul yet, but her stomach churned. He mustn't find her here; the humiliation would be unbearable. She grabbed the figurine and stuffed it into her coat pocket so she could plump up the pillows and straighten the duvet. Then she swept the photos and letters back into the drawer and slammed it shut.

In the hall, she pressed herself against the wall, listening through the soft wood of the door. Annie could hear someone whispering in the corridor. Shaking, she slipped her feet back into her shoes and waited for the footsteps to move away. One minute, two minutes, and then five minutes passed with no further sound, and she pulled the door open, grabbing the keys. She replaced them on her way back through the car park, careful not to be seen.

As she reached the alley to the station, she could hear footsteps coming towards her. Whoever was there would be directly in front of her in moments. She tucked herself into the rear doorway to Tandoori Villa and crouched behind some empty crates, gagging on the stale smell of garlic and spices. Her skin prickled with fear when she recognised the rhythm of Paul's stride. She held her breath and watched him cut across to the apartment block. He paused, head down in front of the door. Annie cringed further back into the gloom, hoping he couldn't hear her rapid breathing among the squalls of wind and rain, but he finally turned the key and entered.

Annie ran down the alley, almost laughing with relief. The sky was a cloak of black velvet, and the wind blew up a troupe of dancing leaves spinning around her. When she reached her car, she flung herself inside and drove home, the blood fizzling and popping through her body like tiny sparklers.

2

FRIDAY AFTERNOON

The humiliation of the afternoon at the office clung to Annie as she entered the bar. Worse, she couldn't see Lauren anywhere. The heavy, glazed door swung shut behind her, and she hovered for a moment, dazzled in the lights. She glanced out into the dark, willing her friend to appear behind her, then turned with a sigh. Her phone showed the exact time they'd agreed, so Annie dumped her sodden coat at one of the empty tables in the window. What she really needed was to move, to fly back down Holborn Viaduct and across the wind-buffeted Waterloo Bridge to release the week's stress and to drown out the chatter in her mind with the thrumming of her own blood. She sighed heavily, feeling the adrenalin still shaking in her breath.

There was already a noisy group being served at the counter despite the early hour. Annie climbed onto a bar stool to wait and let her shoes drop one after the other to the wooden floor. Brass lights hung from the ceiling above the bar and cast a yellow glow that bounced off all the hard surfaces, dulling the headlights that passed in the dark street beyond the windows. Annie watched for Lauren in the mirror on the wall behind the bar, so that she didn't need to keep swivelling on the wobbly stool.

The door to the street opened and a rush of cold air hit her legs as two men burst into the nearly empty room and joined the group beside her. Annie watched as the two jostled for place among the others and added their drinks to the order. The shorter man touched the arm of a sweet-faced woman in a black dress, so lightly and quickly that it could have been an accident. The woman didn't react, but she leant towards the man with a tiny tilt of her head that made Annie's heart hurt. The others didn't seem to notice.

The faint smell of old alcohol unsettled Annie's stomach. What she really needed was a soft drink, but one glass of wine would ease her hangover. She tapped her fingernails loudly on the bar, hoping for one of the other bar staff randomly wiping non-existent marks from glasses to realise that she was on her own. The woman ordering for the group looked around and caught her eye. For one short moment, Annie thought she might offer her a drink, too, but her eyes dropped, taking in Annie's crumpled skirt and noting her swollen, unshod feet. She turned away quickly to pay, and they all moved off like a school of fish. With all the intellectual capacity of fish, too, Annie thought, and then felt bad. They were having fun.

'I guess my invisibility cloak has turned itself off again, then,' she said when the girl behind the bar finally turned to her. The girl's bright smile wavered. 'You know, now that you can see me.' Another bartender appeared and whispered something into the girl's ear before she could answer. They both laughed. Annie wondered what he'd said — it was obviously about her. She put her shoulders back a bit to appear defiant. But the girl didn't make eye contact with Annie again, even when Annie handed over her card to pay. Not so much invisible, Annie corrected herself, as unseen.

At the table, she set down the two large glasses of wine, deliberately putting the second in front of the empty chair, in case anyone thought she was there on her own. An open copy of *The Standard* lay discarded on the table. After another long look through the window for Lauren, Annie flipped to the concise crossword. She worked out at least a corner of answers in her head and then filled them in fluidly. If the bar staff were talking about her, let them talk about that.

By the time all the little boxes were complete, the bar was in full swing, and her glass was nearly empty. The wine had eased her headache a little, and she felt her earlier feelings floating away. Annie looked around the room. Three tables away, there was a man sitting on his own flicking through something on his phone. Annie willed him to look up and catch her eye but, as she watched, a woman approached the table with a bottle of wine and two glasses. The man stood and wrapped his arms around her so that the woman laughed and had to wriggle out to put the glasses down before they were crushed in his embrace.

Annie looked away and pulled out her own phone.

Where are you?

She texted Lauren, twisting the other glass of wine so that the light swam through the liquid as it swirled. She should have walked the long way round, not pressed Lauren to come straight to her. The knots in her shoulders tightened. She took a breath and tried to focus on the positive. *I'm grateful that I don't have to go to work for the next two days.* It was something.

At the next table, the glossy heads of two drinkers drew close across the table so that Annie could almost feel the thrill of the secrets they might be exchanging. Annie's secrets were not for sharing. A roar of laughter burst out nearby, and she looked up, expecting that she was the joke, but no one was paying her the least attention. Her jitters had not completely gone. Paul would be out with the team somewhere, too, his tie slightly loosened to acknowledge the end of the week, pausing over the punchline of a joke for best effect. Annie felt her stomach clench as she thought of him. The noise in the bar had intensified, and she really wanted to get out now. She lifted Lauren's glass, replacing it with her own empty one; the wine would have to do.

Her phone buzzed.

Five minutes away.

Annie sat back and peered out the window, and there was Lauren outside, phone in hand. She was talking to a man who held an umbrella high above the two of them. The cuffs of his trousers were dark with damp and his hair slick with rain. Lauren stepped forward and kissed him on the cheek. Annie dropped her head back over the paper so they wouldn't catch her watching.

Ten minutes later, Lauren cut through the crowd easily, heads turning as she went, and flung herself into the chair opposite Annie. Her hair was beaded with rain and beginning to frizz. Annie took a moment to acknowledge her, as if she was absolutely absorbed in the tangle of numbers and jagged lines around the Sudoku grid in front of her. She was ashamed that she felt so raw and exposed out on her own and tried to hide it, even from Lauren, who wasn't fooled.

'Wow, you're so hard to see here behind this lot.' Lauren shrugged off her coat and waved at the drinkers standing around them. 'Sorry I'm a bit late.'

'It would've been easy to find me if you'd got here on time.'

Lauren pulled her 'forgive me' face, and Annie forced herself to smile. She knew she was being unreasonable; she was the one who'd asked Lauren to meet her for an emergency drink at the last minute. Now that she'd had a glass of wine, she felt a little foolish. She'd just succumbed to her usual booze blues and tiredness earlier.

'Well, at least I've managed to get you out socialising on a Friday evening,' Lauren replied, and the warmth in her smile felt genuine. Annie waited for Lauren to say it. 'You're practically a hermit.' She looked around assessing the scene. 'Surely, you could have found someone to chat to here, while you waited? Widen your network.' Annie stared back at Lauren. They both knew that wasn't likely to happen, because Annie was a social phantom. Deliberately so, she told herself, her chest tight. It was absolutely her choice.

'I didn't come here to chat up men,' Annie frowned. If Lauren picked up any more friends, she'd be able to start her own nation. She was certainly always frantically busy if Annie suggested they might actually go for a meal rather than these quick drinks squeezed in here and there. Annie liked to think that she gave Lauren a welcome break from the maelstrom of her social life. Lauren could just be herself, because they'd known each other for so long. She didn't have to make herself sparkling for Annie.

'Okay, then.' Lauren threw up her hands. 'What's the big emergency?'

Lauren's red lipstick had smudged on her teeth, and Annie noted the pull on the sleeve of her electric blue jumper, but Lauren still looked amazing. *'When you're this tall as a woman, you can't hide,'* she'd told Annie, *'so I might as well go all in.'* Just Lauren's presence made Annie feel better; she was a walking advert for confidence.

The first time Annie had seen Lauren out of school, she'd been startled by the neon eyeshadow and bright lipstick. *'Well, if I just used nice, safe neutrals, you wouldn't see them on my skin, would you?'* Lauren laughed at Annie's expression and pulled her upstairs to her bedroom, past the raised eyebrows of Lauren's older brother who sat on the stairs nodding to whatever music was streaming through his ear buds. Clothes and sports kit and books and make-up of all colours were strewn around the room as if they'd been splattered there by David Hockney. They'd spent hours listening to Nick Cave and the Bad Seeds on loop while Lauren turned Annie into her own make-up doll with purple eyeshadow and teased hair.

'Oh, I just wanted to vent about Paul really. Probably nothing.' It wasn't just that, but now that Lauren was there opposite her, listening, Annie couldn't find the words to tell her the truth about the night before. She'd woken that morning with an overwhelming sense of guilt and foreboding, her stomach sick and brain scrambled, and she hadn't been able to shift it all day. She had a vague memory of speaking to Lauren from the train on the way home, but what she'd said was unclear. She just knew that she'd done something very wrong. Finding the figurine in her coat pocket had brought back the memory of Paul's flat with a rush of remorse.

Lauren sat back in her chair and sighed. Annie had described all the things she liked about Paul to Lauren once, his confidence and smile and the way he swept his hair back off his forehead. Lauren had been so dismissive of him that Annie hadn't called her for a week in retaliation.

'He humiliated me in front of the whole office.'

Lauren raised an eyebrow. Paul had stopped by her desk that afternoon to let her know it would be better if she didn't go to the pub with the rest of the team. He'd leaned in close and said it would make everyone feel uncomfortable after the scene she'd caused the night before. The office had gone particularly quiet while he spoke. It was never that quiet, and Annie burnt with embarrassment. They all knew exactly what he was saying, of course.

It wasn't as if she'd planned to go to the pub anyway, because she never did. Forbidding her was a deliberate act of cruelty. When he'd walked towards her, she'd still harboured a tiny pinprick of hope that he might want to hear what she had to say. She'd imagined him asking her if she was okay and telling her she was right, there was something between them. The disappointment had twisted in her gut, and she couldn't respond. Later, when the others left the office in a loud rush, no one would meet her eye.

'Well,' Lauren said, 'maybe he had a point.' She reached forward and squeezed Annie's hand. 'You know, when you rang me from the train, it sounded like you'd made a proper scene at the conference. I think he was probably right to send you home before you really messed things up.'

Annie stared at Lauren. All she'd done was to try to explain how she felt about him. That she'd noticed his particular kindnesses towards her, and she'd waited such a long time to meet someone she might trust. It had taken every iota of courage she had, but he'd shut her down, told her it wasn't appropriate.

She knew he had to be denying their connection so, while she waited for an opportunity to talk to him later in the evening, she'd fortified herself with the free drinks. It was a bit of a haze now, but she had a vague memory of finding him again and telling him how he'd made her feel, and how hurtful his words were, and then she might have given him a precis of the areas where he himself was particularly lacking in emotional basics. It wasn't her fault if he'd found that hard to listen to. And, yes, the wine had loosened her up a bit, given her a bit of courage, but she could tell from the way people had stopped to listen that everything she'd said was sensible and interesting. It had felt thrilling and liberating at the time and wildly romantic.

'Whatever, I don't think you should have made a play for him at a work event. And look, you were fairly incoherent on the phone anyhow, so just apologise and say you were taking antibiotics and you were drunk.'

Lauren's words hurt. 'I wasn't *making a play* for him. I was trying to talk to him about our relationship.'

Lauren snorted, 'You haven't got one!', and Annie felt a flash of rage. It was all right for Lauren — she had no idea what Annie felt. It had taken a long time, a lifetime in fact, for Annie to consider she might find someone who could care for her.

The sense of guilt and fear that she'd woken up with still zinged through her veins, too. And shame. That was what she really needed to talk about, but clearly Lauren wasn't the right person. She realised that now, but she didn't know who was. In her coat pocket, her fingers closed around the sandstone figurine. It filled her hand, and she felt her pulse slow as she tightened her grip.

Annie tamped down anger. 'Whatever. Tell me about *him*,' and she nodded out the window. Lauren reached across the table and took a drink from the glass Annie pushed towards her. Tony and Lauren were supposed to be on blind dates with other people, but they'd got chatting before their dates arrived and that was that. Lauren laughed with her hands on the table and head thrown back. Annie couldn't help smiling with her, even though she hadn't really been listening to the story. Two men standing at the bar looked over towards Lauren, too, and then away when they saw Annie had noticed them. She felt a small kick of defiance. *Yes, I was waiting for a friend and look at how spectacular she is*, she wanted to tell them.

She stretched across the table to hear Lauren better, the wine in the glass glowing between them. Annie felt a tingling in her neck as her shoulders relaxed and the jangle in her head softened.

'Thank you for coming, Lauren. I do feel better now.'

Annie knew she exasperated Lauren by refusing to join her when she was meeting up with her other, more exciting, friends. It meant Lauren had to shoe-horn her into her scheduled one-on-one, and she was usually on her way to or from somewhere else. *'Well,'* Annie would say, *'I don't feel comfortable around lots of other people, but if you don't have time for me ...'* and Lauren would sigh and fit Annie in somehow. After all, Annie didn't need much.

It hadn't always been like that. When she first moved to London, she'd trailed around after Lauren as she'd floated from bar to bar, but she never managed to join in the conversations, and, gradually, she'd hung back so much that she might have been standing on her own. Nobody ever talked about anything important, she thought, so how was she meant to join in? Anyway, it hurt less not to try.

'Hey, we need some more wine.'

Lauren glanced at her phone. 'Look, I can't stay. Sorry. Tony's waiting for me next door.'

'Oh, of course. I should have known you'd be busy.' Annie pulled her hands away and sat further back in her chair. She'd thought she could rely on Lauren, but, at the end of the day, it would only ever be Annie on her own. She picked at the edge of the table where the wood was rough and cracking. 'Well, you've seen me now. I'm fine.' It bothered her that Lauren thought she was the one who behaved badly when Lauren hadn't even been there. And Paul, he'd smiled and rolled his eyes at Adrian as he steered Annie towards the door the night before, as if she was a fantasist or a tiresome toddler. Bastard.

The bar was hot and crowded now, and Annie longed to be at home.

Lauren frowned. 'Are you fine though? All that talk about going round to his flat to confront him. Please, tell me you didn't do that?'

Annie shook her head. She didn't dare tell Lauren the truth. In fact, the whole thing was a bit like a dream in her memory, all smells and noises but no real images. She wouldn't have been so sure that it'd happened if her car hadn't been parked outside her house and the sandstone figure in her coat pocket when she woke. There was no denying that.

"Course not. I just went home.' Annie crossed her fingers under the table. 'I'd had far too much to drink to do anything else.'

'Hmm,' Lauren narrowed her eyes and tilted her head, considering Annie's answer. Annie held her breath, waiting for Lauren to say that she didn't believe her. Lauren sighed. 'I still think you should apologise to Paul though. You know, smooth things over?'

Annie felt her stomach flip. 'He humiliated me.'

Lauren patted Annie's hand. 'Look, I'm sorry you got hurt, but you do need to put it behind you. He's just not that into you. It's not the end of the world. Nobody died.'

Annie broke off the splinter she'd been toying with and felt it stab into her finger. 'No, nobody died.' She wanted to scream. 'Look, I'm fine, you don't need to worry about me. I just needed to vent. Sorry.'

Lauren was already pulling on her coat.

'Okay, if you really are fine, then I should go.' Lauren waited for Annie to reply until it became clear she wouldn't. Annie examined her nails so that Lauren couldn't see the tears in her eyes.

'God, Annie, don't go all mute on me again.' Lauren's voice

sounded strained. She always complained that Annie used silence like a weapon, but for Annie it was the only defence she had. Sometimes she wondered what would happen if she did tell Lauren what she was really thinking. Probably, Lauren wouldn't be her friend anymore. That was too awful to think about.

Annie put on her perfectly fine and normal smile. 'I'm all right now. You go ahead.' The rain gathered in the corners of the window as the wind blew it along the glass.

'Okay, well, take care!' She blew Annie a kiss. 'Chin up, tomorrow is another day!'

It would be another hour before Annie would be at home, too late for a film and too early for bed. She drained her glass quickly and picked up *The Standard* to read on the train.

As she walked across Hungerford Bridge, a piece of paper picked up by the breeze caught her eye, and Annie watched it flutter into the steely churn of the river. The bulky buildings framing the Thames seemed flattened and pallid against a vast sky that was mobile with clouds, like the swirl of people underneath it who threaded through the throngs towards the West End.

At Waterloo, she picked up a sandwich and stood alone under the glass canopy while she waited for her train to be listed. The evening commuters streamed around her to their platforms, and she felt like a small pebble in a shallow stream, waiting to be flipped and tumbled.

It wasn't until she was sitting in the carriage with her sandwich half-eaten that she turned the paper the right way out and was stunned by the image on the cover.

3

FRIDAY EVENING

T he girl's eyes were wide, her head turned back over her shoulder, as if someone had called out to her. Or as if she'd heard footsteps approaching. The image was fuzzy in print, so her expression was smudgy, not smiling exactly, but a hint of something curling up the corners of her mouth. Annie had no idea who she was, but the station car park she walked through was at Westhurst — population five thousand and Annie's home. The train lurched to a stop at Clapham Junction, and the sandwich box slid from Annie's lap. Fronds of lettuce spilled across the train floor. She collected it quickly and shoved the whole lot into the bin so she could read the story properly.

School girl Chloe Hills, twelve years old, has been missing for nearly twenty-four hours.

Annie studied Chloe's face. Was it possible that Annie'd seen her around the village? Perhaps she'd walked past her on the way to the shops, or maybe she was one of the school kids who hung out in the bus stop by the crossroads at weekends. It made Annie feel self-conscious as they watched her walking too fast and gasping for breath. Generally, she tried not to make eye contact with anyone unless she had to. She preferred to watch things obliquely, seeing a distortion of what was happening but safe from challenge.

Annie didn't really know many people in Westhurst and didn't plan to. That's why it had been so remarkable to her that Paul lived there, too. It had felt like a sign— not a coincidence, but actual evidence of how much they had in common. She pushed him from her thoughts.

The article said that Chloe had been visiting a friend but never made it home. The friend had walked with her to the station, half-way between their houses, where she'd said good-bye. The Hills called the police when Chloe wasn't home by eleven, and their family controls said her phone was switched off. She'd been captured by CCTV walking in front of the station, and then she'd just disappeared before the next set of cameras on the bank could pick her up.

Annie looked out at the wind and rain and pictured Chloe spinning up above the station like Dorothy, hair and arms flying. She half smiled and then remembered there really was a child missing, and an old dread settled on her chest. Annie knew how many children went missing in the UK. The numbers were on the Missing People's website. The charity said 86,000 children, or one in every 200, went missing every year. They would nearly fill Wembley Stadium. Only a little over ten percent were considered to be high risk, and a very tiny number of cases ever made the headlines. Annie studied the girl's face. What meant Chloe's story was picked up rather than any of those others? Annie knew the answer; Chloe was a photogenic white girl from a middle-class town.

Probably, Chloe was just playing a trick on her parents,

trying to frighten them, Annie told herself. Annie could imagine running away from home at Chloe's age. She herself had felt trapped and desperate to get away by the age of twelve, but, then again, she already was a runaway. It really wasn't a lot of fun, the reality of always looking over your shoulder.

She glanced around the carriage. There was a man on his own sleeping hunched over in his seat, his crumpled face reflected in the window of the train. Three women talked animatedly, and Annie wondered if they were discussing Chloe or even knew her, but they left the train several stops before Westhurst. Two young lads got on and sat in their place, laughing and joking over something on their phones. Annie kept an eye on the one man on his own, turning away when he opened his eyes and looked straight at her, as if he'd known she was watching. She shrank back into her seat.

Annie picked at the raw edges of skin where the splinter had pierced her finger. She would never have imagined that anything sinister could happen in Westhurst. It was a nothing-happening kind of place, which was exactly why Annie had chosen to live there. The majority of its residents were commuters — immigrants from other parts of the country using Westhurst as the dormitory for their working lives in the city, flowing in and out through the station like the tide. The shops were nice, and she loved her tiny little house, felt safe within her own solid walls, but it was the train line that mattered. A population of part-time inhabitants provided Annie with the perfect anonymity and freedom that she needed. The idea that there might be something more dangerous there, under the surface, was disturbing.

The brakes screeched as the train came into Westhurst, and Annie winced. She stepped onto the platform, tucking the paper under her arm and lifting her bags onto her shoulder.

The air was cold after the damp fug of the carriage, and a headache pulsed behind her forehead. Another carriage door shut further down the poorly lit platform, and Annie heard footsteps coming towards her, splashing through the puddles on the tarmac. She froze as the other passenger reached her, visible only at the last minute. Their open coat flapped against Annie's legs as they passed, talking very quietly into their phone, and Annie felt fear uncurling in the pit of her stomach.

She listened for anyone else who might still be on the platform behind her and then fished in her bag for her car keys, holding them between her fingers, before she walked out through the empty ticket office. She couldn't see where that one other passenger had gone — they'd just disappeared into the darkness — but she could see her car parked across from where she stood. The drizzle muffled any other sounds in the car park.

Something flapped at Annie's face and she ducked. A piece of paper had been only partially taped to the wall, and Chloe Hills' eyes stared back at Annie. She was pictured at a point just in front of where Annie now stood. Annie looked around for the camera and saw it mounted on the wall of the ticket office. It made her shiver with shock. Was somebody watching her now? Where were they, these people monitoring her movements, and who were they? She hadn't thought there might be cameras watching the front of the station.

Ahead was the metal safety of her car, but she knew she shouldn't drive after the wine she'd drunk. She'd got away with it the night before, but she didn't dare risk it again — especially now she knew about the camera.

The soft patting of the rain stoppered her ears up and blurred her vision, so she kept casting around to make sure no one could approach her without warning. But she was alone. She shook off the uneasy sensation of being watched and took the steps up to the road, holding tight to the wet handrail so that her boots didn't slip on the shiny stone. She'd walked this journey countless times.

At the top of the steps, Annie blinked in the glare of the streetlights and adjusted the keys between her fingers. The building site on the corner loomed above her, dark and empty, but, somewhere inside, the drops of rain tapped on something hollow. Annie crossed to the other side of the road to where the holly and beech reached through the open fencing. Rivulets of water drained and splashed along the edge of the road surface, and Annie picked her way along the curb away from the shaking leaves.

Once home, she bolted the front door behind her and drew the curtains against the dark. The house was warm and dry, and Annie felt her heartbeat slowing. She made herself some tea and curled up on the sofa with the paper, waiting for the throbbing and jangling in her head from the wine and the journey to ease up. Her hair started to spring back off her face as it dried, and Annie could feel the tension in her muscles easing. This was what safety felt like.

She thought of Chloe Hills again. Was it possible that Chloe really had just got lost outside somewhere? The rain hammered against the windows. Chloe would be cold and wet and scared. Were people out there looking for her now? Annie pulled the blanket from the back of the sofa over her legs. But how could she have got lost in her own village? Annie thought of the rat-a-tat coming from the building site and the scratching of the plush hedges of the road, the hungry darkness behind them.

She shook the memory away. Chloe almost certainly was just bunking off with friends. If the police hadn't made it public for twenty-four hours, they couldn't really consider her to be in real danger, could they? Besides, she'd probably already got in touch with her parents after seeing the media appeal.

Annie reached for her tablet to see if there was any news. Her mother had been very clear that she should stay away from social media, that it was a trap for people like Annie, but Annie just wanted to see if she could help. Maybe if she just knew a bit more about Chloe, could find a colour photograph of her, knew where she lived, then Annie could make some sense of it. Maybe she would remember seeing something important. There were five thousand people in Westhurst, someone must know what happened.

She checked the news sites first, but, as she read, her eyes were drawn to the comments underneath the articles and then the comments on the comments. Some were obviously from people who lived in Westhurst, people Annie might have been squeezed next to on the train or queued behind at the newsagent. It was like being in a conversation of sorts, but Annie resisted the temptation to join in. Still, it made her feel good to see that she wasn't the only person to think Chloe could be a runaway. Annie kept reading. Everyone was sharing ideas and knowledge, and it felt hopeful. She swiped and clicked and studied the comments.

* * *

Seeds from the tall grass on either side of the dusty path catch in Lottie's white socks. She picks her way carefully along the overgrown trail. The sun is already warm above her, but she must hurry. The surface of the dark sea below her ripples, bouncing the sunlight off in flashes. Her ears are full with the drumming of her pulse, and she can feel rather than hear the slap of her own steps pushing through the sea carrot. Above her, the distant cry of gulls, gliding on the thermals above the cliffs, drifts down.

The surge and suck of the sea makes her feel uneasy, and her legs burst into a race that urges her faster along the narrow cliff path. The straps of the school bag that she's filled with biscuits and bottled water bite into her shoulders, and she can feel tears starting. She focuses all her attention on moving quickly, trying not to look behind, not to think of the cry that went up as she climbed over the stile from the little path out of the close.

Something her father said about the tide is gnawing at the back of her mind, but she can't think about it. The gulls are up and circling on the thermals, and the sand glitters with puddles below where the tide has retreated.

Lottie's breathing is loud and fast now, and she stops, becoming aware that there are noises behind her. The path is hard to find because it's hardly ever used. There's a sheer drop along most of its length. She daren't rest but presses on until she finds the wooden bench with the broken arm and scrambles from the path. She slips on the rocks as she climbs down to the beach, cutting her knees, but she can't stop. Seaweed and flotsam have been cast high up on the beach in heaps. The decaying and salty smell of it hits her as she drops finally on to the sand. Tiny flies rise from the green fringe. Lottie sees the tidemark is higher up the beach than it was the day before, and she runs as fast as she can towards the cave entrance, kicking up sand and broken shells behind her.

A voice shouts out from the path above her, but Lottie is focused on her footing as the sand turns to smooth rock near the mouth of the cave. She kicks fronds of bumpy bladderwrack (that she would normally pause to pop) to one side and has to slow to stop her shoes sliding on the wet surface. A voice calls out behind her from the beach now, and she pushes herself forward, dropping onto her hands and knees under the shadow of the cliffs. She pulls aside a sheet of plastic that has been cast up by the tide overnight and slips in the salty water that's puddled there. She should've stopped to take her school shoes off — her mother will be furious, but it's too late now.

The waves hiss over the sand, dropping debris and tokens from the seabed as it goes. Lottie wonders if the tide is going in or out. It's important to know that, but the thought makes her feel cold and wobbly in her tummy.

The smell is stronger inside the cave, damp and rotten, and a wave of terror makes her pause. She can hear more people calling along the beach, and she knows they've seen where she is. She forces herself forward into the darkness and the cold, praying to the Piskies for safety.

* * *

Annie woke with a dry throat. There was no way she was going to get back to sleep until she'd drunk a lot of water. It took her a few moments to come to properly and shake off the dark wings of the dream that still flapped in her head. Fear twisted in her stomach as she swung her legs out of bed, and she listened hard before removing the wedge that held her bedroom door shut. The familiar ticks and sighs of the house ambushed her anew as she stepped down the stairs and into the kitchen, bracing herself for the bang of the pipes as she ran the water. She left the kitchen light off so the outlines of plants in the garden were visible, but no one outside could see in. The bones of the honeysuckle trembled along the fence under the rain that still fell. The furry catkins of the pussy willow she'd planted the year before jumped in the feeble moonlight that leaked through the racing clouds. Annie refilled her glass a second time, the spray spattering droplets down the front of her dressing gown.

The lonely hours before dawn exposed her old nightmares and sleep was unsafe. She couldn't risk sinking back into those dreams again and being trapped in the wild disorder of images and noise. Instead, she had to sit and nurse the fainter tangle of decades old memories: sunshine, wet rocks, shards of glass throwing rainbows on the carpet, and hiding in the footwell of a speeding car with a blanket over her head. They tumbled over themselves calling for her attention.

This morning it seemed that the shadows were more insistent, more nagging, and she fought to control her panic as anguish flooded her mind. She knew there was something wrong now, too, but the details were murky. This was how her brain acted. It tapped into a lifetime of guilt so that she couldn't unravel her latest failure from the first.

Annie checked the bolts on the front door reflexively as she passed and picked up *The Standard*. She climbed back into the hollow she'd left on the sofa last night to read it properly. There was something about that picture of Chloe that had been flickering in and out of her dreams all night, spurring them on again when she thought they might subside. The girl was walking away from the camera. They'd chosen a still when she'd turned her head to the side, arcing her hair back over her shoulder to reveal her pale face and the direction of her gaze. As if she'd been checking a noise behind her. Annie caught her breath. In her head was the sudden image of another child looking back at her. The thought of her whispered across her mind like so many other images that she couldn't shut out.

Now that Annie had seen numerous photographs of Chloe in colour, she didn't need to study this dull imitation of the girl's face. She knew her eyes were blue and the tips of her long hair were lighter than the rest, as if she'd dipped them in a pot of paint. The headlights of the car behind Chloe created a dazzling halo effect, so that her features were blanched and indistinct anyway. It was as if Chloe was already fading away when the image was taken. Annie blinked, the pain behind her eyes playing with her vision.

Carefully, she smoothed the paper out on her lap and looked at the whole picture. She'd been so focused on trying to recognise Chloe that she'd concentrated on the face of the girl alone. The curve of Station Parade in the background was lit up by the streetlights as it bent around the small island of grass and up towards the main road. If the camera had panned a little to the left, it would've picked up the alleyway through to Paul's apartment block. Some mornings, Annie would slow her walk to the ticket office hoping to see him emerge so they could travel on the train together, but it had never happened. She felt a moment of pain as she thought of him joking with the others in the pub after work, wondered what he'd said about her, how much they'd laughed.

She pushed the thought away and concentrated on the image, searching for whatever had triggered this particular night of broken sleep. The headlights of the car behind Chloe obscured its registration plate and left the windscreen a blank, so that the driver was invisible. Annie assumed the police would already have spoken to that driver anyway.

And then she knew they hadn't.

The glow from the streetlights along Station Parade behind was just enough to outline the distinctive shape of the car's nearside mirror. It stuck out at an awkward angle from the tangle of masking tape that held it together. She dropped the paper.

It had taken her nearly half an hour to wind enough tape around that mirror to keep it in place.

4

SATURDAY MORNING

D awn finally arrived and Annie opened the back door
and stood outside as the fragile light crept up the sky.
The frost was still layered on the grass, and her breath curled
into the steam rising from her cup, smudging the view across
the small garden.

It didn't seem possible that she could've actually been
sitting in her car — directly in front of Chloe — and have no
memory of it. Her entire journey home was a series of disconnected images and events in her mind, but any record of
Chloe was missing. Annie knew she'd argued with Paul at the
conference drinks, and he'd sent her home. She also knew that
she'd called Lauren on the train, because Lauren had told her
that. And Annie knew she'd gone into Paul's flat. Remorse
filled her as she remembered his living room, the sharp smell
of coffee, washing her face in the bathroom, and then having
to leave in a hurry. The little figurine was still nestled in her
coat pocket.

She sipped the tea, her head clearing like the darkness
lifting from the night, but her memories of Thursday evening

remained sticky and hidden. Would Annie have noticed if a girl had stepped out in front of her car? She felt ashamed that she couldn't remember her journey home, that she'd clearly driven in that state. Her heart sank as she realised how close she'd been to having an accident. Was it possible that she'd hit Chloe? If she hadn't seen her, was it likely she could have knocked her over without noticing?

Of course not. She hadn't hit the girl because someone would have found her, even if Annie herself hadn't noticed. But the thought that it was possible ... She certainly had no memory of the drive home. The more Annie dwelt on it, the more she felt the familiar sensation of guilt hollowing out her stomach. She desperately wanted to check her car, to reassure herself that there were no signs of damage. If only she hadn't drunk that second glass with Lauren last night. If only she hadn't left it parked where she had.

She sank onto the doorstep and clamped her dressing gown between her knees, catching her phone as it slipped from the pocket. There were no messages for her. She thought about texting Lauren, but it was too early in the morning, and it would make her cross. There was something in the scraps of images from Thursday evening that teased at Annie. It was as though there was some piece of information that she could see but couldn't understand, like someone whispering too quietly. Annie shook her head and tossed out the dregs of her tea. It was just the bad dreams again.

Chloe was probably hiding out with friends, Annie told herself firmly. She tried to picture her happy and oblivious to the worry and trouble she was causing her parents.

If Annie disappeared on her way home, the first people to notice her absence would be her work colleagues. She wondered how long it would take them to stop leaving sarcastic messages on her mobile and begin to think about contacting her family or friends. Assuming they knew how to. There must have been a next-of-kin box on one of the many forms she'd completed on her first day, but she couldn't remember filling it out. There was only the one name to put down anyway.

Stepping back inside, she made a piece of toast and settled at the table picking bits up and chewing them slowly, trying to work out what to do. The fact was she hadn't seen anything useful, so there was nothing she could add to the police investigation. She knew nothing. She couldn't even be sure which train she'd caught or how long she'd sat in her car. And she had no idea how long she'd been in Paul's flat. How would she explain the gap between her train arriving at the station and the time she actually drove home? *'I was sitting in my car waiting to sober up, officer?'* There was no way she could tell them where she'd been.

So, contacting the police to say she was there would just be wasting their time and hers. It was a bit of good luck that the registration plate wasn't clear, and maybe they wouldn't notice the broken wing mirror. She should collect her car from the car park as soon as possible though, just in case, and she could at least satisfy herself that she hadn't hit anything on the way home.

Besides, she always went to the supermarket on Saturday afternoon. Saturday was Annie's chores day, and she loved the satisfaction of ticking off each task on the list. The very first task was to write the list itself on the pad she kept specially taped to the fridge door. There was no real need for her to put it on paper because these were the same things she'd done every Saturday since she'd moved in, but it gave her pleasure, anchored her in the empty house. Annie tied her hair back and got started.

. . .

By the time the phone rang, there was a load of washing in the machine, the fridge had been tidied, and Annie had made her shopping list and was running the bath. She'd ticked off half of the items on her list already. Once she collected her car, she would do the shopping, clean the house, and check her bills were up to date. She liked to sit down on a Saturday night with everything freshly cleaned and put away.

Seeing Westhurst in the paper had thrown her off balance, but the action of restoring order to her own little place in the world was calming, and she could feel her emotions coming back under control. Also, she liked everything to be perfect in case someone decided to visit. It didn't matter that nobody would just drop by, but the feeling that she'd be ready pleased her. Maybe Lauren would visit her at home one day. Or Paul.

The phone ringing interrupted her planning, and she answered without checking the number.

'Why did you take so long to answer?' Annie's mother never started with hello. 'I read about that girl, the missing one. Do you know what's going on? Do you know her?' Annie's mother didn't wait for an answer. The nightmares rushed back, disturbing the peace she'd found in her house-work. Eventually, her mother paused to take a breath, and Annie broke in to disrupt the flow.

'Of course, I'm fine. It's nothing to do with me, is it?' It wasn't a question.

'Annie, don't take that tone with me.' Annie sighed. 'You know I'm only looking out for you. You know if you need help, you can ask.'

For a moment, Annie was tempted to tell her about being in the car park when Chloe went missing. But she didn't dare. Sometimes, Annie didn't think her mother would ever trust her, so she kept her fears to herself.

'I do know, but you don't need to worry about me. I'm fine. Tell me about your week.'

'Well …'

Annie put her mother's voice down onto the sofa and walked through to the bathroom. She poured in some bubble bath and turned the taps up to full so that the water fell into the pink puddle and dispersed it in foamy eddies. Then she returned to the phone and told her mother she had to go out.

'Oh, but you're not going into Westhurst are you? Promise me you'll stay away.' The stress in her mother's voice grated on Annie's nerves.

'Bye, Mum,' Annie said firmly, and she disconnected. She put the phone on silent and went into her bedroom to lay out some warm clothes. She needed to walk into town to pick up her car. Besides, how could she avoid Westhurst when she lived there? She carefully tore Chloe's picture out of the paper and stuck it to the fridge with a magnet at each corner.

As she lay in the bubbles, she wondered whether Chloe was home yet. She closed her eyes and tried to let the week wash away in the warm, scented water, but she kept seeing Chloe's grey face.

Annie tried to dismiss her own unease. The girl's just run away, she told herself again. Just another teenager in a fight with her parents. She probably hadn't realised they would call the police and then seeing her own picture in the news must feel overwhelming. But if Chloe didn't come home soon, her mother would probably never let her out alone again. Annie turned the hot tap on again with her toe.

It was very rare for a child to be abducted by a stranger, Annie knew that, but the thought made her shiver. Had there been someone waiting in the car park for an opportunity to abduct a stranger? Had she, herself, just been lucky to avoid being taken? The thought was terrifying.

Surely it was a coincidence that she was there.

People who took children didn't also take adults. The guilt overwhelmed her, and she sank under the water, the bubbles popping in her ears, and wondered how long it would take for her lungs to fill up. Her chest ached and then burned, and she couldn't hold herself there any longer. She came up gasping for air, her eyes pricked with flashes of light. This wasn't helping. She had to think about Chloe; she had to make up for her stupidity.

Statistically, it was more likely to be someone who knew Chloe. Annie dragged her thoughts to Mr and Mrs Hills. The police would have already crawled through her home, pried into all their secrets. They would be overwhelmed with fear and hope, haunted by whatever their last words to Chloe were, desperate to do something. Annie was anxious to help, and yet she couldn't. She wished she knew where Chloe was, that she could at least tell them that Chloe looked happy when she left, that it wasn't their fault. She wished she could tell them Chloe was safe. She closed her eyes and imagined their relief. The person who brought that news would be a hero to them, she thought. She could atone for her failure.

'Well, of course, I had to help. It was nothing really, just what any normal person would do.'

When Annie got out of the bath, there was a rolled-up piece of paper poking through her letter box. She tugged it out gently and took it with her into the bedroom.

Volunteers needed at the railway station 10am
Saturday to form a search party for Chloe Hills.
Any time you can give would be amazing.
Please help #BringChloeHome.

So, Chloe was still missing. Annie checked her watch. She would have to move fast if she wanted to collect her car before the search party gathered. She dressed quickly and scanned her phone to check the local news. A live bulletin showed a reporter standing in front of the Westhurst ticket office, a small group of people visible behind him. She grabbed her rainproof jacket and headed out.

She'd seen other search parties, of course, the camera panning across the backs of a crowd, a single spokesperson for the family picked up and interviewed by a journalist vibrating with suppressed excitement. They would say how shocked everyone was, how ordinary the missing person was. Annie knew the drill. It was the sound, though, that bothered her most, the voices lowered self-consciously and the soft shuffle of feet that was so unnatural and hardest to bear. A small dark stone of dread settled in her stomach.

Annie lengthened her stride to take in the incline, regretting the wine she'd drunk the night before and the way it stung her stomach. The sky was not much brighter than it had been hours earlier when she sat on her back step, and the wind blew drops of water from the curling leaves above her. She blinked as they fell into her eyes.

When she reached the crossroads, she saw a couple of girls tying yellow ribbons around a sheet of paper on a lamp post. She recognised the face of the missing teenager bent out of shape around the metal. #BringChloeHome was written across the bottom. This poster included the telephone number for the Missing Person Helpline and the name of a Facebook page set up to share information about the search. The girls were chatting quietly, utterly absorbed in their task. Annie wanted to tell them she knew what happened to Chloe, but all she could offer was encouragement.

She stopped to look at their work more closely, and they

both fell silent, watching her with glassy eyes. The taller of the two, slouched shoulders and hair pulled back in a tight pony-tail, fiddled with the knot she was tying, her fingers purple and swollen. The other stared at the ground intently, avoiding Annie's gaze. She had a roll of ribbon in one hand and a wedge of posters tucked under her arm.

'So, this is Chloe too, is it?' Annie put on a broad smile. The photo was a new one, Chloe in school uniform. 'She looks a bit younger wearing that, doesn't she? In the CCTV image you can't really tell how old she is, but I guess this is to make us realise how vulnerable she is.' She smiled at the girl holding the ribbon who stared back at Annie, her mouth dropping open slightly. 'So, I guess your parents have sent you out to do this? Bet you'd rather still be in bed.'

The taller girl stepped around to the front of the lamp post and folded her arms. 'Everyone's helping. Besides, she's our friend.'

Both girls were red-eyed and pale and radiated taut nerves and hormones. Something about their expressions jarred, and Annie wondered why. Most likely, they were fed up with Chloe running off and leaving them. Or maybe they knew something that made them anxious.

'So, what do you think has happened to her?'

The tall girl tossed her long hair back over her shoulders. 'Are you from the press?'

Annie heard the coolness in her tone. She understood that caution completely and didn't take offence. The other girl looked away.

'Oh no, I live locally, so I have a genuine interest. Espe-cially, if there's a mad axe murderer on the loose, ha ha!' Annie knew straight away that wasn't quite the right thing to say and blushed. She nodded at the posters. 'Good job.'

She felt herself diminish as both girls stared at her. Annie couldn't quite meet their eyes, two against one wasn't fair. Did they know how rude it was to stare like that? The expression on their faces was particularly unfriendly, too, she thought. Sullen, her mother would say.

'Do you want some posters to put up?' The taller one was wearing make-up, failed camouflage for the sprinkle of acne around her jawline. The other one looked as if she was desperately trying to shrink behind her friend, her head retracting into the collar of her parka and one leg twisting around her other like bindweed. Annie filed every detail away, because who knew if they really were Chloe's friends or just pretending. There was something about them that piqued her curiosity. A car sped past hooting its horn, and a fine spray of water speckled Annie's boots. She realised the girls were waiting for her to leave, and she searched around for the right thing to say in parting. The thing that might help Chloe.

'Oh no, thanks. Someone will know something, and they just need to come forward, right? No matter what promises have been made.' Annie gave them both a long look and then checked her watch. 'Well, I'd better get a move on if I want to get away before the search party kicks off!'

Behind her, she could hear the girls whispering. She cast a glance back as the road turned and saw them in furious discussion, the shorter waving her arms. Their raised voices fractured in the wind.

Annie saw more and more ribbons and posters. It was like walking to a macabre village fete. The damp had already started to curl up the corners of some of the paper, and it wouldn't be long before the ribbons sagged under the weight of responsibility and rain. Annie really did hope they wouldn't be there long. It was all the waiting around that was so diffi-cult. Nobody ever seemed to start looking in the right places.

She bent her head against the weather and closed her

fingers around the keys in her pocket. Annie didn't think her registration plate was readable on the CCTV image, but she wanted to get the car away as quickly as she could in case there were questions. Talking to her would just be a huge waste of police time, and, besides, she had her cleaning and washing to do and the quiet rituals of her life.

Lauren was never free on Saturday nights to meet up. Annie knew that now, even when she hadn't just seen her the night before. It would be nice to catch her on the phone for a chat about Chloe, though. Annie felt off balance, and Lauren was her touchstone for normal. Lauren would tell her it was not surprising that Annie felt disturbed about Chloe, that was to be expected when it was so close to home. She would tell her that other people would have more going on in their lives, a sort of perspective coating that Annie lacked, and then she would give Annie 'the talk' again. The one about trying a bit harder to meet people. Annie smiled to herself, thinking that Lauren would paint her a picture of a possible future with dinner parties, theatre dates, and walks through twinkly lit towns to little restaurants that no one else knew about ... and all Annie had to do was start with one new friend. *'Who knows,'* Lauren would joke, *'you might even find you don't have enough time for me! And that would be fine.'* For Lauren, it was only a case of Annie trying a bit harder. She was always trying to persuade Annie to get to know more people. Annie knew it worked for Lauren, and it was a nice daydream, but Annie only needed one friend.

It had taken years for Annie to persuade her mother that she was ready to move into her own place, and it was only because her mother saw how committed Annie was to solitude that she finally agreed. That and the fact that Annie knew her mother was torn between keeping an eye on her daughter and her own itchy feet. One day soon, her mother would just take off, disappear entirely, but, for now, it was enough for her to be sending Annie instructions, warnings, restrictions. It was the deal they'd made. Annie would move to her own place, have her own life, but she would live according to her mother's tried and tested rules. That was fine by Annie — she wasn't like other people, always wanting to put down roots and entwine their lives with others. Unless it was Paul. She shook the thought from her head.

Whenever Annie had thought she might share her secrets with someone in the past, something always stopped her. Always. It was her cross to bear, alone. It did bother Annie that she'd never told Lauren about her childhood back when they'd first met. But, while Lauren might have asked questions about Annie's past from time to time, she didn't take it personally that Annie kept her secrets to herself. If Annie had told Lauren straight away, there was a possibility that Lauren would have given Annie away, and Annie was desperate to avoid moving again. Now, it was too late. She couldn't risk losing Lauren. She was her only friend, and she had no idea how she could explain it without Lauren hating her. Lauren would have no time for someone like Annie, if she knew. No one would.

Annie reached the steps down to the station car park and stopped abruptly. Below her, in front of the station, was a swarm of people gathering, newcomers joining from all directions like bees. The air was humming with anticipation.

Annie's car was just visible right in the middle of the crowd. There was no way she could discreetly move it now. Behind her, a middle-aged couple coughed, startling her, and she hurried down the steps she'd been blocking.

* * *

Lottie scrapes up the cut grass with her fingers and piles it around the base of the cherry tree on the front garden. Her fingers are stained green, and she loves the fresh, clean smell of them. The cuttings feel cool and damp and are easy to mould into shape. She creates a large cave with grassy walls and puts an empty toilet roll in a gap, covering it with a sprinkling of glossy blades, to make a little entrance tunnel. When she finishes, she will balance a little piece of cardboard, cut from a cereal box, so precariously that it will fall and block the tunnel when any Pisky passes through the toilet roll. It will be the best Pisky trap she's built yet.

Lottie sits back on her heels and picks off bits of grass from her knees. The shoebox she's carried down from her room is open beside her, ready for duty. The contents have been scrounged and foraged, some that day and some she'd been collecting forever. Everything slides around and tumbles over each other as she tips the box to and fro. There's a little table she'd made from Lego, and she plucks it out and sets it up carefully near the knobbly bark of the tree trunk. Then Lottie finds an acorn cup and pours a tiny drop of water into it from her beaker and places it carefully on the table along with two Parma Violets. The little cup wobbles but doesn't spill over. The blush-pink petals that have fallen from her mother's roses become little blankets for some Playmobil plastic hospital beds. She adds tiny wads of cotton wool as pillows.

When the cave looks welcoming enough, she ties some wool to the end of a twig and then passes it over a low branch to make a little swing, her tongue poking out as she concentrates on the fiddly knots. The swing bounces backwards and forwards when she taps it. Lottie wishes she could have a real swing in her garden, but Dad says there's no money for that sort of thing. She doesn't want to ask him again, because it makes him quiet and sad.

She kneels down and peers through the toilet roll to check what any little visitor to her den would notice first and then adjusts the position of the table. An ant tickles her leg, and she brushes it away *carefully before pulling a couple of small figures out of her dress pocket. They feel warm and solid in her hand. She has her two favourite bronze Piskies with pointy hats and grinning faces that she stands up by the table and a wooden mouse with a leather tail that her parents bought for her on a rare trip to Mousehole. They'd all played in the sand in the harbour basin and then bought an ice cream and walked back up to the rock pool to paddle. She places the mouse on the little bed and curls his tail around his body. Then she pulls some glittery ribbon out of the box and leaves it in the den as a gift. The sparkle really does look a little bit like gold in the sunshine, like a true Pisky treasure cave. Lottie claps her hands. Everyone knows Piskies love shiny treasure.*

When it's done, she lies back on the grass, looking up through the branches, noticing the serrated edges of the leaves and the little veins on the undersides that arrow towards the clusters of dark red fruit. Her head fills with thoughts of tiny sweet fairies in cherry blossom skirts, lounging on the glossy leaves and dancing along the branches or swinging on the little twig.

Lottie wouldn't dare to try and catch a Fairy and risk frightening them. But Piskies can be naughty and mischievous, too, so she hopes they'll understand. She closes her eyes and conjures up the image of a tiny little man who would fit in the palm of her hands. She tries to imagine all the things she will ask him to do, once she has him.

She dreamt of a Pisky who would grant her wishes. If Lottie could do magic, she would fill the freezer with ice cream and pizza and buy Daddy a new car so he wasn't always trying to get it fixed and running late for work. She'd make her mum's back better and tell her to give up her job stacking shelves so she'd have time to sit with Lottie, and they could paint their toenails like that time when mum's friend, Jan, came over and Jan had opened a bottle of wine at lunch time.

But more than anything else, she would wish her parents enough money so that they would be happy and she could have a baby brother or sister. Lottie and her dad are always badgering her mum to have another baby, but her mum just huffs and puffs. 'There's more to life than Trehaven and bringing up babies,' she says. 'There's a whole world out there to see. Besides, who'd look after another kid between both our jobs? It's not like we can survive on your salary.' Lottie can see her standing with both fists planted on her hips and her dad slumping a little under her glare. Lottie is going to fix everything just as soon as she's captured her Pisky.

She imagines a little baby with chubby cheeks that she would carry everywhere and look after and love. And the baby would love her back and always be there when she needs a friend, and she'd be able to tell the baby everything and never ever be alone.

Lottie snaps her eyes open at the sound of small feet padding across the lawn. Her breath hisses out in annoyance when she sees little Tegen dragging her Paddington Bear behind her. Paddington has a dirty patch on his face where Tegen feeds him marmalade sandwiches, and it is grey with fluff and dust, however often her mother wipes it clean. Which Lottie's mum thinks is probably not enough.

Lottie gets to her feet and crosses her arms, blocking Tegen's path to the Pisky cave, because last time she'd tried to build one, Tegen had messed it up. She doesn't even want Tegen to know what it is, in case somehow the Piskies hear about it. Secrets are important in magic.

'What are you doing?' Tegen squints a little as she looks up at Lottie, and the sun hits her eyes. Lottie shrugs.

'Secret stuff. You wouldn't understand.' She waits for Tegen to go away, but she doesn't. Behind her, Lottie can see Tegen's mother sitting in her front garden chatting to one of the Hancock women. Lottie's mother says you can't turn round in Trehaven without bumping into a Hancock or one of their friends. They are like the mob.

Usually, Lottie likes to pretend Tegen is her baby sister, but, now *that she's hit on the idea of finding a Pisky, she doesn't want to be distracted.*

Tegen tugs at Lottie's dress. 'Wanna hold Paddington?' Lottie shakes her head. 'He really, really likes you, Lottie!'

The little girl thrusts the tatty bear towards Lottie, and she sighs and sits down on the grass. She pulls the little girl down onto her feet, rowing her backwards and forwards as they sing the silly song, and, when they reach the crocodile bit, they both scream so loudly that Tegen's mother looks across. Lottie and Tegen wave back to her and then carry on.

'Row, row, row your boat ...'

5

SATURDAY AFTERNOON

A nnie had never seen so many people at the station. The air was congested with their breath and their chatter, and her passage across the car park was slow. She peered through the crowd and saw a uniformed police officer at the entrance to the station car park turning cars away. Even if she could manoeuvre her car through the crowd without creating a scene, she would need to pass the officer on the way out. The taped wing mirror seemed less obvious with the commotion all around, and there was no obvious police notice on her car, so Annie stayed away. The little Honda was in a different space than it had been Thursday night, so perhaps it hadn't been seen yet. Now that she knew where the CCTV camera was, Annie could avoid its range, but her image would be captured if she tried to get to her car.

She looked around to see if there was anyone she could talk to about when the car park would clear, but it was becoming impossible to see through the mass of bodies. Her head swam with the sensation of too many people so close to her that she could smell their deodorant and perfume and the damp wool of their hats. She searched #BringChloeHome on her phone for any information and discovered the police were planning to make a statement before the search parties left. There were floods of notifications from people pledging to help, many more than were already there, Annie thought, though a steady stream was still arriving. She sighed heavily and a couple nearby stopped talking to look at her. The woman's expression was sour. Annie rolled her eyes at her to convey her own exasperation — they were probably as trapped there as she was. Perhaps the crowd would clear once the police had made their statement and everyone's curiosity had been assuaged. A few of them, at least, would leave with the search parties.

'Sorry, love.' A man jostled her, and she noticed that the crowd was now moving with purpose. A small area had been kept free on the grass opposite the station entrance, and Annie could make out a few people with cameras in a horseshoe in front of it. A woman in a tightly belted navy raincoat was holding her microphone directly into the face of a young man at the front of the crowd. He was waving around at the people behind him as he spoke, and the navy coat woman nodded encouragingly. Some teenagers pushed forward behind him. They were trying to get on the TV, desperate for a moment of fame. Annie shook her head and checked she was well away from those cameras, too. The people around her were speaking in hushed tones, sharing secrets and gossip about Chloe no doubt, and Annie felt apart and exposed, despite the elbows that jostled her and the clouds of breath around her head.

She tried to push her way towards where she'd seen a white marquee and trails of people coming out with plastic cups billowing with steam. If that was the control centre, then someone there might know how long this would all take. A discarded water bottle tripped her, and she nearly went sprawling among the boots and trainers. She reached down to pick it up and stood too quickly. Her vision swam and she wobbled until someone put out a hand to steady her and then tried to pull her back. She was about to complain when she realised the burble of the crowd had faded, and Annie heard car doors open and shut.

Bodies condensed around her to create a pathway, and she took a gulp of air in relief. Then she noticed the focus of everyone was on the man and woman coming towards her. Annie recognised Chloe's parents from photos that she'd seen online. Their heads were bowed, and exhaustion made their gait awkward and hesitant. She barely noticed the police officers who flanked them, so raw and arresting were Mr and Mrs Hills' own expressions. Nobody in the crowd spoke, but for the reporters whispering quietly into their microphones.

Someone tugged at Annie's arm, and she managed to step out of the way just as Chloe's parents passed. A tall man with dark thinning hair and a waxed jacket released his grip on Chloe's father for a moment and reached for Annie's hand. He clasped it between his own, and Annie started to shake because he knew that she was an imposter in that crowd of well-wishers. He leaned in close to her, so that the smell of his jacket was pungent in her nostrils, and Annie became aware of the strength of the hands enveloping hers, trapping her where she stood. Was he going to expose her? Her pulse raced.

'Thank you so much for coming to help us find her.' His eyes burnt into Annie. She blinked as flashbulbs popped around them, and then she pulled her hand away. The man crossed to the other part of the crowd and knelt to speak to a young girl and the cameras whirred again. Annie let her lungs empty, still dizzy from his attention.

He set off after Chloe's parents, and Annie noticed the two

girls she'd spoken to on the way there standing near the microphones. They seemed fixated on the progress of the Hills but melted away into the crowd behind them as the tall man reached where they'd been standing. It seemed a little odd to Annie, as though they were hiding from the Hills, or even the police. Why would they do that if they really were Chloe's friends? She looked to see whether either of the police officers or the Hills had noticed, but they were chatting to each other close to the microphones. Only the man in the waxed jacket scanned the crowd as if sizing up the response. She could still feel the force of his urgency in her hands.

The silence vibrated in the shortened breaths of those assembled as Mrs Hills lifted a sheet of paper in front of her and looked up. Annie found herself unable to move as she waited for Chloe's mother to find her voice. Someone behind her coughed, and a few heads turned. Mr Hills moved closer to his wife and tightened his hold around her shoulders, as if they might both crumple to the ground if he let go.

Annie wished she had something tell them, something that would help, berating herself again for not paying attention, for drinking too much, for not being able to risk talking to the police. Without consciously moving, she allowed herself to be carried forward so that she was near the front when Mrs Hills started speaking. The silence vibrated with anticipation. Annie imagined being able to step forward with the answers they needed. How good it would feel to be able to answer all those calls for information she'd seen online. It was only a matter of time before the mad conspiracy theories started and the recriminations.

The crowd waited patiently, respecting Mrs Hills' bravery and willing her to speak. Just when the atmosphere began to spoil, she read out their thanks for everyone's support and made an appeal for Chloe to come home. She described their last morning with Chloe and the clothes her daughter was wearing. The mass fidgeted uncomfortably, and no one dared look at each other in the face of her pain. Chloe's father stared at the ground in front of his feet. The other man, the tall one, stood behind them both, watchful and nodding at everything Mrs Hills said.

While Mrs Hills spoke, the cameras kept up a barrage of flashes, and the staccato sound of the shutters popped in the silence. A plane hummed rudely overhead, and Annie would have swatted it from the sky if she could. When Mrs Hills finished speaking, there was a hiatus as her audience awkwardly avoided clapping, because there was no joy in this speech and no relief in its ending.

One of the police officers introduced herself as Detective Superintendent Thomas and reminded the crowd of the different ways they could phone in with information. Those wishing to help with the search needed to register at the marquee, so that they could be briefed. When she finished, people began stamping the cold out of their feet and chatting in low voices as they shuffled away.

A woman with a brightly striped bobble hat turned to Annie and said, 'The poor love. You've just got to help, haven't you?' Annie didn't know if she meant Chloe or Mrs Hills.

'Oh, how could you not?' a small man with a cagoule pulled tightly under his chin said.

'I wish I could,' Annie whispered. She could still feel the sensation of that man's hands holding hers and the startling way he looked into her eyes. Despite the twist of fear in her stomach, she found herself standing in front of the marquee.

They did need help after all, and perhaps this was something that she actually could do. If she couldn't remember seeing Chloe on Thursday night, she could still help search. It was a sort of penance. Besides, she glanced to where her car was parked, she wasn't going to get to the supermarket any time soon. It would be impossible to extricate her car from where it was parked without attracting a lot of attention. There was no way she would risk that if she could avoid it.

'Annie Marwood,' she told a broad-shouldered man with a clipboard when she reached the marquee. It felt reckless and exciting to tell this stranger her name, like stepping into the sea as the tide turns. The man wore a large yellow ribbon on his jacket. One of the tails had #BringChloeHome handwritten in blue. The tips of it bounced on his chest as he spoke.

'Is that for the police?' Annie gestured at the clipboard. 'I mean, are our names recorded then? Do they get sent anywhere?' She tried to read the information at the top of the page. The man pulled the clipboard away and flattened it against his chest, so she couldn't see clearly. He shook his head, his forehead wrinkled.

'It's just so we can keep track of who's doing what.' He made a note on the paper and then looked at her properly so that she pulled the collar up higher around her neck, her eyes skittering away from his gaze. She shouldn't have come. She hadn't thought it all through, especially that the police would have her name now. She considered retracting her offer to help, but there was a queue behind her now. 'Okay, Annie, you can join that group.' He pointed to where three men and two women stood in conversation nearby. 'You could be out for a couple of hours, so I suggest you grab a hot drink on your way. Oh, and thank you for your support.'

So, Annie was part of this now, and, even if she was only a tiny cog in the machine, she might help find Chloe and put things right. Despite her misgivings, it felt only fair that she would give up a few hours to do this, especially when she couldn't tell them what had so obviously happened right in front of her own eyes. She shook the guilt away, and a tiny kernel of warmth replaced it.

Annie picked up some watery looking tea and considered the people she'd been directed to join, still feeling a little uneasy and exposed. There were two older women in cold-weather jackets with small backpacks. They looked like they could be setting off on a hike, and Annie imagined them standing on a stile to survey the fields ahead with a carefully folded Ordnance Survey map in one hand and a thermos flask of tea in the other. A middle-aged man with a hard face and shoulders almost as broad as he was tall was pointing something out to two younger men, one of whom looked particularly ill-dressed for the weather.

Annie hesitated, wondering how best to break into the group. 'Hi,' she said, 'I've been sent to join you. I'm Annie.' The second young man turned and smiled at her, and she felt her cheeks colour under his open regard. 'Like the orphan but not actually an orphan. Ha ha! Anyway, hi!'

Thankfully, he didn't appear to notice her clumsiness, but she felt her stomach turn. 'Hi, I'm Sam. This is Alex, that's Kieran …' The older man looked up from his watch and nodded, '… and this is Moira …' The softer faced of the women smiled '… and Jan. We've been asked to stay here until they tell us where to look.'

'I hope we don't have long to wait. Let's get it over and done with, right?' Annie smiled back at Sam, who seemed entirely relaxed and easy. In contrast Kieran, behind him, bounced from foot to foot and clapped his arms round his body. The others said nothing, and Annie was relieved when the man with the clipboard walked over. He held out a photo-copied map and showed them an area that was boundaried by the path between the railway track and the back of the resi-dential roads behind the shops.

'I'll need a main contact and phone number.'

Everyone looked awkward until Sam straightened and gave the man his details.

'Right, remember what you were told in the briefing?' He looked around at everyone and Annie nodded with the others, though she wasn't sure what he meant. 'If you feel there's anything you need to report immediately, the phone number's on there, too. Good luck.'

The other young man, the one called Alex, put a hand on Sam's shoulder. 'Looks like you're in charge then, mate.' They must be friends, Annie thought, though Sam was dressed in a waterproof jacket and a thick roll neck. Alex looked like he was going into town. Well, she hadn't planned to go out on a search in this weather either. Perhaps, he'd just become caught up in the fever of the crowd like her.

Annie turned to Sam. 'You look very appropriately dressed, Sam.' She gave him an encouraging smile. 'You know, for the weather. I hope I'll be warm enough, but I wasn't really planning to come … it's just that, once you're here, it's all kind of exciting, isn't it?' She threw a look at Alex that she hoped was the right side of rueful and laughed. 'Not like Alex here. Bet you feel like a bit of an idiot in comparison.' She laughed so he'd know it was the way she felt, too.

Alex didn't respond. Annie turned back to Sam who seemed to be hiding a smile. 'Anyway, I do hope we're the ones to find her.'

Sam looked a little surprised, but he just nodded at Kieran and the women. 'Right, shall we go then?'

The marquee was emptying out as other groups headed off in different directions, the high visibility jackets of police obvious among them. Annie followed the others around the marquee, but she stopped to check her car before it was lost from sight. Chloe's parents were being led away by the tall man. She recognised their robotic walk, propelled on the invisible strings of necessity. They had to feed the media. Annie hoped the deal would work out for them.

As she watched, a journalist approached them, microphone thrust out, but the tall man in the waxed jacket put his hand up and blocked the way. His attitude towards Chloe's parents looked too familiar to be a police officer, so he had to be a close friend of the Hills. The journalist stopped in his tracks. Mr Hills tightened his arm around his wife, and the three were led to their car by a uniformed policewoman.

'Are you coming, Annie?' Jan called out to her.

Annie poured her tea away and threw the cup into a bin bag. She watched after Mr and Mrs Hills for a moment longer and then had to run a little to catch up.

'Okay, looks like we should start here,' Sam said, holding the map out for everyone to see. Kieran set off poking at weeds at the edge of the path with a stick he'd found. The women started calling out for Chloe, which Annie found odd — as if no one would have called for her since Thursday. She must have pulled a face, because Jan glowered at her.

'She might have hurt herself. You know, not be able to move.'

Annie flushed and looked away. A spray of rainwater blew onto her from one of the scrawny hawthorns along the path, and she flicked the drops off her sleeve. On a normal Saturday, she'd be nearly finishing her supermarket shop by now, having ticked off the meal plan on her shopping list. Two lunches worth at the weekend and seven dinners, except when she saw Lauren, when she might order a bowl of nachos and cheese in the bar as a treat. This change to her routine felt slippery and dangerous.

'Hey,' Sam spoke loudly enough to stop Kieran and the

women. 'Has anyone ever done this before? I mean, I haven't, and I don't want to be a liability here.'

It was nice the way he did it, kind, she thought, a little bit like Paul with his jokes and smiles. Her chest ached. Annie shook her head. Strictly speaking, she had never actually taken part in a search before. Alex shuffled his feet and looked at the ground. No one replied.

'Okay, well, maybe we should agree a plan?'

Alex nodded. 'Of course, we should. The girl's already been missing for two nights, and if she's out here in this weather, God knows what state's she's in.' Alex looked pretty cold himself in his fancy outfit. Annie predicted that the weather would be on Alex's mind all day. 'I think we should just work fast, whatever.'

'Poor child, she'll be cold and starving,' Jan said, tapping the flask in the outside pocket of her backpack, 'so we've brought soup.'

Moira sniffed loudly and nodded at Jan.

'Oh, that's what I forgot to put on my shopping list,' Annie murmured. 'Tomato soup. This whole thing has really thrown my day out.'

Alex turned to her. 'What was that?'

Annie hadn't realised she'd spoken out loud. 'Oh, sorry, just talking to myself. Just something I forgot. It was nothing.'

Alex frowned at her, and Annie closed her mouth firmly and concentrated on smoothing down the stray bits of hair that had sprung up around her face in the damp.

Sam snapped the map. 'Okay then, team, let's get organised.'

He split Kieran and Annie to different sides of the path, sent Moira and Jan to knock on the doors of the houses within their area, and he took Alex to check in the scrubby areas at the back of the gardens and in all the alleys. Annie was disappointed that Sam hadn't chosen to partner with her. She'd immediately warmed to him, but it was simple work. Although she was itching to get to her car and get on with her Saturday chores, there was something calming in focusing on the one task. She just had to sweep her eyes across a section of paving stones and weedy grass verge, clear the area, and move on. Kieran didn't say much, so he was a perfect companion. In fact, he'd made it quite clear that he wasn't that interested in chatting after Annie had tried to strike up a conversation about Chloe. Whether he knew her, what she was like, how she got on with her friends. Which was exactly what she wanted, really. A relief in fact — there was no reason at all why they should chat to each other while they searched. None at all.

She watched Sam walking alongside Alex. Annie pictured him living in one of the little Victorian cottages behind the shops on Christchurch Road with a fat and loyal Labrador. She often wondered if she should get a pet. That way she would always have someone to come home to. It wouldn't be fair though, if she suddenly had to move. She couldn't picture Alex with a dog, even though the two seemed to be friends. How do people make friends outside of school, Annie wondered. She hadn't made any at work.

Alex looked more suited to a slick apartment than a cosy cottage. Her stomach clenched as she thought of the sandstone figurine that she'd taken from Paul's flat and which was still in the pocket of her coat at home. She wondered if he'd noticed that the little figurine was missing. He had so few decorative items that it must have been important to him. It hurt her a little to think that there was a chance he might not notice.

She directed her attention back to Sam. His head tilted in a funny way when he smiled. Maybe he and Alex were just casual acquaintances who'd bumped into each other in the car park that morning. She wondered whether they'd got caught up by accident, like her, or whether they'd set out to come. Maybe that was the sort of person Sam was. The old ladies looked like the sort of amateur sleuths on the daytime TV detective programmes. They'd clearly prepared well for being out all day. Annie had to stifle a snort of laughter as she pictured them interfering away in an Agatha Christie mystery.

Kieran stopped what he was doing and turned to her. 'What's that?'

Annie shook her head. 'Sorry, just thought of something funny.' Kieran frowned at her, his chin jutting out from his chest, and Annie felt momentarily intimidated. 'No, not about Chloe. Of course not. Something else entirely.' She held her breath, but he turned back to the patch he was searching.

Sam bounded backwards and forwards between the path and the houses, keeping them all motivated and delivering a steady stream of updates from their teammates. Annie found herself looking forward to his appearances, hoping to have something to show him. She wondered why he and Alex had nothing better to do on a Saturday morning. She imagined that Sam's usual Saturday involved lunch with a group of friends after a morning playing football or cycling, rather than scrambling around in the rain on a wild goose chase. He could've been in some of the groups of friends she saw in the Piccolo on a Sunday when she walked past. People who looked like Sam were never alone. Annie felt the little hollow place inside her ache.

Kieran paused, so Annie slowed her pace, but she didn't make the mistake of asking if he was okay again. It was really best if she said as little as possible. Everything she said came out wrong. Kieran poked at a pile of take-away cartons on the path, and Annie stepped over to pick them up and shoved them into the plastic bag she always carried in her pocket.

'Yeah, why don't you pick 'em up, love. Someone should.'

Annie looked at the cigarette butt that Kieran had just dropped on the path but said nothing. Still, his appreciation cheered her.

It occurred to Annie that picking up litter might be the one useful thing she could do. None of them had found anything that looked like it could belong to Chloe, and, after all, the CCTV footage had clearly shown her heading in the other direction. Annie wondered why no one had mentioned that. It was almost enough to make her laugh as she looked at them all, desperately searching for a girl who most likely hadn't come that way at all.

Still, as much as it was an exercise in mass delusion, Annie found pleasure in spending her morning in the open air, the cry of crows wheeling in the sky, and the sense of common purpose binding them together. She tugged a plastic bag off the wire boundary of the embankment, and the shredded edges danced and wrapped themselves around her hand.

Of course, it would be much better if she could only remember what she'd seen on Thursday night. If she only knew which way Chloe had gone, they might all be able to go home and she could get on with her shopping. Had there been someone else in the car park, a shadowy figure watching for Chloe? The sense that she was in some way to blame returned. She had the faintest memories, a sliver of footsteps and puddles and fear, that raised goose bumps on her arms. Guilt crept across her skin like the shadows of the clouds when she thought of Paul's flat.

Annie cursed as her gloves caught on the hawthorn again and exposed her skin to the bitter cold. They'd been out in the soft drizzle for over an hour now, and an ache bloomed at the base of her spine. She looked ahead to where Sam and Alex had stopped to chat. A train rattled by on the tracks behind them, startling her, and she heard a shriek. Alex turned back to stare at her. The draught from the train sent the brown leaves of a dripping chestnut shivering and sprayed droplets of rain onto the men's trousers. For a moment, she was convinced they'd been talking about her. Just her imagination, that's all.

Yet another train rumbled passed, the weak daylight bouncing off the windows and setting up flashes through the hedgerow. The drizzle had stopped, but the air smelt damp and dank, and the group barely made a noise as they concentrated on their own patch. No one had found anything useful.

Annie set her rubbish bag down for a moment and rubbed at the hand that was streaked with purple welts where the plastic bag handles had cut in. She couldn't possibly collect any more litter. A twig snapped on the path behind, and Annie jumped. She breathed a sigh of relief when she saw it was just Jan and Moira.

'Well, we've finished our bit now,' Jan waved back at the neat back gardens along the path. Annie wondered if Jan thought she and Kieran should have been working faster. She looked around for Sam and Alex, but they were out of sight now, and Kieran clearly hadn't heard anything. He was up ahead of them, staring into the tangled branches of the hawthorn.

'Wow, you two work fast. We're trying to be really thorough, aren't we, Kieran?' she called out, hoping he'd stop and join them. 'I mean we don't want to miss anything by going too fast — it's not a competition. Less haste, more speed, etc.' She tried to smile, but Jan narrowed her eyes at her.

The silence stretched taut between them, and Annie was

about to say more when Jan asked, 'Do you know Chloe or her family?'

Annie was taken by surprise by the question and felt her hand lift to tug at her hair. 'No, but I couldn't get my car out of the car park, so I thought I might as well join in while I waited.' Kieran had started walking back when Annie had called him, and she felt herself blush as he reached them. 'I mean, I'd seen the news. Those bloody yellow ribbons are everywhere, aren't they? And that man with the Hills, he stopped and shook my hand in the crowd. Made me feel, I don't know … seemed like a sign, anyway. Seemed like he wanted me to join the search.' She felt herself flush in embarrassment as she heard her own babbling.

Jan looked confused, but Kieran nodded. 'Ah yes, that's my mate, Jason Berman. If he asks you to do something, you do it.' He tucked the stick under his arm like a comedy soldier. 'The Hills have been right there for him since his wife left with the kids six months ago. Nasty bit of gossip about him, there was.' Kieran tapped the side of his nose. Annie had never seen anyone do that except on TV, and the gesture made her want to laugh, until she heard his tone. 'If you come for Jase, you deal with me.' He puffed his chest out a little. So, that was why Kieran was here.

Annie felt disconcerted by the force of Kieran's response and turned back to Jan. 'Did you know Chloe?' Moira made a small choking noise that Annie ignored. 'I mean, I'm guessing that you did because of your question, and you're here, obviously. I mean, I guess random strangers just turning up would be odd but, you know, nice, too, because the more people the better for the search, right?' Jan's face was stony. 'I mean other than me, ha ha!'

'*Did* we know Chloe? Don't you mean *do* we?'

Annie felt the sting in Jan's tone and immediately realised

her error. She could feel the strength of Kieran's sudden interest, too. If Chloe wasn't bunking off somewhere, then after two nights away the statistics weren't good. She bit the words down.

'Oh, yes, I see what you mean!' Annie tried to laugh despite the twisting in her gut. 'Yes! That's how they always catch the murderers in the TV programmes, isn't it? They're the ones who know the victim's dead before the body's even found.' Annie knew she was gabbling, wished she hadn't said that word out loud. She could feel her guilt staining her cheeks as she spoke and had to bite her lip to stop herself saying anything more.

Moira dabbed at her eyes with a tissue that she pulled out of her cuff, and Jan fixed Annie with a look that might as well have been a slap to the face.

'Chloe is in Moira's granddaughter's year at school. Moira's terribly upset.'

Moira's shoulders shook.

'Oh dear,' Annie said, 'I don't suppose your granddaughter's one of those girls who was hanging up posters, is she?' She wondered what Chloe's friends might know about her disappearance. 'Could it be a prank? On Chloe's part? Kids that age might do that for a dare or to scare their parents, don't you think? I mean, I'm sure she's fine, probably just run away.' Annie made herself stop talking and crossed her fingers in front of her face.

'I don't think so.' Jan put her hands on her hips and frowned at Annie. 'Her parents said she isn't that sort of girl, didn't they, Moira?'

Moira nodded. 'They did, Jan, they did.'

Well, parents never think their child is capable of something terrible until the evidence is put before them, Annie thought. For a moment, Annie could see her father's face with his sun-bleached hair falling over his forehead.

'Oh,' Annie couldn't think of the right response. 'So that's why you thought, hoped maybe, that she might have had an accident?'

Kieran was still listening intently, and Annie turned so she could see him clearly. There was something coarse about his expression that set Annie's nerves burning.

'A sprained ankle maybe,' Moira whispered, her red eyes narrowing, 'something minor.'

'Oh, because you don't want to think someone's taken her?'

Moira's face crumpled, and Jan gave Annie a cold look. Moira allowed Jan to turn her away from Annie, and, when Kieran snorted, they moved off.

Kieran put his face close to Annie's. 'So, do you think she's run away or do you think she's dead?'

Annie opened her mouth to speak but couldn't make any sound come out. It was more than he'd said to her all morning, and the aggression in his tone shocked her.

Kieran's eyes were bloodshot, and Annie could smell stale smoke on his breath. 'Whichever it is, bit weird you're here, isn't it?'

She glanced back, but Sam and Alex were still out of sight, and she didn't dare call out to Jan and Moira.

Kieran burst into laughter. 'Gotcha! Cheer up, just having a laugh. Those women are a bit uptight!' He set off after Jan and Moira and then turned around and called back over his shoulder. 'Get on with it, shall we?'

Annie took a long breath and cursed herself for being so stupid. Stupid for being there, stupid for letting her mouth run away with her. *Just be normal, Annie.* Sam and Alex were catching up behind her, so she bent over, apparently absorbed in searching through the grass.

'How are you doing?' Sam asked. Annie stood up and tried to smile. 'Fine. Well, not fine. I mean, I haven't found her. We haven't found her. The others went ahead.' She bit her lip so she didn't have to explain why they weren't walking with her. 'You?'

Sam shook his head. Beside Sam's open face, Alex looked pale and dull. She focused on checking down the embankment towards the track to appear committed to the task. The boys fell into step beside her, and she was acutely aware of Sam, his gait easy despite the freezing weather and the tedious job.

'Do you know Chloe or her family?' she asked, carefully checking her tense.

Sam turned his brilliant smile on her and shook his head. 'We're just doing our good deed for the week or something, aren't we?' He deferred to Alex, who nodded.

'Oh, you're not worried about people thinking you're suspects then?'

Sam looked confused.

Annie tried to elaborate. 'Helping at a search but no real connection to the person we're searching for. *Is it a real sense of community or just guilty conscience?* I can see the headlines now.' She laughed to show them she was joking. It was ridiculous to think they might be involved in Chloe's disappearance. She hoped it was as ridiculous to think she might have a sinister reason for being there, too, but Sam answered her seriously.

'We've lived here all our lives, Annie. It's just what you do.'

Annie felt a stab of envy. She glanced at Alex, who didn't look like the picture of civic duty that Sam described. She wondered how Sam could be friends with him, but maybe he was just being kind.

'Where are you from, Annie?' She felt a little glow inside that Sam was interested in her. Maybe it hadn't been such a mistake to come.

'Oh, nowhere exciting.' It was too complicated to explain even if she wanted to. 'I wonder if anyone else has found anything? Should we join the others, do you think? Moira seemed a bit upset.' She pointed towards Kieran and the women.

'Actually, you know, we've been out for hours.' Sam looked at Alex, who was rubbing his hands together. His lips were blue with cold, and Annie was grateful for her gloves. 'We've pretty much covered our patch. I think we should go back and check, grab something to eat, maybe. And, hey, Annie's going to need a new bag for rubbish.' He waved at the bag Annie was carrying, the corners of his mouth tilting up in amusement. He was letting her know he was impressed. She felt a rush of gratitude.

'Oh yes, we've definitely done our bit now,' she said, 'and we need to get Alex warmed up before we have a casualty on our hands.' Alex gave her a dirty look, which felt unfair. She was only trying to be friendly.

The women hurried past at Sam's shout, Moira keeping her eyes firmly on the ground, and went ahead. Annie found herself walking on her own on the way back. Behind her, Kieran weaved from side to side as if he didn't trust a single one of them to have searched properly. She concentrated on not letting any of the litter drop out of her bag. The path already looked better, so that was something.

The sky was a grey wash of rain-filled clouds. Annie wondered if the search would be called off if it rained, or whether they'd have to keep going, however damp and chilled they were.

It was strange that there were so many people out looking, such a large group working to one end, and yet they'd not seen or heard anything about how the other teams were doing. She half imagined that Chloe had been found, and they'd return to discover the marquee being dismantled and the posters taken down. If they were in a film, they'd return to find the whole village missing, a lost mobile phone ringing on the ground, a car engine still running, and no explanation for what had happened. They'd have to learn to rely on each other, bonded by whatever catastrophe had happened, and would be the only people left to put things right.

She smiled to herself as she got caught up in the fantasy. Anyway, it had been an unexpected lift to spend some time around other people on a Saturday. She mentally rearranged her chores list, squeezing her usually leisurely timetable to compensate.

Sam's laugh rang out ahead, and she glanced up just as Alex turned round to look at her. What were they saying? It was ludicrous that she'd taken part, the very worst thing she could have done. She should have listened to her mother; she wouldn't find Chloe. There was no way she could fit in with these people, even if they welcomed her. Perhaps, she should slip away now, though, if she really wanted to disappear, it was going to be pretty difficult with Alex watching from the front and Kieran keeping an eye on her from the back.

She'd managed to get herself trapped. She shook the thought away. Just paranoia.

6

SATURDAY EVENING

There was no real news at the marquee. The atmosphere was fractious, the eager anticipation of the morning replaced with frustration and a creeping sense of unease. A thin-faced man in a high visibility jacket shouted for attention and gave what, Annie supposed, was meant to be a pep talk. There was no news of Chloe. That all the teams had covered so much ground was a mixed blessing. Yes, they'd worked fast, but it meant Chloe was further from home. Annie searched the upturned faces listening for any sign they understood that it was now as unlikely that Chloe had had an accident on the way home as it was that Chloe was staying with a friend and oblivious to the search.

Even Sam's sunny face looked grey in the hard light of the halogen lighting hung from the marquee's frame. Annie checked her watch. If she could get her car out now, she would still be able get to the supermarket with plenty of time spare for the rest of her chores. She considered leaving the search.

But, though the group was not entirely friendly, there was something compelling about being part of this movement of people, all acting with one purpose. The man finished speaking, and Sam looked around, catching Annie's eye, and smiled. Maybe she would stay and try a bit harder not to say the wrong thing.

After a sandwich and a hot drink that barely warmed her up, they'd gone back out and quickly fallen into an urgent rhythm, making a fast sweep to check for the girl herself and then a more meticulous search for any items that could possibly have belonged to her. As it would soon be nightfall, the search felt more serious, like they'd had their opportunity to be social in the morning and now it was time to work. That was okay; Annie was good at working. Surprisingly, Kieran was the one who seemed to take the most care, muttering to himself and answering regular phone calls. 'No, Jase, nothing yet.' 'Mate, I'll call you as soon as I know.'

It was Sam who kept the group going, his easy chatter keeping their spirits up when the cold started to bite and the task felt more and more hopeless. Whenever he was nearby, Annie felt her back straightening and the incessant nagging in her head to get away, get on with her own business, quietened. It soon became clear that Moira and Jan — with their backpacks that contained a flask, a tub of biscuits, and two notepads with pencils attached with string — were particularly well suited to knocking on doors and asking the occupants, many of whom they seemed to know, to check their own houses and gardens. Everyone insisted they'd work better split up, and so Annie was partnered with Kieran again. They were like the silent clean up team, Kieran poking around and dislodging litter and Annie picking it up.

They'd all been given posters, too, with a new photograph of the missing girl smiling directly at the camera. On her shoulder was the hand of someone who'd been otherwise cropped out of the picture. It gave the image a slightly macabre feel. Printed on it, along with Chloe's name, her height, and a description of her clothes, was the police hotline number. Emblazoned across the top was #BringChloeHome. Annie had folded hers and tucked them into a pocket, importantly pulling them out and peeling one off when she came across someone the backpack ladies had missed. She'd picked up a spare bin bag and tied one of the handles onto the belt hooks of her jeans to make it easier to carry. Sam patted her shoulder and gave her an encouraging wink, and she'd felt a glow of unexpected pride. There was something in the gesture that reminded her of her father. Her back straightened a little, and she attempted to collect every wrapper and empty plastic bottle she could find. It was a task that almost completely absorbed her. She knew she was looking for any signs that Chloe had come that way, too.

'Silver lining, I suppose,' Annie beamed at Sam, but he looked confused. 'You know, one good thing about the search.' She pointed to the bin bag that now bulged with cans and wrappers. Sam looked a little puzzled, and Annie wished she'd said nothing. Still, she recovered a little when she noticed the others collecting litter. They were passing along the land, clearing the ugliness and dangers away, leaving a cleaner, safer place behind them. If there was a bogeyman hiding in the shadows, then they would flush him out, too. She felt lighter the harder she concentrated on that.

By the end of the search, Annie was chilled and sore, but she felt good. She'd served a purpose. She'd been part of a team, and it felt nice, as if she belonged, and she realised she'd barely checked on Facebook to see what Paul or Lauren were up to. She wondered if Paul was part of the search. She struggled to picture him scouring Westhurst for a lost little girl. He might think of Annie differently, though, if he knew she was there. She checked her hair was tidy and pulled back her shoulders at the thought of bumping into him. It would be nice to have someone to talk to about her day. Still, for once, she would have something to say if she did manage to catch Lauren before she went out. She wouldn't have to bore her with the usual Saturday chores.

When they reached the marquee, they found the air muggy with the smell of damp wool and steamy breath. There was no news about Chloe, and the conversations were muted, but Annie felt buoyant. She hadn't felt so useful, so needed, in a long time. The others looked beaten. She knew they weren't just tired and miserable, but that each one of them was painfully aware that a twelve-year-old was still missing. She wanted to lift their spirits, let her team know that what they'd done together was worth something. Annie wished she knew about the good stories of children being found, the survival-against-all-odds tales, but those weren't the ones that stuck in her mind.

'Well, I think we should feel pleased with ourselves for our efforts today,' she said instead, thinking about the way Paul spoke to the team when he wanted to encourage them to work harder. 'I really hope we're all together again tomorrow, and we can smash this searching thing. Team Chloe!' She punched the air.

Alex turned to her. 'We're all hoping that Chloe is found before then, Annie. I mean, look at the weather.'

Through the opening of the marquee, Annie could see a light rain. She couldn't help smile that she'd known the cold would be bothering Alex. Moira and Jan turned away, and Sam shoved his hands in his pockets and frowned.

They were all exhausted, of course. That was it. 'Well, of course,' Annie frowned, 'I just meant that it feels good to be helping. That I want to keep helping. As a team.'

Kieran snorted. 'Depends whose team you're on, love.'

I know that, Annie thought, *of course I would know that.* He didn't need to joke with her. But she comforted herself with the thought that, actually, it wasn't as if Chloe was a very small child. There was nothing on the CCTV to suggest someone had taken her, was there? Or they wouldn't be searching like this. Clearly, Chloe had walked out of that car park under her own steam. Annie quashed the voice at the back of her mind telling her that it'd already been too long since she went missing. She cleared her thoughts and looked around. She was on her own.

If Chloe didn't come home overnight, Annie decided that she, at least, would be back in the morning. That would show how much she cared. She didn't notice the uniformed police officer standing near her car until it was too late to turn away.

'Is this your car?'

She nodded and gave him her name. Just being spoken to by the police made Annie's throat close up in panic. She concentrated on a loose thread on the collar of his jacket so that she didn't have to meet his eye.

'Was your car parked here on Thursday evening?'

She nodded again.

'And have we already spoken to you?'

Annie felt the confidence she'd gained from the day. 'Of course, I mean, I've been here since this morning searching for Chloe today myself.' She waved back towards the marquee. 'Wish I had seen something useful, but I didn't. Look, I'd definitely be telling you all about it if I had. It's not like I'm trying to hide anything. Why would I do that?' She tried a little laugh, but it snagged in her throat, and she had to turn it into a cough.

The officer looked up from his notebook and studied her face long enough for the blood to rise and warm her cold cheeks. She held still and tried to stop her eyes skittering away.

'Are you all right?'

She slapped her hands together. 'Yes, of course, just tired. And freezing. Sorry. I mean, I know you're cold, too.'

He nodded. 'Yes, miserable, isn't it? By the way, you want to get that wing mirror fixed soon as you can.' He gestured for her to go.

She drove straight out of Westhurst to the superstore in the next town. There, she could pass through the aisles as just one more stranger. As nice as it had been to spend time with the others, she craved the sanctuary of her own company now. She picked up a huge bunch of flowers, a plump chicken breast, and some green salad along with her other shopping. She wanted to recapture those feelings of satisfaction she'd experienced during the day.

At home, she put the poster with the smiling face of Chloe on the fridge next to the newspaper clipping and set the chicken to marinate. The flowers were a luxury. Every bit of her income went on the rent for this house, so she could stay tucked away. She separated the stems between several glasses and took one into each room. Then she cleared away everything that was out of place and swept off the dust with tissues. And before she ate, she set her alarm and put out her clothes for the morning. It had been a long time since she'd taken such trouble for herself, and it felt good.

Then, when she was sitting down to eat, she turned on her laptop and watched the coverage of the search. While she was there, they hadn't really known what else was happening, but now she could just search #BringChloeHome and find a world of information. It felt weird to think that she had actually been out in the heart of it, but might know less than someone reading about it at home. Maybe one of those watching online knew something useful. That was stupid, she thought, someone always knew something. She felt a shiver of fear as she imagined all the people watching from their armchairs and their kitchens, poring through the articles and the images. Were they watching the crowd, too, analysing the faces of the volunteers in the search parties?

There was an article about Chloe's family. Annie hadn't realised that Mr Hills was the owner of the lettings agency on Christchurch Road. She'd only been in there once — before she'd found her house. The website had a photograph of Mr Hills and his partner, Jason Berman, Kieran's friend. Annie wondered why he'd chosen her hand to grab that morning. That moment seemed like a lifetime ago.

She squinted at the image of Berman again and realised that she'd actually spoken to him when she'd first arrived in Westhurst. He'd laughed at her tiny budget and tried to steer her towards a pokey studio flat in the same block as Paul's apartment. There were always empty flats there. 'Best you can do for the money, love.'

Annie didn't want a flat. She'd wanted her own front door with minimal chance of having to make small talk as she fumbled with the door key. Her house was perfect. A little shabby, but it was on the edge of the town and overlooked fields at the front. At the back, dense hedging perfectly created her own little enclosed world in her overgrown garden.

She thought back to that meeting with Berman. The door had opened just as Annie was about to reply that she really did want to look for a house, but she'd lost his attention entirely as a very young woman with glossy hair and perfectly applied make-up walked in. Berman straightened his back and stood up, smiling with his teeth, and Annie took the opportunity to slip away.

Outside, she'd glanced back through the gleaming glass.

She was sure that Berman hadn't even noticed her leave. He had his hand in the small of the other woman's back as he steered her towards his desk. Had she left him her details so he could do vetting checks?

Annie wondered why he'd chosen to grab her hand at the police conference, and the thought caused her anxiety to flare up again. Her mind roamed across all the possibilities, until she panicked as she remembered the flash of the cameras behind her. She searched quickly for any copies of that photograph and breathed a sigh of relief to find that the media were using one of him bending over to talk to a small child. The little girl's face was turned toward her mother, whose hand she gripped tightly.

Annie cursed herself for not keeping to the back of the crowd. If her mother saw that photograph of Annie, she'd be likely to turn up on her doorstep with an empty suitcase and an expression of martyrdom. There was something a little gleeful about the pleasure Annie's mum took in packing up, clearing out her house, scything away the memorabilia. As a small girl, Annie had loved collecting things; tiny shells from the beach, beads, small figurines. Over the years, she'd learned to let go of so many things. She walked to her coat and withdrew the little sandstone figure from the pocket. It felt warm and solid in her hand. She would return it as soon as she could, but for now it felt comforting right where it was.

* * *

Lottie rests under the cherry tree in the front garden. The Pisky trap survived Tegen's visit, but Lottie doesn't want to risk leaving it in case she comes back. It's so hot that even the trunk Lottie leans against is warm through her T-shirt. Bronnen and Gwen wheel past on their bikes again. Lottie watches with interest as they skid into the curve at the end of the close. When she's their age, Lottie wants to be able to go out on her bike by herself, too.

'What's that supposed to be?' Bronnen pauses, splendid in a bright pink T-shirt with a neon cat cartoon on the front and striped leggings, and taps one foot on the curb of the pavement. Lottie feels colour flooding into her cheeks. She doesn't know what to say. Bronnen and Gwen are not the sort of girls Lottie normally talks to. They are at least, she counts on her fingers, three years older.

Gwen jumps off her bike and pokes at the piled-up grass. She grabs one of the little figures. 'Look, Bronnen, Piskies! Isn't that sweet?' Gwen tosses it to Bronnen, who drops her bike on the pavement and walks over to Lottie. She holds the Pisky up to the sun and says,

'Don't you know how dangerous it is to play with Piskies?' Gwen giggles behind Bronnen. She's rolled her black leggings up to her knees, and Lottie can see where she's drawn cats on her leg in pen.

Bronnen sweeps her hand through Lottie's work, sending the Playmobil and toilet roll and wooden mouse flying. Lottie starts to cry. 'Silly girl, you might conjure one up.' She hunches over and pulls a face at Lottie.

'That's what I was trying to do!' Lottie won't have time to rebuild it before dinner now.

Gwen tugs at Bronnen's hand to pull her back to their bikes. 'Leave her, Bron, let's go down to the harbour.'

But Bronnen's eyes are sparkly, and her face breaks into a tight little smile as she tells Gwen they need to help Lottie. 'We've just rescued you from making the Little People angry, you should be grateful.' She sits down in front of Lottie and sighs theatrically. 'Looks like we need to take you under our wings before you do the magic wrong.'

Gwen rolls her eyes but allows herself to be pulled down to help flatten the grass.

The three of them sit close together in the shade. All that remains of Lottie's Pisky trap is the little twig swing. Gwen pushes it back and forth.

Bronnen swats Gwen's hand away. 'If you want to see a Pisky, you need to join the Pisky Society.'

Lottie still feels upset about her trap, but she risks a glance at Bronnen to see if she's serious.

Bronnen smiles broadly. 'Ah, you are interested. Only thing is that you can't join, because it's a Secret Society.' Bronnen swings her face into Lottie's. 'The first thing you'd have to do is prove you can keep a secret.'

Gwen nods. 'Keeping secrets is the most important thing. But she's probably too young, Bron.'

'I'm not!' Lottie wants to find a Pisky more than ever, and they owe her, she thinks. If they'd left her trap alone, she could have caught one on her own.

'Of course, you're not,' Bronnen says, and she puts her arm around Lottie tightly. 'We should test her first, shouldn't we, Gwen?'

Gwen picks up the wooden mouse and throws it up into the air over and over.

Lottie feels a bloom of unease building inside her. Magic is one thing, you're not supposed to tell how it works, but her parents are always telling her not to keep secrets. 'No lies, no secrets, and then there'll be no trouble,' they say. The twisty feeling in her tummy makes her feel anxious, but she definitely wants to hear more about Bronnen and Gwen's Pisky Society, too.

'Can you keep a secret, Lottie?'

Lottie considers it and then nods.

'We need to make a vow, then.' Bronnen puts her hand over her heart and nudges Gwen. Gwen closes her eyes and puts her hand over her heart, too. 'Okay, repeat after me.' Lottie screws up her own eyes so that she can just squint through her lashes. 'I promise to always keep the secrets of the Pisky Society.'

'I promise to always keep the secrets of the Pisky Society,' Lottie and Gwen repeat. Bronnen has opened her eyes and is playing with an empty Maoam wrapper in her hand.

'And if I tell, then all the vengeance of the Piskies and all the Little People will come down on me and my family.'

'And if I tell, then all the vengeance of the Piskies and all the Little People will come down on me and my family,' Gwen and Lottie say. They open their eyes, and Bronnen flicks the sweet wrapper into the grass.

'Well, we've got to go now.' Bronnen pulls Gwen up. Gwen's sigh is loaded with relief.

'Where are we going?' Lottie stands up too, but Bronnen pushes her back down.

'Not you, silly. We've got stuff to do that you wouldn't understand.' She links her arm through Gwen's and pulls her towards their bikes. Lottie jumps up.

'Can we play again later? Will you tell me some more about the Pisky Society?'

Bronnen doesn't even turn around, just waggles her hand in the air. Gwen gives Lottie a little smile and shrugs. Her baggy T-shirt billows at the back as she cycles away.

7

SUNDAY MORNING

Throughout the night, the wind had picked up, and it whistled in and out of Annie's sleep like a stalker's breath. The fence below her window creaked and rattled, and the rain smacked on the glass like handfuls of gravel. The stone baby lay on the pillow next to her, and she wondered if Paul had been woken by the storm, too.

Long before the sky cleared, Annie got herself a mug of tea and returned to her bed. She reached for her phone, rubbing the sleep from her eyes. Chloe was still missing. The #BringChloeHome campaign had released more family photographs and memories overnight. The girl had been a pudgy toddler, her smile as lopsided as the tufty ponytail on top of her head.

Nobody should ever leave a child that age alone. They're too vulnerable, too trusting.
A child that age might go off with anyone.

Annie felt the panic rising in her chest as she thought about what could have happened. She pushed the worst thoughts away and brought her mind back to Chloe. She tried to go over the events of Thursday night, the ones she could remember, but there was nothing there but a wisp of guilt and shame.

There was another photograph of Chloe in school uniform, a tight smile on her face and her hair neatly brushed. How many times are parents asked to provide these photographs? A picture of an uncomfortable child, looking the least like their usual self, seemed an odd image to use. Annie assumed it was for the media, created the right framing around the child that was missing.

Annie read a piece written by a body-language expert analysing Mr and Mrs Hills' demeanour at the press conference. The expert considered it significant that Mrs Hills had paused for so long before she spoke, that Mr Hills had held on to her so hard.

Could Mrs Hills have been struggling to remember the story she wanted to tell?
Was her husband trying to make sure she kept to an agreed message?

Annie sighed and scrolled down.

She knew all about the cases where the parents had made heart-rending public appeals but had later been found guilty of their own child's kidnapping or murder. There were enough to keep the media columns fat with easy conjecture and the reading public fascinated. They compared the blankness of expression of the Hills with Berman's earnest appeal to the crowd. Annie spilled a drop of her tea when she saw the photograph of Berman holding her hand in his but took a steadying breath when she realised it just showed the back of her head. The focus was on his smiling face. She could still feel his hands on hers and smell the waxed jacket he wore.

The article generated a storm of comments. Annie watched as new ones popped up from around the world. People arguing with the content, arguing with each other, throwing about their own theories as though it might help. She found herself compulsively reading the responses, until she could almost hear the shouting in her head. Annie studied the photos of Mrs Hills, too, but could only see a mother frantic with worry and only just holding herself together, desperate to find her lost child. But the world seemed obsessed with her clothes and the way she stood. It was so unfair. Annie wanted to tell her how sorry she was. Annie was so very sorry.

There were rumours that Chloe'd been arguing a lot with her parents lately, spending more and more time at her friends' houses than her own. But at the age of twelve, who didn't argue with their parents? Unless you only had one parent and absolutely no one else in the entire world. Annie pushed the memories away.

Besides, Annie had Lauren now. She really wanted to call her to go over the details of the case. Lauren would know what was normal. Her family home had been loud and messy and always felt like safety to Annie, even when Lauren complained the most.

Most of the messages wished for Chloe's safe return, but some took Annie's breath away with their vile views. She felt her insides knot with the impulse to respond. People should mind their own business unless they actually knew what was going on. Annie needed to stop reading now.

'Where are you, Chloe?' Annie took one last look at the press conference photo. Behind Mrs Hills, one of the two girls that she'd spoken to hanging posters was peering through a gap in the crowd. Annie noticed her because she wasn't watching Mrs Hills — she was staring at Berman. It struck Annie as odd. It was the quieter of the two friends, Annie thought, and she wondered if the girl knew something. Maybe she was trying to work out if she could talk to Berman about what had happened to Chloe, but it didn't look like that. Annie searched the picture for the other, more confident girl. Berman was staring at the back of Mr Hills' head, unaware that he was being watched. Annie couldn't make out the taller girl in the crowd. Perhaps she'd left, and her friend was looking for an opportunity to talk to Berman alone. There was something about the girl's expression that troubled Annie.

She wondered if anyone else had noticed. Could she leave an anonymous message on the missing persons line? It was out of the question. She couldn't bear to speak to anyone, knew that she'd gabble and mess it up, and it was probably nothing anyway. On some level, though, she trusted her instincts, and she felt afraid for Chloe. Her hands started to shake, and she had to force herself to get dressed and eat breakfast.

Annie took unusual care to tidy the house up, immersing herself in the satisfying process of marking off the tasks she'd completed. A tiny nugget of hope grew that, if her search party came near her house, she would be able to invite them in. She knew it wouldn't happen, but what was the harm in being ready just in case? A girl could dream. She straightened the cushions on the sofa, ran a duster around the half-empty shelves again and tied the curtains back. It didn't take long; the house was small, and she didn't have much stuff.

She was just pulling her coat on when her phone lit up with notifications, and she saw that the police had issued another statement. They said they were gravely concerned for Chloe's safety. Her parents had discovered her latest prescription of asthma inhalers untouched in her bedroom and believed she only had a few days left in the inhaler she carried with her.

'Without her preventer, Chloe could suffer a serious attack,' her mother said.

'She's been admitted to hospital twice in the last two years when it's got really bad,' her father added.

The BBC were interviewing a medical expert who warned that asthma sufferers were particularly vulnerable to serious attacks in cold weather. #BringChloeHome burst into action as she spoke. This, they said, proved Chloe was no runaway, because she would never have gone anywhere without her inhalers. This was proof that someone must have taken her. Annie felt her stomach turn over. It did look like Chloe must have intended to go home after all. It was certainly an answer to the theories that she'd just run away.

Mrs Hills still pleaded on the television.

'If anyone knows where Chloe is, please make sure she has enough medication.'

Annie zipped up her coat and pulled on a scarf. She'd thought she was having an asthma attack once. Even now she could feel her throat closing up, the blood rushing into her head, her hands fluttering uselessly to pull the material of her T-shirt away from her chest. It was as if her own lungs refused to let her live, repulsed her breath. In the end, it had turned out to be a panic attack.

Torn posters were mulched on the roadside and grubby yellow ribbons hung from hedges. The wind had blown itself out, but fallen twigs and leaves were scattered across the pavement, slippery and shifting beneath Annie's boots. She stopped twice on the way to the station, certain that she should turn around and go home. She could busy herself with ironing, but, if she did, she knew she would spend the day wondering if anyone else had noticed that one girl, Chloe's friend, looking the wrong way at the press conference. Annie was sure it was important. Like the tiniest sensation of footsteps approaching her on Thursday evening that kept surfacing in her memory. Was it on the platform or was it in the car park? Annie couldn't unravel it in her head, but she felt the fear creaking deep in her bones. She carried on up the hill under the bare branches.

By the time Annie found her group, she was chilled to the bone, despite the extra layers she'd put on that morning. It was so bitterly cold that their breath clouded in the air around them as they waited. Annie thought of Chloe, damp and freezing if she was still outside, and felt dismay again that she hadn't seen anything. Thursday night had been this cold, too. Her breath had filled the car, the condensation on the inside of the windscreen running down the glass. She had a memory of wiping it off with her coat sleeve, too impatient to wait for the heater to clear it.

The atmosphere in the marquee where they gathered was muted. Annie wondered if there were fewer people there than the day before. Her own back ached, and the day of searching seemed to have yielded nothing of any value. The chances of finding Chloe well seemed to have slipped further away overnight with the storm. The organisers reminded everyone that Chloe had been gone for three nights, and the searchers pulled their gloves up higher on their wrists and stamped their feet thinking about the girl and what they might find.

Annie's little group eased back into their roles of the day

before with little discussion. She was grateful for Sam's smiling presence, lifting them all up. An hour into the search, Jan dropped back to ask Alex and Sam a question, and Annie saw her chance. She caught up with Moira.

'Moira, has your granddaughter said anything about Chloe's friends?' Moira looked tired. Her soft face was pale, and the strain showed around her eyes. 'Has she said if she thinks any of them know where she is?' Annie bit her lip. She'd forgotten to ask Moira how she was first, just jumped straight into it, and Moira looked offended. 'Oh, sorry, I meant to ask how you were first. Are you okay?'

'What do you mean?'

Annie glanced back to Jan, who wouldn't hesitate to call her rude or nosy.

'I mean, could they be up to something? One of them seemed to be hiding from the Hills and the police at the press conference yesterday. It seemed suspicious.'

Moira turned and looked Annie in the eye. 'Look, Dawn's not really a friend of Chloe's — she's a good girl, my grand-daughter — so I don't know much about Chloe's friends.'

'Oh? What's she like then, Chloe? Was she in trouble a lot?'

Moira drew herself up straight. 'I don't know. What it's got to do with you?'

Annie flushed. The tone in Moira's voice was disapproving, and she wished she'd asked the question a different way. 'I was just trying to work out what her friend was up to. You know, young girls aren't always kind to their friends. I was wondering if someone should say something?'

Moira glared at her and walked off towards Jan. Annie turned back to the verge along the path and grabbed at a beer can. Her hand shook as she shoved it into the bag. She was sure that the girl had been up to something but, then, perhaps that said more about her. She tried to breathe.

'Have you checked this bit?' Sam broke into her thoughts, and she realised she'd been staring at the bin bag.

She looked guiltily at the ground in front of her. 'It's all a waste of time, isn't it? We're looking for a human-sized girl in undergrowth that doesn't reach our knees. I mean, if she was here, she'd have been found by now.' Her fingers felt raw with cold, and the thought of actually finding Chloe here by the path now made her feel queasy. 'We might as well be searching for the Little People.'

How could anyone survive so long in this weather? She checked herself. It would do her no good to imagine what might have happened. How could no one have seen her though? How could Annie not have seen her?

'What?'

Annie shook herself out of her thoughts to look at him. He looked shocked.

'Oh, nothing, sorry, I was thinking of something else. But surely we won't find her along here?' She rubbed her hands together. 'She would have been found by now if she was hurt. People use this path all the time. I can't help thinking that she's really just run away. Or hoping that she has, anyway. What do you think? This could all be a waste of effort.' Annie could hope that Chloe had just run away, couldn't she? Or think that they were looking in the wrong places at least. That was the best she had. 'I just want to believe it's a waste of time, that's all.'

'If we're wasting your time, maybe you shouldn't be here. I'm sure the rest of us can cope.' Alex appeared at Sam's elbow. It was like he appeared every time she spoke to Sam, always with a little put down or a snide comment.

'Sorry, I just meant —' Annie searched for the right thing to say '— she's not likely to be here.'

Moira pulled out another tissue from her cuff and dabbed at her eyes again.

'We just can't take that risk though, can we? The slower we are finding her ...' Alex's voice trailed away as Moira blew her nose loudly beside him.

'Of course.' Annie returned to her search of the embankment, determined to concentrate on what she was doing. She wondered where Kieran was — she really hoped he hadn't overheard her exchange with Alex, and then she saw him ahead swiping at the undergrowth with his stick.

8

SUNDAY AFTERNOON

The sun had barely broken through the lowering clouds all day, and the early chill had melted into rain. They'd spent hardly enough time to warm up in the marquee, the disposable cups of tea and coffee scorching their frozen hands. It was clear to Annie that the number of volunteers was falling away quickly, and she felt proud of her own group as they zipped up their coats and pulled their gloves back on. She nearly said something to Sam about it, how well they were doing to stick together, but thought better of it when she saw Alex glued to his side.

Annie had put on an extra layer under her jumper, and even Alex was wearing a warmer coat, but they were a sorry-looking little group as they set out again. She scanned their search area hard for any sign that Chloe, or any girl for that matter, had ever passed this way. As much as Annie wanted to be part of finding Chloe, she hadn't thought the search would take this long, eat up her Sunday, too. But each time she thought of packing it in, she saw Sam pressing a shoulder or making a friendly remark to each of them. It was a consolation to watch him gently chivvy them along. Paul relied on his status more, she thought.

Annie straightened up as Sam reached her and found herself patting at her hair to move it off her face. She caught Alex's eye and awkwardly stuffed her hand in her pocket, suddenly unable to think what else to do with it.

'Well, at least we're clearing up the litter as we go, ha ha! Something positive, isn't it?' She wanted Sam to see that she could support his efforts at keeping their spirits up.

'We were wondering whether we should suggest that Moira and Jan go on home,' Sam said.

Annie looked to where the two had paused and were leaning against a faded wooden fence, their backpacks at their feet. They did appear cowed, now that Annie looked at them. They were the oldest in the group, and Moira didn't look as if she usually walked much further than the cafe, Annie thought. She dismissed the mean thought straight away — Moira did have all the walking gear. Jan was another matter. Annie was quite sure she could go on indefinitely, but if Sam thought it was the right thing, she was okay with that. If Jan and Moira were struggling though, Chloe would be in real trouble in the cold. The CCTV image had shown her wearing a bomber jacket and jeans. It was hard to see how she could survive in this weather. No one ever feared the natural world as much as they should, Annie thought. She shivered as she considered the way beauty could conceal danger.

'Right, yes,' Annie said, 'I mean we should probably all go home.' Sam's smile wavered on his beautiful face, and Annie stopped herself. 'She's surely not out here.' She gestured at the empty path. It was almost as if they'd just been sent off to get them out of the way. Annie wondered what the police knew. No one ever looked in the right places.

'Have you got a better idea, then?' Alex sounded frustrated. Of course he did; they were all hoping to find Chloe.

'Well, I just think someone must know where she is, so the police would be better off talking to people rather than have us poking around in the weeds at random. You know, at the press briefing, one of her friends was acting a little strange, I thought. I wish I knew what her name is, the one who turned up and seemed to be staring at Jason Berman all the time? What's her name?'

Alex frowned at her, so she turned to Sam. He would want to help.

Sam shook his head. 'I didn't really notice, Annie.'

'But she was looking at him in a really funny way. I really think someone should talk to her. Don't you know these people?'

Alex coughed, and Sam looked from him to Annie. He sighed. 'Look, Annie, there are a lot of people asking questions at the moment, and I'm not sure how helpful it is. I'm sure the police know what they're doing.'

Earlier, she knew she'd said something wrong when she'd asked Moira whether her granddaughter thought Chloe really needed her inhalers. Annie's lips were already cracked and fraying in the cold, and this had to be the worst weather for asthma sufferers. She'd only questioned whether it was really true that Chloe had been hospitalised. Her friends would know that. Obviously Moira's granddaughter wasn't really friends with Chloe at all. If Annie was a more sensitive person, she'd think that Moira had been avoiding her since.

Sam and Alex turned towards Jan and Moira, closing the conversation down.

'You know, Jase knows Chloe and her mates pretty well.'

Annie jumped when Kieran spoke behind her and spun around.

'So, it's not so strange that they'd be looking up to him to help find her.'

The look Annie had seen wasn't admiration, she was sure of that.

'But it didn't look —'

Kieran stepped a little closer. 'You ask a lot of questions, Annie Whatchamacallit. Why's that?'

Annie felt her mouth drop open, but Kieran had already turned back to his side of the path. Annie poked about in the weeds a bit on her own, the bag of litter bashing at her legs, while she bit back a sob of fear. There was something unpredictable and dangerous about Kieran.

The group was so far from the station now that the hawthorn had turned to weeds, and the other side of the path was barbed wire that ran along a field of ponies, who snorted clouds of steam in the cold air and swung their heads to watch as Annie moved to their side. One white-faced old girl walked loosely towards Annie and stuck her head over, snuffling out of friendship. Annie froze. She put a hand out slowly and then jumped as the pony shook its head and snickered.

'I have nothing for you,' she whispered.

'Do you ride, Annie?' Kieran reappeared at her side. He'd been asking questions all morning.

'Um, no, I haven't really been around horses much. Not everyone has been, have they? Weird thing, one animal riding another, when you think about it like that.' She took a deep breath and tried not to let her discomfort at Kieran's attention show in her answer. The last thing she wanted him to think was that she had anything to hide.

'By the way, Annie, where did you say you were from?' Kieran cocked his head to one side as he waited for her response.

Annie had to be careful now. She wasn't used to anyone

showing this much interest in her, and it felt strange. She flushed. 'Westhurst. I live here.'

He rolled his eyes. 'Before that?'

'Reading. Near Reading. Mostly.' She couldn't look at him, knew he wouldn't believe her. 'Shouldn't we check whether Chloe's been found yet?' The light was beginning to fail.

Kieran gestured back along the path, and Annie stretched her pace to fall into step beside Alex and Sam. She hoped Kieran would be put off from his questions by their presence. Instead, the others looked towards her too, curious.

'So, what do you do, Annie?' Sam said.

Annie flushed at his interest. It would be nice to chat to him some more when Alex and Kieran weren't listening in. 'Nothing interesting, I'm afraid. I work in sales support for an IT company. Passing on sales leads, tracking sales made, that sort of thing.' She shrugged. 'Pays the bills, I suppose. What do you do, Sam?'

Sam opened his mouth to answer, but then his phone rang with a piece of music that Annie recognised, but which jarred in the silence among the fields. He turned away to take the call, and Annie noticed the way his head tipped forward and his shoulders lowered, exposing the back of his neck to the rain. She nearly stepped forward to raise his collar, but caught herself just in time.

'Yes, I see,' Sam said. 'I'll tell them.' He suggested they return to the station where there were hot drinks.

Annie walked back beside Sam, the pleasure of companionship warming her as much as the prospect of a hot drink.

'Well,' Sam said. 'I hope this is good news.'

'Probably just the rain,' Jan said, but everyone looked chilled, and a second day of searching in the cold had left them pale and weary. Nobody picked up the conversation as they walked, and Annie's mind turned to the lonely evening ahead.

The atmosphere in the station car park was thick with the weight of collective dismay. It was clear that all the search parties had been called back. The search was being called off, and all the volunteers were released. All search activity was being taken over by the police and other emergency services going forward. The area in front of the station itself had been cleared for another press conference to announce this to the public. They were no longer needed, but for all the wrong reasons.

Annie wished she didn't have to say goodbye to the group, Sam mainly, and she felt a pang of regret that they'd all have to return to work in the morning.

'Oh, I wish we could get together and do this again,' Annie said, feeling already a little lost and empty. 'Perhaps, we could all go for a quick drink? To celebrate meeting?' Annie missed the shock in their eyes as she looked down to fish out her phone, but she heard Jan say:

'I hardly think that's appropriate.'

When Annie looked up, she saw that more searchers had returned, and Sam had somehow been separated from her. The rest of her team had also melted into the crowd, and, though Annie pushed her way to the refreshments, she couldn't find them again.

Suddenly, all she could hear were the voices of strangers speculating on what the press were about to be told. She felt tired and her legs ached. The tent was stuffy, and she looked out and saw only tight groups of people chatting together and walking away from the station. She felt cut adrift and self-conscious.

The rain had worsened as they'd been in the marquee, and Annie pulled her hood tight around her face. A cordon across the car park in front of the station forced her to walk up towards the road the long way around. On the other side of the barrier were the press with their booms and microphones and umbrellas, and she had to weave through numerous TV vans and police cars and clusters of onlookers to get to the road home.

Standing in front of the station was a girl with hair blowing around her in the rain like mist. Annie blinked and, for a moment, her insides lurched, as she thought it was Chloe stepping casually back into the world in front of this rage of crowd and media. It was a while before she noticed that the cameras were moving on their tripods to follow her, and she realised it was a reconstruction. Pretend Chloe walked alone across the car park and paused in front of where Annie's car had been parked to look behind her towards the steps up to the road, recreating the still from the CCTV. Then she carried on towards the row of shops. If Annie had been paying attention that night, Chloe would have been right in front of her car. She would have seen whatever Chloe had turned to look at, too. She kicked her boot into the jutting edge of a raised paving slab in frustration.

Pretend Chloe turned and walked back towards the ticket office, and Annie spotted the two girls who had been tying up posters with yellow ribbons the day before watching from a distance. Their heads were bowed together as if they were whispering to each other. Would the police officers talking to the press notice that now?

Annie tried again to think of anything she'd seen. How could it be possible that she was right there and should be able to help this time, wanted to help, but she just couldn't? Chloe's friends looked agitated. The taller one hooked her arm through the shorter girl's arm and pulled her back into the crowd. As they disappeared, Annie noticed Berman pacing near where the girls had been. His hands were shoved into the pockets of his coat, and Annie could almost feel the tension in his shoulders, the seams of his jacket stretched, as he watched Chloe's stand-in waiting to see if she was needed again. She looked around to see if Sam or Alex were nearby, so she could point it out to them, but she was standing on her own.

There was a mist thickening as Annie reached the road, and she almost fell straight into Paul.

'Look out, Annie.'

Typical that she would be on her own, after a day spent in the company of others, the one time she bumped into Paul in Westhurst. And at the end of a long day. She'd made some effort with her hair that morning, even putting on a little make-up, but it would all be ruined now.

'What are you doing hanging around the station car park on a Sunday night?'

'Is there a law against it now?' She tried to inject a tone of humour into her voice, but it didn't work. She thought Paul nearly smiled though.

'I guess that depends what you're doing, doesn't it?' He glanced down into the car park and saw the police cars and TV vans. 'Not that you'd be able to get away with much criminal activity tonight.'

Could he know about his flat? Annie smarted at his tone but then noticed the girl with him as she tightened her fingers through his. Annie's heart pinched a little.

'Hi, I'm Claire, and you are?' the girl asked, stepping in closer to Paul.

'Just someone I work with,' Paul cut in.

Just. The rain dripped from her hood and splattered down her front. Paul took in her chilled appearance and then looked down to the station. He raised an eyebrow and laughed.

'Don't tell me you've been out with that lot? I wouldn't

have put you down as the dutiful citizen. I mean, aren't you always telling me that crowds are too difficult for you?' Paul's eyes narrowed. 'Do you actually know the girl?'

It was unexpected to walk into Paul. Even considering they lived so close to each other, it almost never happened. Annie had dreamt that they might bump into each other sometime, close to the pub or the cafe so they could laugh and suggest a quick drink. Paul would be different with her away from work, more relaxed.

Annie looked from his face to Claire, whose head was now tilting back under her fur-fringed hood, her slick lips curling up. She looked immaculate, unlike Annie, whose hair was plastered around her face and lips chapped from the cold. Her stomach clenched, and she took a deep steadying breath.

'Well, it looks like you underestimated me then. I'm surprised you wouldn't have wanted to help, living so close.' She waved towards his apartment block. 'Doesn't it feel at all upsetting to you that a girl seems to have disappeared right beside where you live?'

Paul frowned at her. 'No more upsetting than the thought of someone breaking into my flat.' He seemed to be waiting for her to say something. 'Or bumping into my car.'

Was he trying to tell her that he knew she'd been in his flat? How could he possibly know? Annie sifted through her scant memories of the evening, but her head hurt too much to work it out. There was something unusually cold about his eyes in the streetlights, though. She really needed to get that wing mirror fixed quickly; not that he would ever notice that her car was damaged, too.

Claire shuffled and tugged slightly at his hand.

'Look, I've got to go and get warmed up, Paul. I'm as cold as if I'd been out all day.' She shot a look at the girl in her fur-trimmed hood. 'Which I have.' Annie felt the cold curling around her bones. If she could just get home and climb into a hot bath, she would still have a little bit of her weekend left. She raised her hand and turned to go. 'I'm tired, Paul. See you in the morning.' The woman beside him stiffened, and Annie felt a pulse of pleasure at her discomfort. Although, really, she should probably feel sorry for her.

'Yes, off you go.' He stepped closer and whispered in her ear. 'You're much safer at home.'

Was that menace in his voice or a warning? She cast her eyes around to see if anyone else was nearby. She glanced at Claire to see if she'd noticed, too. The curl in her lip suggested she had.

Annie saw the pity in her eyes and felt a lick of anger in her belly.

'Yes, I will, because, as an important witness, I have to look after myself, you know.'

The amusement on Paul's face wavered.

'Yes, I was in the car park when Chloe was captured on CCTV.' Saying it out loud felt good. 'So, you know, I might have been the last person to see her before she disappeared.'

The woman's eyes narrowed, and she moved closer to Paul who tucked her in close and laughed.

'Ah yes, is that what you were doing on Thursday night?' Paul looked up at the clouds as if there was a message for him there and sighed. The contents of Annie's stomach shifted as she remembered the sandstone baby she'd found in her coat pocket the next morning.

'So, did you see anything?' Claire's tone was sceptical, and, when Annie looked at her properly, she saw that she was older than she'd expected. Annie shoved the hair she knew would be tangled back into her hood. This wasn't how she wanted Paul to see her. Annie shook her head.

'I can't say. Look, I've got to go. I'm meeting friends.' He didn't need to know she'd been separated from her group.

Paul screwed his eyes up, studying her face, but Claire was tugging at his arm now. He sighed. 'Oh well, I do look forward to hearing more about that at work.'

Annie stood for a moment, watching them walking away towards Christchurch Road, wondering what she would say if Paul remembered to ask her about it in the morning. Her head throbbed. What had he said about Thursday night? Did he definitely know she'd been in his flat? How could that be possible? It was unlikely that he'd noticed the figurine was missing, but she needed to return it somehow. She put her hand in the pocket of her jacket, but the figurine was in her coat at home. Besides, there was no way of knowing how long Paul and this new girlfriend would stay out. Even if she'd had it with her, she couldn't risk going back into his flat now.

Her feet were stiff with the cold as she set off again, and, as she walked past The Cricketers, she slowed down and looked greedily into the warm room. She stopped altogether when she saw her own little search party sitting near the bar. So, they had liked her suggestion after all. They'd just got separated in the crowd. Her heart jumped a little and she walked in. This would shake Paul and that girl right out of her head.

'Oh, you did come! Did you think I'd gone on ahead?' she said when she got to the table.

The group stopped talking, and Annie felt happy when Sam stood up awkwardly. She knew he wouldn't have meant to leave her out. She looked around for a spare chair in the busy pub, but no one made space for her at the table.

Alex sighed heavily, and she felt doubt spoiling her pleasure at finding them.

'Look, Annie, the group felt that ...' Sam's eyes sort of flicked away from her as he spoke '... Well, it's just that we are all connected to Chloe in some way. We didn't think you'd be interested.'

It was a blow to the stomach. She knew a lie when she heard it.

Annie kept smiling, even though she knew it wasn't appropriate anymore. Moira and Jan both sat back in their seats with their arms tightly folded across their chests. Kieran was shaking his head.

'You ... you deliberately left me out?' Her voice faltered. 'But I worked just as hard to find her as any of you!' Annie said, thinking of all the pieces of litter that she'd picked up and feeling a rush of hurt blossoming on her cheeks. She could see the rest of the group watching.

Sam grimaced, as if he was trying to tell her he felt worse about this than she did. Her chest ached.

'Yes, but none of us can work out why you joined the search, Annie.' Alex crossed his arms as he spoke. 'You don't seem to give a damn about Chloe.'

Moira sniffed.

'And you've always got another bloody question.' Kieran made his hands snap like crabs.

Annie stared at them. Had they all been talking about her behind her back? She did care about Chloe, she told herself. Every time a child went missing she cared, and Westhurst was her home, her chosen home.

'I just wanted to help,' Annie said.

Jan lent forward over the table. 'By trying to dig up dirt for whichever grubby little outlet you work for? Did you think we'd be fooled by that IT firm story?'

'What?'

Sam took her gently by the arm and led her away from the table. 'Look, think about how you would feel if you knew her.'

How dare they think she wouldn't know what it feels like.

Behind him, Annie saw Jan mouth a word to Moira, and a surge of anger overtook her. Words burst into her head, *evil, freak, devil child*. She shook Sam's arm off and walked back to the table leaning over into Jan's face.

'Do you know what?' she shouted. 'I've more business here than most of you. I was in the car park when she was taken, you know. That's why I came. I'm a key witness.' The words slipped out, hot and slick, before she could stop them, but it wiped the smirk off Jan's face. 'I'm more important to the search than any of you!'

'Christ, Annie, what did you see?' Sam asked, his tone part olive branch, part challenge.

Annie had the sensation of a thousand eyes in the pub boring into her. A huge vacuum swallowed up the noise and held her trapped. She couldn't think how to answer. The blood that had flooded to her face drained away just as quickly.

'I can't tell you,' she said. She just wanted to leave now, too many people were watching her.

'Goodness, sorry Annie, we thought …' Moira looked at her as if Annie might be able to produce Chloe from her pocket, hope and surprise and disbelief shining in her eyes. Kieran raised his eyes at Annie and shook his head. He was not so easily fooled. She felt her insides twist with the deceit of it, the hope she'd created in Moira gnawing at her, but, when she looked at Jan, she saw nothing but disbelief and contempt. Jan could probably see through the gloss into the devil's own soul.

'But have you actually spoken to the police?' Kieran's voice cut across Moira, too low for the rest of the pub to hear but loud in Annie's ears.

Annie backed away. She felt the prickling of a hundred

eyes on her back and turned for the door before her anger turned to tears.

Sam jumped up and followed her. Was he trying to let her know that he, at least, believed her? No, he just pulled the door open for her to go through. His expression was still and cold, and she felt it like a slap. 'You have told the police, Annie, haven't you?'

9

SUNDAY EVENING

The rain and tears mingled on her face as Annie ran from the pub, her jacket flapping where she'd left the zip undone. She pulled her hood close to her head, muffling the sound of the conversations that had restarted as she left. The humiliation of the moment cut into her as finely as the cold, like little shards of ice to her heart. All the time that she'd been thinking they were a team, a little force for good, working together to help Chloe, the others had been talking about her, judging her behaviour, assuming what exactly? She couldn't believe it. She'd gone the extra mile to pick up the litter. They were right that she didn't know Chloe, but didn't that make her more worthy of respect? That she would spend her weekend searching for a complete stranger?

What did they think she was there for? Gathering information? Why would she do that? It hurt to think that even Sam might doubt her intentions. It wasn't unusual for her to experience the dislike of others but, just for the last day, she'd begun to hope it might be different. She put her hands to her head to block it all out.

A horn blared and the driver lowered his window to shout at her. Annie hadn't even looked up before she stepped into the road. The hazard lights flickered around the building site in the rain, but Annie couldn't hear anything except the rushing of blood in her ears. She pushed the hood off her face and let the rain trickle down the back of her neck, her hair clinging to her cheeks. At the lamp post where she'd spoken to the girls the day before, the ribbon was plastered against the metal, and the poster itself was soggy and streaked with ink that no longer made any sense. Annie pulled another sheet from her pocket without thinking and tucked it under the ribbon with clumsy fingers. The paper rucked up and tore in several places and disintegrated before her eyes.

Chloe's eyes stared back over her shoulder at Annie, mocking her. 'I want to go home, Annie.' The paper buckled and sagged as the rain rolled down and soaked through, sliding Chloe's face from the page. 'Don't leave me here, Annie.' She stared at Chloe's erasure until a passing car sent a sheet of muddy water over her legs from the puddle swollen over the drain. She continued down the hill, slipping from one pool of lamplight to the next under the murky sky. The headlights of passing cars jagged out from puddles to shiny pavement. Above, the dark sky was vast and distant through the mist.

Annie had tried so hard, been so determined to help. How could they have all turned on her, even Sam? What did they mean she was digging up information for work? That made no sense. Unless Paul had said something to them. Maybe he knew them, was just pretending surprise when he saw her. He'd probably just left the pub. That made more sense. Paul had been poisoning them against her. She pushed the wet hair out of her eyes.

Of course, he hadn't, that was just the paranoia. How would he even have known she'd been with them? That woman didn't look as if she would have spent time hanging around while Paul's attention was elsewhere either. Claire probably wasn't the sort of girl you could just brush off.

What could any of them really have said about her anyway? Nothing true. None of them really knew anything about her — no one did. She made sure of that.

Annie should be warning people about them, not the other way round! Kieran with his aggression and Jan and Moira wilfully misunderstanding. It was the thought of Sam that hurt the most. He was probably too influenced by Alex, who shadowed him everywhere. Perhaps Annie should try and talk to Sam on his own about that. That kind of friendship can be dangerous, where one person was trying to control others. First though, she had to prove to Sam she wasn't whatever they thought she was.

A branch, cracked and gnarly with age, had sheared off an oak on the other side of the road and a car swerved to avoid it, almost mounting the pavement in front of Annie. Her heart rattled against her ribs. It was the only warm part of her body. She needed to concentrate on getting home.

The light was on in her neighbour's lounge, and she could see the backs of their heads silhouetted in front of the flickering TV screen. How wonderful it would be to join them. How special it would be to have someone to ask about your day, who listens when you need to talk and is happy with silence when you don't. She walked up to their front door, her body shaking with rage.

They were nice people. In fact, they were the only people she spoke to with any regularity other than Lauren and her mum. She paused. They'd let her in if they knew how upset she was. She felt so deeply sorry about everything, but mostly that her attempt to do the right thing had backfired, made everything worse. But she saw her reflection in the glazed panel. She looked back at herself, wild-eyed, bedraggled, shoulders slumped in defeat, and her hand couldn't press the doorbell. What if they saw what the others saw? What if they decided she was a fraud and a freak, too? She turned away and walked up to her own front door.

She left her wet clothes lying on the floor by the door and poured herself a glass of wine. There was a message on her home phone from her mother. The only person who ever rang it.

'Are you there? I'm worried about you. Pick up, please.'

Annie deleted it.

* * *

'Well, did you take it?' Her mother's face is screwed up, and Lottie steps back a little. She shakes her head, keeping her fingers firmly crossed behind her back. 'I had five pounds in here and it's gone.'

Lottie knows her mother would be furious, because there's never enough money. Even if her mother still had the five pounds, it wouldn't be enough. But she says nothing, because she's given her word to the others. And her parents are bound to be so pleased with her if she comes home with Pisky gold that they'll forget all about five pounds.

Her mother crosses the kitchen and bends over so that she is Lottie's height. Her breath smells of the KitKat that she and Lottie have just shared. 'I'm sick and tired of things going missing around here.' Lottie backs herself up against the kitchen units. 'You'd better not be going to tell me it was the bloody Piskies again, because I've had enough of that, too. It's like some kind of built-in excuse around here, and I don't like it.'

Lottie keeps her mouth shut and concentrates on thinking about the Pisky gold. It might even be enough to take that holiday her mother always talked about.

In her bedroom, Lottie checks that the rolled-up five-pound note is still hidden inside her slipper. She slides it carefully inside the spelling book in her school bag, so that she can hand it to Bronnen and Gwen in the morning. She can hardly believe they know how to contact the Piskies and will help her. It's like a dream come true.

She waits for her mother to say she can go back downstairs for dinner, but she never comes. Lottie feels a little sick that she's upset her mother so much. She wishes she could tell her what she's doing, but Bronnen said it would spoil everything if she did.

When her dad brings in a plate of toast, her stomach churns with hunger. She stands up on the bed and hugs him. He gives her a quick squeeze back and sits down, moving Purple Ted out of the way.

'Please, tell me the truth, Lottie.'

She puts some toast in her mouth quickly and shrugs.

'The thing is, if it wasn't you that took the five pounds, then your mum is going to think someone at work took it out of her purse. What if she goes into work tomorrow and accuses someone there of stealing? It's a serious thing for a grown-up to ask.'

'Maybe she just lost it.' Why can't her mum just believe that? Her father watches her carefully. He has dark patches under his eyes, and the crinkly lines around them sag with tiredness. 'Or it might have been the Piskies, Daddy. They're always up to something.'

Her father frowns. He's the one who told her the stories about the Piskies and the giants and the mermaids. He tells excellent funny stories, and everyone loves to hear them. Once he'd told her he thought Piskies were more real than the tooth fairy. She throws herself into his arms, so he won't stay cross with her for long.

'Is everything all right, Lottie?' He picks up Purple Ted and tucks him into bed beside her when he lays her down. 'Mum says that Bronnen girl has started turning up to walk you to school. She's not bullying you, is she?'

'No, 'course not. She's my friend, actually.' Lottie sticks her chin out and her dad nods.

'Okay. It's just a bit unusual for an older child to hang around with a much younger one.'

'I have to hang around with Tegen, and she's practically a baby.'

Her Dad picks up her hand. 'Is it possible you picked up that money by mistake, sweetheart? Maybe we could have a quick look in your room?'

'No! Why don't you ever believe me? You never listen to me!' Lottie pretends to screw her eyes up tight, so he won't keep asking. She hears him sigh, and then the bed creaks as he gets up and walks to the door. Lottie opens her eyes just in time to see his back walking out.

If only she could tell them what she's doing, they would be so proud. She clasps her hands together with the thrill she'll give them when she brings the Pisky gold home. But Bronnen and Gwen had been very clear that it wouldn't work if she told even one person.

'It won't be a proper trial of your faith otherwise, right?' they said.

* * *

Annie sat in the dark and watched the downpour bending the smaller branches of the acer outside. As the rain landed, the boughs slanted towards the ground until the drops gathered and rolled off, sending the twig flying upwards only to be weighed down again and again. Annie's phone pinged on the sofa beside her as the threads she followed reacted to the televised reconstruction.

Her whole body ached despite the hot bath she'd had, and her eyes felt dry and raw from tears. The evening seemed to last forever. Annie snorted and took another glug of wine. She picked up her phone and flicked through the news reports. Neither Chloe nor any of her possessions had been found during the search. Police were now working on the theory that she must have left the area in a vehicle. They were appealing for any witnesses near the station at the time of her disappearance to come forward so that they and their cars could be eliminated from the enquiry. Annie shot her hand up — 'Yes, me! I was there!' — and then sagged back down onto the sofa. The CCTV image of Chloe walking across the front of the station was shown again. The outline of the broken wing mirror taunted her.

She closed her eyes, trying to remember the journey home on Thursday night. There'd been a conference with those awful networking drinks afterwards, waiters wandering around carrying trays of drinks that sparkled as they moved. Annie hated networking drinks. It wasn't even her job really, but Paul had insisted that the whole team show their faces. She'd found a little spot near the door, so she could catch the fresh drinks as they were brought through and watch the rest of the room. It was precisely her idea of hell, and Paul knew it. Lots of people, faux happy faces, and an obligation to talk to strangers. If she hadn't been so determined to please him, she would have sneaked off without telling anyone. Now and then, she'd caught sight of Paul, smiling and shaking hands as he wandered around the room.

She'd just grabbed another glass of something fizzy, the bubbles popping in her head, when Paul appeared beside her.

'You're supposed to be talking to people, Annie. The company is sponsoring these drinks, and you need to get out there and get some leads.'

Adrian was standing behind him looking through the business cards in his hand.

Annie took a deep drink and smiled at Paul. 'Why don't I talk to you? Or better still, you could talk to me?'

Paul sighed and glanced back at Adrian. 'Annie, God, not now.' He stepped a bit closer so that only Annie could hear what he was saying. 'This really isn't appropriate. You're a good worker. Reliable. And I don't want to lose you.' Annie put a hand out towards his chest, but Paul stepped back quickly. 'But I don't want a relationship with you, and this is inappropriate.'

'Is it?' Annie waved her glass at Adrian and a little swirled over the sides. 'Maybe we should ask what Adrian thinks.'

Paul grabbed her elbow and started walking her towards the exit. 'Jesus, you're drunk. Time to go home.'

Annie yanked her arm out of Paul's grip and tottered back in her heels tipping up a table. Glasses fell and little rivulets of wine and orange juice dribbled over the edge. She grabbed for purchase and her hand came away sticky.

Jenna and the others had joined Adrian. They were watching her with wide eyes. Good. It was about time they found out what was going on. All the times he'd invited her into his office on her own for a chat about the numbers. All the times he'd sat on her desk while checking the sales reports, chatting and joking. Sure, he chatted with everyone, but she could see it was just a front. He knew Annie wasn't the sort of girl to mess around with. She was serious. It was deceitful to pretend otherwise. And now he was being cowardly. Hadn't he manipulated her affections? She caught a sob and blinked at the ceiling. She didn't want them to think he'd got to her, but she wasn't going to let him get away with it, even if it destroyed her, because wasn't she destroyed already?

Then, Paul was right in front of her holding her by the shoulders. 'You will not do this here, Annie,' he breathed in her ear and, putting an arm around her shoulders, held her up as he walked them both to the door.

'Is she all right, Paul?' Was that Jenna? Another woman would recognise what he'd been doing. Paul muttered something about Annie and medication, and the woman went away again.

'Wait, don't leave me with him!' she shouted, and then Paul had propelled her out to the pavement and someone put her coat around her and he bundled her into a cab. 'Waterloo!' he called to the driver and clicked the door shut.

Annie rang Lauren from the train. She really needed someone to keep track of this. 'I'm not going to let him just wave me away, Lauren. It shouldn't be allowed.' Lauren sounded far away on the phone, as if she was disappearing down a long tunnel. 'I'm going to confront him, even if I have to turn up at his bloody flat!'

Annie could only really remember snatches of their conversation. She burned at the thought of the team watching her stumble over and tip up the table because they would dismiss her as a drunk, but she didn't regret confronting Paul.

The rest of the journey home was a bit of a blur. Sounds on the platform, drinking coffee in Paul's flat without him, footsteps coming towards her. Speeding out of the station car park.

The lights of her car had been pretty much pointed straight at where Chloe had walked. If someone had picked her up in front of the station, then Annie would have seen it. If she could just focus, maybe she did know something that would help. She lay down and breathed deeply. Didn't they used to hypnotise people to uncover hidden memories? Perhaps that would work. Perhaps she should find out.

The girl had walked right across the front of her car when she was sitting in it. The headlights were very clearly on in the picture, the dazzle obscuring her registration plate, but the shape of the wing mirror, with the tape wound around it was silhouetted in the light from the streetlight behind.

She wished she could be the person who helped the police

find Chloe Hill. She closed her eyes and imagined how elated her parents would be to see their daughter, and how grateful they'd feel toward whoever brought her home. That tall man, their friend, would be pleased, too, but how sweet it would be to tell Sam. It would be good to tell Paul, too. Perhaps he would see her in a completely different light. Then she remembered the woman with him earlier. She angrily wiped the tears from her face and scrolled down her contacts for Lauren.

'You didn't find her then. I've just seen the news.'

Annie sobbed.

'Oh, come on, Annie, it isn't your fault. You've been out there all weekend with a bunch of strangers looking for her.'

'They think I'm a freak. I was just trying to help, I really was, and I thought I might have made some friends, but they shunned me, Lauren. They didn't want me near them, went out of their way to exclude me. Humiliated me in front of the whole pub.'

Lauren listened to Annie for a few minutes and then broke in when Annie took breath.

'For goodness sake, Annie, take a breath. Sounds like you're taking this way too personally. They're probably all just tired and stressed out.'

'The thing is … I panicked, and I told them I'm an important witness.' Annie needed Lauren to understand.

'What? Are you?' Lauren's voice rose. She sounded really intrigued, and it gave Annie a little moment of warmth. She wasn't usually the interesting one.

'Well, I don't know. I was there, so I could be the last person to have seen her.'

'Did you see her?'

Annie felt the shame of her blank memory again.

'I'm not sure, Lauren. I can't remember. But you can clearly see the lights of my car in that CCTV image.'

'Well, you know you should at least tell the police. You do know that, don't you?'

Annie nodded into the phone.

'You know they'll think it suspicious if you don't contact them?'

Yes, she did know. She'd been hoping they might not have noticed.

She lay back down on the sofa, her head aching. The headlights of passing cars created a moving band of light across the ceiling, one, two, three.

No one could have seen Annie in the station car park, or she would already have been contacted by the police. There was no reason to draw attention to herself, and she had plenty of reasons not to. She made tea and watched the tea bag stain the water, trails forming until she swirled it with the spoon and topped up with milk. The mug moved slightly on its own, as if recoiling from her hand. Somebody had once told her it was just water trapped underneath. She stared at the mug; it was one of a cheap set she'd bought when she first moved in.

She had the clearest sensation that things were slipping away from her no matter how hard she reached. The search party, her own team, had pulled away. It hurt. That woman with the fur round her face had pulled at Paul's hand until they left. Paul did pause though, when she said she knew something. There was a flicker of interest in his eyes when she said she was a witness. That was something. A flicker of interest. Like Lauren's.

Annie wondered what she could do to see that again. She would have to step out of the shadows and stop hiding. The curtains in the lounge were not quite pulled. As she walked over to tug them shut, the slick of limescale on her tea slid around her mug as it tipped. She turned and stopped.

'Of course, I'm happy to help as much as I can. That poor girl, if only I'd realised what was happening at the time.'

It felt okay, like she was taking control, making a brave stand.

She placed the mug down carefully and smoothed out the fabric of her trousers as she sat. Her reflection in the polished wood of the table looked back at her. Her eyes were wide, a tight smile stretched her lips, her mother's face.

'It's just that it's taken me a little while to realise that what I saw might be relevant.' She shook her head a little. *'No, no,'* she murmured, *'that I could be of the tiniest bit of help is enough.'*

She sat back in the chair and pulled her telephone towards her. She held it in her left hand as she pressed each number from the poster carefully.

'Hello. Yes, yes, I do have some information. Annie Marwood. Yes. 29 Oak Lane. Lane, yes. Yes, the number I'm calling from, yes. Well,' she took a breath, 'I think I'm the last person to see Chloe Hills.'

10

MONDAY MORNING

The alarm pierced Annie's dreams, and she rolled over to hit snooze, wishing she could ignore it altogether. Her back ached from spending the weekend bending down to search the paths but, at the back of her mind, like a lingering dream, was a small, warm feeling. She'd spent the weekend doing something useful, purposeful, and she had put her own fear, safety even, aside to call the missing persons helpline. She swung her legs out of bed. If she bumped into Sam or Paul on her way to the station, she could now tell them she really was part of the investigation.

In fact, the woman on the phone had sounded grateful for her call, said it was important that they knew who was in the car park that night, even if Annie didn't remember seeing Chloe. They'd come back to her if they needed anything else. Annie had done her duty, and it felt good. The woman hadn't pressed her for any more information, and Annie had felt a little foolish for worrying that the police might be suspicious of her. Of course, there wasn't any reason why they should be.

They wouldn't be interested in anything other than finding Chloe.

She flicked through her phone as she ate breakfast, half hoping there would be an announcement.

A vital piece of information has come in from a member of the public that police believe will crack the case wide open.

It was a nice dream, all these people desperately worried and searching for Chloe, and she might be the one to help. She imagined telling Sam, watching his smile spread. Maybe he would put an arm around her shoulders as he told the others and welcomed her back into the team. She shook the image away and dressed carefully.

Overnight, more yellow ribbons had been tied to the trees and fences along the route, and they fluttered gaily in the last wisps of wind. Annie enjoyed the bracing temperature, knowing that she would soon be packed onto a stuffy train.

When she reached the platform, though, the atmosphere was tense, and her buoyant mood deflated. Annie considered her fellow passengers, as careful to avoid eye contact as everyone else was. She wondered if anyone standing here now in their suits and working clothes had been in the search party yesterday. Perhaps they shared the stiff legs and sore back that she had. Or had any of them been on that same late train home with her on Thursday night? Or been in the car park while she sat in her car and looked away while Chloe passed and then was spirited away? Her cheeks flushed with remorse for her lack of attention.

That was not going to happen again. To her left was a white man, chubby, about 5'10 in a grey suit, and beside him a black lady, almost as tall as the man, in a long green skirt and black puffer jacket. Annie would memorise everyone she saw from now on, just in case. She scanned the platform resisting the urge to put her head in her phone for the latest news, despite the noise of her notifications.

At the office, Annie dropped her bag under her desk and slipped into her chair. There was a companionable hum around her as colleagues exchanged the highlights of their weekends. Annie was a ghost — the effort to keep her past out of sight left her present invisible, too. She told herself that all she really missed was a bit of inane chatter, but, in that moment, that morning, with news she could share, the loneliness overwhelmed her. When Paul had told her not to go to the pub on Friday, not a single one of them had been able to meet her eye.

She'd watched the morning rituals enough to know they centred around hot drinks. Eventually, her desire to show them all Good Annie, who'd volunteered in the cold all weekend and overcome her own fears to step up as a witness, won out.

'Would anyone like tea?' she offered, and a few surprised faces turned towards her. She lingered when she delivered each mug hoping to be drawn into conversation. Eventually, she announced, 'Of course, my weekend was spent looking for that poor lost schoolgirl. You know, Chloe Hills.' She kept talking as she returned to her desk. 'There was quite a crowd there! Westhurst is a very community-spirited place.'

'Have you told everyone that you're a vital witness, too?' Paul strode past with his coat billowing behind him and an amused smile stretching across his face.

It didn't matter how long they worked together or how long they lived in the same village, Annie never travelled on the same train as Paul. She wondered if he kept watch for her out of the window of his flat to check she was safely past before he sauntered down to the station to get the later train each morning. Another little twist of the knife. Annie rolled her eyes at his back in a way that she hoped was scornful and dismissive. Today, she wasn't going to waste time on Paul. She turned back to her screen.

But when Jenna from accounts walked by Annie's desk later, she paused and asked about Chloe Hills, and Annie told her what a marvellous sense of community there'd been, how wonderful it was to be part of such a collective effort for good.

'What did the police say? Do you know anyone who knows her?' Jenna was full of questions.

When it got too much, Annie remembered to ask Jenna about her weekend, too.

'Oh,' Jenna said, 'just the usual. Drinks with friends on Friday, a party on Saturday.' She wandered back to her desk, and Annie returned to her work, a little warm curl of something uncoiling inside her.

She risked checking her phone when Paul went into a meeting to see if there was any more news. There were reports that people were leaving asthma inhalers in different places and posting images of them on Instagram and Snapchat, like some kind of geocaching game. There was another argument raging online about whether kids might find them and be in danger of overdosing on Salbutamol. It seemed daft to Annie. If Chloe could get to one of these places to pick up the inhaler, then she could get home. It would be quite a job to clear them all up, too.

Then she read the message from Chloe's mother.

If you have Chloe, it's very important that she has an inhaler. We know you don't want to hurt her, but Chloe needs medical help if she has an attack, so the best thing is to let her come home. Or you can just call the helpline and let us know where she is.

Mrs Hills thought Chloe had been abducted. It was a sobering thought. If someone had taken Chloe, would they care enough to make sure she had an inhaler? Perhaps, if they wanted her to live. Annie shuddered. Had the police already ruled out the possibility that the girl had just run away? Annie wondered what they knew.

There was a report that the police were visiting Chloe's school to talk to her classmates, and right there was a photo of two girls in uniform who Annie recognised as the girls hanging up posters. Their names were Hannah and Megan, and it was Hannah's house that Chloe had been to on the night she went missing. Annie looked closely. Megan was the one who had spoken to Annie, the more confident of the two, and it was Hannah who'd hidden behind her. There was a quote from another child describing the three friends as 'often in trouble recently' and 'always whispering in corners'.

It was about time the police got around to talking to them. Annie thought of the nervous way that Hannah had coiled her leg around the other and their reluctance to talk. Chloe's friends were bound to know something. Annie felt the cold seep back into her stomach. The police should have talked to them first. Annie hoped they were being watched, felt an urge to tell the police to take a closer look, see past their fake concern. Annie closed her eyes and tried to place the girls in the station car park on Thursday night. A tiny fragment of information seemed to be just out of reach, but she couldn't retrieve it however hard she tried. The next article included a reverent interview with the head teacher about the special measures the school had put in place and the number of counsellors they'd brought in to help Chloe's classmates cope.

Another slew of experts and commentators fell over themselves to talk about the emotional damage to the children as they waited for news.

Wait until they find out what really happened. If they ever do, Annie thought.

11

MONDAY AFTERNOON

T hrough the windows, the world seemed drained. The sky was the greyscale of any winter afternoon; the promise of sun already broken. In the nearest corner of the frame, Annie could see a cobweb only by the glassy drops of water beading along its strands. She was trying to listen to the monthly sales report, but she was distracted absolutely by the little pearls of light that danced erratically around the struggling fly.

Her focus was brought back into the room as Adrian knocked his stacked reports off the table. Annie bent down to help pick them up to avoid Paul's stare. He'd been watching her on and off all morning. Maybe he could tell her mind was elsewhere. She'd kept thinking about those girls, Hannah and Megan, Chloe's friends. Annie's sixth sense was afire with warnings about them.

The door to the meeting room opened and Jenna called her out.

'Very important phone call, Annie.' Jenna's eyes were wide,

and Annie immediately thought of her mother. She swept her pen and pad off the table and rushed out.

'Miss Marwood? This is Detective Sergeant Miller from the Chloe Hills missing persons team.'

The small dark hole waiting in Annie's stomach expanded, and she felt her face flush with shame. She hadn't wanted them to call her back. It would be a terrible waste of their time. Of course, somebody must know something, and she really wished it was her, but it wasn't. Miller's voice sounded loud in the quiet office.

'Yes, hello,' she whispered into the receiver.

Jenna stood watching, and Annie flapped her hand at her in a bid for privacy.

'You rang to say that you were in the station car park the night Chloe Hills went missing. We'd like you to come into the station to make a statement.'

'No!' Annie could feel panic rising. She pushed her knuckles into her forehead and tried to think.

'Oh, is this not Annie Marwood?'

'Yes, sorry, this is Annie.'

'But you didn't call?'

'No, yes! I did call but,' she whispered, 'I can't come into the station. Uh, I want to help obviously, I mean why else would I call? I just can't come to the station.' She scratched at the marks on her desk. 'It's a phobia thing.' Painful memories surfaced and her stomach reeled. The small boxy rooms and the bright lights and the smell of disinfectant and the nausea and the shouting.

DS Miller was silent for a moment. 'Like agoraphobia?'

'Yes, sort of.' She glanced up to check that Jenna had gone back to her desk. 'I do want to help, but, you know, I didn't really see anything anyway. I just thought I should say that I was there.' She took a shaky breath. 'You know, so you can eliminate me from your enquiries. That's what you do, isn't it?'

'We really do need to interview you. It's possible that you noticed something that you don't realise is important.'

Annie glanced towards the conference room. She couldn't ask the police to come to the office, however impressed the others might be. She couldn't risk Paul, or anyone else, telling them how drunk she'd been on Thursday night, because she'd driven home from the station. She cursed her stupidity. She should never have called.

'Hello? Annie?'

She needed to say something. Annie checked her watch and looked across to the meeting room. The meeting hadn't finished, and she really should go back in, especially as she didn't have anything useful to say to the police. Through the strip of glazing in the door, she saw Paul sit back and laugh, his hands behind his head.

'Could you come to me instead? Is that allowed? I can get home for six o'clock if I leave now. It's just it would be so much better for me.' She heard someone whispering in the background.

'Okay, we can come to you. Six o'clock?'

'Yes, thank you so much. I can do that.'

Jenna came rushing over as soon as she put the phone down. Then, Annie remembered that she'd left the sandstone figure on the table in her lounge. There was no reason to think that Paul had even missed it, but she felt desperate to get it out of sight, just in case.

'Look, could you tell Paul that I have to go? That was the police.'

Jenna nodded, wide-eyed. Annie never left early, never took sick leave, never did anything noticeable really.

'Tell him it's about that missing girl, something I saw. Obviously, it's urgent.'

Annie's hands shook as she turned her screen off, pulled her bag out, and left the office, conscious of Jenna's eyes prickling at the back of her neck. She flew down the stairs and strode down Holborn Viaduct towards Waterloo, too highly strung to wait for the bus. As she crossed Waterloo Bridge, the wind hit her in the face and slapped her coat back around her legs. A river bus appeared from under the bridge, and, for a moment, Annie thought of soaring off the wall and letting the currents carry her away out to sea. Just for a moment.

The train carriage was almost empty, and Annie kicked off her shoes and curled up in the corner to send Lauren a text.

God, Lauren, the police are actually going to interview me.

Annie wasn't often on the train at this time of day. The emptiness of the carriage felt strange. The dirt on the windows was more obvious, and it turned the pale sun into a mustardy smear. She closed her eyes, trying to sort out what she would say.

In the first place, she had to explain why she'd rung them when she hadn't seen anything. Could they charge her with wasting police time? Obstruction of justice or something? How would she make them believe that she really hadn't seen anything, even though Chloe had been right in front of her? She really didn't want them to know she'd driven home drunk, because she'd lose her licence. She needed her car. What if she needed to escape again? She put her shoulders back and tried to slow her heart down. There was no need for them to know she'd been drinking.

Why, what have you done? Only kidding! Well done.

Annie wished she could talk it all through with Lauren, but Lauren was so busy. And how could she explain the uneasy sensation of guilt she felt about that evening? The fact that there was a blank where the memory of Chloe should be? She tried to remember exactly what she'd said on the phone about her car. If DS Miller turned up in uniform, she'd probably fall apart, so she had to have a plan. It wasn't about having a story, just about not messing it up. Everyone always says they feel guilty when they see a police officer, but not everyone actually is.

The door connecting to the next carriage clanged open, and Annie jumped. A young man, can of beer in hand, walked past her, staggering a little as the train lurched on the tracks. When he reached the rear of the train, he swore loudly, and Annie could feel him looking around. She sank a little further back into her seat. Was there anyone else in the carriage with her? She could hear nothing but the man, muttering unintelligibly. He paused when he reached Annie again.

'You'd think there'd be some bloody toilets, eh?'

Annie waved to the sign with the arrow pointing back the way he'd come from. He swore again and went back through, letting the door slam behind him. Shaking, she stood up and looked around. She was completely alone as far as she could tell.

Had she been alone when she got off the train on Thursday night? Surely, she would have noticed if no one else had got off the train at Westhurst? It was a busy station. But she hadn't even noticed that she was alone in the carriage just now until that man burst through the door. It was daylight, though, she told herself. She would have been more alert late at night. The platform was lit at intervals, but anyone walking the full length of it would have been stepping in and out of the shadows, hidden one moment and there the next. Annie would have noticed normally, been finely attuned to any possibility that someone might be watching her, except she'd been drunk. As hard as she tried, all she could remember was sitting in her car, the fury racing through her veins, and then she was in Paul's flat. She was definitely alone then.

Annie needed to come up with an explanation of how she was clearly in her car when Chloe passed in front of it, but she hadn't seen the girl. She didn't want to say that she'd been too drunk to remember, so inebriated that she'd broken into her supervisor's house and carried out some unintentional thievery. What could she say?

If there was someone else on her train, then they must surely have come forward, too. Annie's hands shook as she realised they might have seen her, maybe had already given the police a good description of Annie or her car. Maybe she'd phoned the police just in time before they'd tracked her down. She glanced over her shoulder, checking that no one had appeared behind her. At least she had made the phone call herself. If there had been somebody else there and that other person hadn't come forward, then Annie would assume they were hiding something. The hairs on the back of her neck stood up. Of course, if the other person had been focused on Chloe, they might not have noticed Annie.

There was another gate from the platform that was also open after the ticket office closed. Annie never used it because it came out at the far end of the car park where the lighting was poor and the branches of the trees hung down, shaking in the wind. The CCTV wouldn't have picked up anybody waiting in the dark down there, and Annie wouldn't have noticed them either.

The train pulled in. The lights shone dimly in the twilight

and flickered in the puddles. Leaves blew up around Annie's ankles as she walked, and she scanned the empty platform. She was alone now. She glanced towards the far end of the car park as she left the station, and a shadow moved in the corner of her eye. By the time she reached the road, she was almost running.

MONDAY EVENING

'So, Annie, why don't you tell us what you saw?' DS Miller settled back into the cushions of Annie's sofa and crossed his legs. 'Take your time.' He seemed completely at ease, his sweater a calming blend of blues and in direct contrast to the business-like posture of DC Singh, who had pulled out a chair at Annie's small table. She'd laid out a notebook and watch in front of her and sat, pen in hand, poised to write down everything Annie said.

Annie took a deep breath and tried to shut off the voice in her head that told her to run. They were in her home, on her terms; it was as good as it could be. She thought about Sam and imagined telling him that she'd been interviewed by the police, and that helped. He'd look at her differently then. Maybe he'd tell the others, too, and if she saw them another time they'd invite her to join them.

She tried to take herself back to Thursday night. She could still feel the sickening humiliation of Paul pushing her out of the conference hotel in front of her colleagues. The journey home was then a surreal jumble of images. The lights flashing past the train window were streaky in the dark.

'Annie?' DS Miller shifted a little, and she realised he was still waiting for her to speak.

'Yes, sorry. Well, actually I don't really remember seeing Chloe as such, it was just that I was in the car park at the same time.'

The pen that DC Singh was using made a soft rasping noise as she made notes. She lifted her head to look at Annie, waiting for her to continue.

'Oh, I just mean that I was in my car at the time Chloe was there. I assumed you might just need to rule me out as a suspect, ha ha. I'm sorry to have wasted your time.' Annie raised her hands, watching the pen moving across Singh's pad. 'Look, I really wish I could help. I joined the search party, you know.' Annie bit down on her lip to stop the stream of words.

Miller smiled and lent forward. 'Shall we go back a step or two, see if that helps jog your memory? It's possible you noticed something that doesn't seem important to you but will be crucial to the investigation.'

Annie nodded, clasping her hands together to mask the shaking. It was possible there was something useful among the snatches of memory she was aware of.

'Where had you been?'

Annie described the conference, how she was responsible for getting all the promotional materials there and for looking after all the salespeople, and that Paul had made her attend the drinks afterwards. 'I told him it wasn't really my thing, but he insisted.' She carefully omitted her altercation with Paul. 'It was all pretty tiring, actually.'

'And had you had much to drink?'

Singh looked up for Annie's answer, so she just shook her head.

'How much would you say, Annie?'

Annie had calculated the drink-drive limits earlier. 'Two small glasses of wine, but I'd finished my second more than an hour before I got off the train.' She tried to smile at both of them, as if she was habitually that precise about such details. In fact, she usually was able to be absolutely precise about what she did, as her days followed the same structure, and even the tiniest deviation from the norm would stand out. 'It's difficult not to have anything at all to drink at these things.' She smiled. It wasn't relevant to the hunt for Chloe if she'd been over the limit when she drove home, she told herself.

The focus of DC Singh was unnerving, and especially the way she seemed to be recording much more in her notebook than Annie was actually saying. Was she adding her own thoughts about Annie? DS Miller shifted and nodding encouragingly. Annie focused on him, counting the different shades of blue on his jumper to slow her thoughts. One slip of control and she'd start gabbling and end up confessing to abducting Chloe. The words bubbled at the back of her throat. *I'm guilty, I'm guilty.'* But she wasn't, was she? Focus.

They asked about her journey to Waterloo and the train home.

She took a taxi. (*They're only doing their job, Annie.*)

Yes, she'd caught the next available train from Waterloo. (*I've done nothing wrong.*)

She didn't remember who else was in her carriage, because these journeys all merge into one when you take the same route every day. (*I'm only trying to help.*)

'And what time did the train arrive at Westhurst?'

Annie felt her forehead screw up without her permission. If Chloe had left her friend at the station at about 10pm then that had to be when Annie was in her car. Presumably, they already knew this. 'About 10pm, I guess? I don't remember checking.'

'Did you talk to anyone on the train or at the station, Annie? Who could confirm you were there?'

'No, who talks to people on trains?' Her laugh was a little shrill, and then she remembered. 'Oh. Not anybody on the train, but I made a call to a friend from the train. We just had a gossip, you know. She likes to know what I get up to. I mean, what I'm doing. Obviously, I wasn't up to anything.' She gasped for breath and tried to smile.

'We'll need her mobile number then, Annie.' DC Singh spoke for the first time.

Annie reeled the numbers off.

'Did you notice anyone else getting off the train with you at Westhurst?' DS Miller sat forward now and put his elbows on his knees. Annie could see how much he was willing her to have seen something useful. He looked like he was poised to leap up and rush away with her information so he could rescue Chloe from whatever trouble she was in.

Annie closed her eyes and tried to remember. There were always plenty of other people getting off the last train, but this was earlier, too late for commuters but too early for those who'd been out for the evening. It seemed unlikely that she would have been the only one to get off, but, then again, today she had been.

'It's so dark on that platform, but I think there were others. I just can't remember. I mean, not Chloe. I think I'd have remembered a young girl in the dark, ha ha.' Was that true? Annie always tried to make herself as invisible as possible. If Chloe had been doing the same, would she have been able to slip past in the shadows? Would anyone have noticed Annie even? 'If there were other passengers there, they must surely have got in touch with you too?' Annie frowned as she wondered what those other passengers might have told the police. 'I mean, unless you're thinking they took Chloe?'

Miller didn't reply for a moment. 'What makes you think there were other people there, if you can't actually remember them?' His expression shifted, and Annie was sorry she would have to disappoint him.

Annie shook her head. 'Well, it's just that there usually are. Honestly, if I wanted to abduct a girl, I wouldn't choose the station car park when a train had just got in. There are so many people around then. It's far more likely Chloe has just run away. Have you thought of that? Are you sure her friends don't know where she is?'

'We're just interested in what you saw right now, Annie. Did you notice anything when you got to the car park? Anybody waiting there, any voices, any car engines?'

'It was dark. I was in a rush to get home. Sorry.' Annie looked at their faces: Miller's seemed expectant and hopeful, but Singh frowned at her notebook.

Miller sat back among the cushions again. 'The thing is, Annie, in my experience, women travelling alone at night are usually hyper aware of those around them. It's not fair, but there it is. Is it possible you saw or heard something, but discounted it because you'd subconsciously ruled them out as a threat to yourself?'

Annie remembered hearing steps in the short cut to Paul's flat, but that couldn't have been somebody from her train. It was much later. But still. 'Yes, maybe. Footsteps, I don't know.'

Miller frowned. 'Okay, and how long were you in the car park?'

Singh lifted her head to wait for Annie's answer. Her expression made Annie uncomfortable, and she couldn't think how to answer.

'I'm really not sure. Sometimes I finish the crossword in

the car. Maybe that's why I didn't see anything.' She made herself shrug as lightly as she could. 'I'm a sucker for the crossword. Probably have the paper somewhere. If it's finished, that will be why. Usually only get three quarters done on the train.' Why hadn't she thought of that before? She got up to fish *The Standard* out of the basket by the fireplace.

'But you said you were in a rush to get home?' Singh spoke.

Annie blinked at her. 'Yes, yes, look, I'm sorry. I've been trying to think of reasons that might explain why I didn't notice Chloe when she was right in front of me. I would have called earlier, but I really didn't want to waste your time when I can't explain it.'

'How can you be so sure you were there at the same time?'

Annie fetched the poster from the fridge door and pointed out her car.

Miller shot a look that Annie couldn't decipher at Singh. 'The car with the headlights on?'

Annie nodded. There was silence for a while.

'I see. Well, thank you, Annie.' Miller uncrossed his legs and only just stopped himself from standing. 'Right, do you have any further questions, DC Singh?'

Singh made a show of reading back through her notes. Annie could feel her nerves stretching to their very limits in the silence. She needed them both to leave quickly before she lost it.

'Yes, you said that you left the conference drinks after eight and your boss saw you leave? Can you give me the name and contact details of your boss, please?'

Annie wondered if she should confess how much she'd really drunk before they spoke to Paul. Maybe they wouldn't ask though. They just wanted to confirm what time she left, didn't they? She looked up his number on her phone and handed it over. Singh made a note.

'I really do think you should speak to her friends.' Annie leant towards Miller, and he raised an eyebrow. 'You know, the two girls hanging up the posters. Hannah and Megan, I think. I spoke to them, and they seemed a bit off. Then, they were there at the reconstruction, skulking around a bit. Struck me as odd.' Annie looked at the two of them, waiting for them to say they were already investigating the girls.

Instead, DS Miller asked Annie to sign the notes DC Singh had taken and that they would be in touch again if they had any further questions. Annie's hand shook as she picked up the pen, and she almost forgot the way her signature went, completely unable to focus on the content of the form itself. She could feel Singh's steady gaze on her as she finished.

Miller walked to the front door with her while Singh gathered up her notebook and watch. Annie turned back in time to see Singh pick up the sandstone figure from where Annie had shoved it behind her handbag when she got home. She put it down carefully when she saw Annie looking and went out ahead of Miller.

'Well,' he said, 'we're so grateful that you've come forward. If you think of anything else, please call me at any time.' He passed a card to Annie, and she stood and watched them through the window as they got into their car.

* * *

Lottie sits on the bottom rung of the fence, resting her forehead against the top one. Bronnen and Gwen sit up above her, their legs swinging. They say she has to stay where she is until she's earnt her way up to the top with them. Lottie is too excited to be with them to mind; they're like Gods to her. Real life members of a secret Pisky Society. Besides, whatever they ask her to do is bound to be better than hanging around with little Tegen all day.

Everyone is frightened of Bronnen and Gwen at school, but here they are letting her join their gang. Lottie swells with pride.

Bronnen has tight red curls and freckles, and Lottie thinks she looks like a sunflower.

'You do know, we can't talk to you if any of our other friends see us?' Bronnen says. 'It's just the way things are.'

'Yes, you'll understand when you're older,' Gwen adds. Gwen has a pinched face and an older brother who slouches around down by the harbour with the other teenagers, getting in the way of the tourists and ruining the view, Lottie's father says.

Lottie watches the smaller pony grazing near a clump of lurid dandelions. Its tail swings through the air, trying to sweep away the flies that buzz around. Lottie wonders what ponies think about. They don't seem to do much, as far as she can tell.

'Tell me again what I have to do?'

Bronnen jumps down and stands in front of Lottie. 'So, Lottie, you have successfully completed the first challenge by bringing us tribute of five pounds.' Bronnen speaks in an important, boomy voice, and the curls shake around her face. 'This will be the second of the three challenges you need to complete to join the Trehaven Pisky Society. Your instructions are to wait until we have gone and then give these ponies their freedom, like any real Pisky would. You must tell no one what you've done, on pain of never being accepted into the society. You can only ever say that the Piskies did it.'

'And then will I be in the Society?'

Gwen makes a snorting noise, and Bronnen glares at her. She jabs at Gwen until she jumps off the fence and they both face Lottie. Gwen chews at a bit of skin on her finger and stares at Lottie's shoes.

'The secret rituals must be completed. We will tell you when a judgement has been made.' Bronnen dips her head formally, so that the sunlight fizzes off her curls.

Gwen takes her finger out of her mouth and lowers her face to Lottie's. 'And we never forgive tell-tales. Never.'

Lottie watches as the girls walk back down the road towards the village. They turn to salute before taking the footpath off the road, and Lottie gives them a wave. She wonders if there might be a real Pisky nearby. If there is, will they recognise what she's doing? The small pony shuffles over to the fence and thrusts its head towards Lottie. She can see herself reflected in the shiny globe of its eye.

'I have nothing for you,' she whispers.

The bolt on the gate is stiff, and she has to use both hands and put her back into it, as her dad would say, before it loosens. The smaller pony stops chewing and watches her, shaking the flies from his eyes as she swings the gate open.

'Well, go on then,' Lottie says. 'You're free now.'

13

TUESDAY MORNING

Annie slept badly, her dreams full of darkness and slippery rocks. Men searched around her and called out to each other. They were looking for something, something small and precious, but it kept disappearing so that they could never reach it. Annie could still see it, however far away it was. Annie could always see it, but she couldn't help the men. She'd promised not to tell.

In the small hours, Annie gave up trying to sleep and went downstairs. She poured a glass of the port someone had bought her in a Secret Santa the previous Christmas and sat in the dark. The silence was full, the fridge motor whirred, and the rain fell softly against the windows. She hugged her knees hard and tried to remember the conversation with DS Miller, picking at and turning over what she'd said.

The screen of her tablet threw out a hard light that made her squint. Annie searched the #BringChloeHome tag and scanned the messages for news. Chloe's family and friends sounded increasingly desperate. They'd recorded a fresh appeal to Chloe or her abductor and a small video walking around Westhurst pointing out the family's favourite places, stopping to look at the posters and ribbons that now covered lamp posts and fences all around the town. Annie recognised the waxed jacket and thinning hair of Jason Berman. He was always nearby, a hand on Mrs Hills' arm or a shoulder pressed against Mr Hills.

Annie studied their faces. She knew the police would have already looked at them closely, searched their home, probed their private life, and interviewed their friends and neighbours for any small detail that might show what sort of relationship they'd had with Chloe. It was hard for relationships to survive that sort of scrutiny and exposure.

Online, the recriminations were building up, the whispers of conspiracy and the accusations. The newspaper forums were full of sickening judgements about Chloe and her family.

I wouldn't let my twelve-year-old out that late without checking on her.
Look at her make-up!
They didn't even go and pick her up.
Look at the mother. She hasn't found her daughter, but she's found time to have her hair done.

Since the publicity of the search, a number of Facebook sites discussing the case had appeared. Amateur sleuths popped up on various online news fora, analysing every police statement and spinning theories about what had happened. Annie had to skim past the comparisons with previous cases, the Girl in the Suitcase, the Funfair Boys, The Babes in the Cave, and all the images of lost children laid out for entertainment. It was a sick way to sell advertising. There were actual discussions about visiting Westhurst to look at Chloe's home, the train station, and the places she went that sent shockwaves of fear and guilt through Annie. She wondered what kind of person would do that. Misery tourism her mother called it. *Don't ever get caught up in that sort of thing, Annie. Don't look back.*

Annie walked to the window and peered out. The road outside was empty and quiet. Chloe's family lived on the other side of town. Annie wondered if Mrs Hills was standing at another window looking down the street, hoping Chloe would appear.

Annie returned to the screen and searched for Hannah and Megan. They didn't seem to be commenting much on the #BringChloeHome group. Private message groups, probably, Annie thought. Or they already knew what had happened to Chloe, a little voice in Annie's head whispered. Perhaps they were too scared to speak. Annie wondered if DS Miller had listened to what she'd said about the girls. Perhaps, they'd already told him something useful and Chloe would be found today. That would be something to feel good about, Annie thought.

She dressed warmly and left for work before her usual time to make up for leaving early the day before. She didn't want to give Paul any chance to complain. It was hard applying for jobs with a birth certificate that showed a different name, and she didn't want to have to do that again. She slipped through the dark, heavy at the thought of how long the day would be. How would she bear it? The thought that she had to keep going until the evening, without sleep and without knowing what happened to Chloe, made her feel feverish. The girl could be anywhere. Annie pulled her coat a little closer and kept her arms free as she passed the deep hedges and dark building site.

There were only a few other passengers waiting on the platform. Annie felt the tension between them all, warily checking each other in the poor light. Was Chloe's abductor one of the people stood there that morning, casually going about their day? Had she already sat next to a murderer on a previous day? She felt taut and awkward.

When Annie got to her desk, already exhausted, Jenna jumped up to make her tea.

'Go on, then.' She perched on the edge of Annie's desk and looked around at the others, their faces turned to Annie for the first time. 'Tell us what happened with the police.'

Annie smiled at Jenna, trying to find some small pearl of information to offer up to her colleagues. They would all know she'd been called away by the police, that sort of gossip went around fast, and she struggled to find an answer.

Paul appeared behind Jenna. He smiled without crinkling his eyes. 'Yes, do tell us, Annie, what was so important you had to rush out of our meeting yesterday?'

Annie wondered if he felt hurt that she hadn't told him first. He might deny it, but she was sure they had a connection. After all, he'd taken a chance on employing her when she had nothing really to say about her life other than a couple of A Levels and a driving license. It wasn't just because he lived in Westhurst that she felt it, but that was part of it. They must like the same things. It occurred to her that she hadn't asked him if he knew the Hills. She would take him a coffee later and they could chat about the case and what they knew. It would be a start.

'I had to talk to the police about the Chloe Hills investigation. That's my car in the CCTV image, the one with the lights on. She walked right in front of me.'

Jenna's mouth opened. 'Well, you kept that quiet!'

'You drove home on Thursday night?' Paul's voice held a note of disbelief that caught Annie out, made her feel sad and sorry about that evening all over again. She remembered the way Claire had put her hand on his arm possessively when Paul had spoken to Annie on Sunday evening. She and Paul should be friends at least. She smiled at him cautiously. He cared that she'd been in danger, even after their fight.

'But what did you see? Do you know who took her?' Jenna's eyes were wide open, and Annie couldn't conjure up a face that was less suited to her own life of smoke and mirrors. She looked around at the faces turned towards her for once and felt an unfamiliar moment of pleasure. It was a bitter-sweet moment. The enjoyment of finally being seen was cut through with guilt. Annie felt like a butterfly pinned to a board.

'Yes, do tell us, Annie.' Paul locked eyes with her. 'Seems there was a lot going on in Westhurst on Thursday night.'

Annie heard the sarcasm in his tone that rang alarm bells. He was probably going to complain they were wasting time chatting, so she knew she couldn't speak for long. But now everyone was waiting for her to cough up some little detail they could share with their friends later. She licked her lips.

'I'm not allowed to tell you anything really, I'm afraid.' She smiled, hoping this made her sound important to the investigation but cut her off from further interrogation. Annie could have been telling this sort of story for years, she realised. Was it really that easy to be interesting, just by making things up? She could have painted a picture of an entirely different life if she wanted. Maybe that's what they all did. She pictured Jenna at home on Saturday nights, probably in a onesie, dreaming of the parties she'd describe on Monday morning.

'Do you know Chloe?'

'What's her family like?'

Annie sat down and took a sip of her tea as the questions continued. Paul rolled his eyes and stalked to his office. Annie waited until his door was shut. She wanted to enjoy this brief moment of feeling connected to her peers without worrying about him.

'Well, um, they seem to be a popular family.' Everyone waited for more. 'I mean, there were a lot of people who knew them in the search party.'

'What was it like?'

'Was everyone really sombre?'

'What did you have to do?'

Annie couldn't remember when she'd ever properly joined in the morning gossip. It was almost overwhelming. The relief of not being apart from everyone warmed her sore body, like the feeling she'd had being part of the search party. Then she remembered the way they'd looked at her, even Sam's look of pity, in the pub. They'd been judging her all along, measuring her up as not good enough, not upset enough. Whatever she did, she was never accepted. She could feel the sting behind her eyes. Were her colleagues about to find her lacking, too?

'Look,' she said, 'I need to get back to work.' And she turned away.

She was nearly late with the sales figures and had only just saved the spreadsheet when Paul called her into his office and gestured for her to shut the door. Her lack of sleep was beginning to itch behind her eyes, and she hoped he didn't want to go through it all in detail. She placed the report on his desk and waited for him to speak.

'We need to talk about your behaviour on Thursday night.' Paul sighed. 'You made no effort to help the sales team, never mind talk to the customers. It was not a "free drinks for Annie" event. And —' Annie opened her mouth '— before you say it, I know you're sales *support*, but I asked everyone to pull together.'

'You know I'm not good at that. Crowds, talking, all that stuff. And it's not my job. As you said, I'm just support.' Well, she wasn't going to ask him if he knew Chloe now. She wasn't going to apologise either. He was the one who should apologise for throwing her out of the event like trash.

Paul pushed the hair out of his eyes. Little streaks of grey showed through the russet near his temples. She used to find that gesture endearing, but now she realised it was how his annoyance leaked out, like a poker tell.

'Annie, you were drunk and behaved inappropriately towards me. If it had been anyone else, they would be pressing for disciplinary action against you.' He sighed, and Annie found she couldn't speak. She didn't know how she'd cope if she lost her little house, and she needed her job to keep it.

'I just wanted to talk to you.' She felt small. All he'd had to do was treat her with courtesy and acknowledge her feelings. He waited for her to carry on. 'Sorry.' Annie couldn't look at him, but she heard him sigh.

'Do you have friends, Annie?' The question startled her. Paul's tone was part exasperation and part, what was that, sympathy?

She shrugged, not trusting her voice to sound normal. Her earlier euphoria drained away, and she felt exhaustion sucking at her bones.

'Look, I really should take this to HR, but you're reliable and competent, and I'm prepared to put it down to the alcohol this time.'

He wanted her to stay! For a moment, she thought he might start the conversation she'd wanted to have on Thursday night, but he gestured to the door and started reading through the sales report.

'Oh, by the way,' Paul called to her just as she reached the door, 'you didn't see anyone dodgy near the alley to my block of flats on Thursday night, did you? I had the strongest sensation that there was someone in the car park when I walked through, and, when I got into my flat, I'm sure someone else had been there …'

Annie stiffened. 'As you said, I was a little worse for wear. The truth is, I didn't really notice very much at all.' She pulled the door open quickly and walked out before he could call her back.

14

TUESDAY AFTERNOON

At lunchtime, Annie slipped away and walked through the tourists and into the quiet side roads so she could breathe. The sky was sludgy and damp looking, but the rain held off. Puddles still speckled the ground, reflecting the browns and greys of the buildings, occasionally disturbed by a fat pigeon flapping down to peck at some discarded food. She didn't want to risk staying in the office to eat. Her initial feeling of joy at being part of the group had dissipated, and she felt overwhelmed by the attention and the pressure. She knew she had to be careful to remember what she had and hadn't said to the police, and now she needed to be careful at work, too. She wondered whether DS Miller had contacted Paul yet. She'd already lied to them about how much she'd drunk, but, even if Paul told them the truth, could they prove anything?

She wondered why he'd asked her about his flat. She'd been so sure that she'd been careful to replace things, apart from the sandstone baby, and that had been half-hidden behind the clock already. If he really did think there'd been a break-in, surely he would have called the police, but there was no reason for him to report it. There was no damage and no harm done. Especially if she put the sandstone figure back as soon as she could. Her skin prickled at the thought of someone in her own home, and she had a pang of regret. She hadn't wanted to scare him. She'd just yearned to feel close to him.

Annie bought a sandwich and took it into the little walled garden, spreading a plastic bag onto the bench before she sat down. A child in a polka dot raincoat was calling for her mother from the top of the slide, so Annie popped in her earbuds. The memory of her conversation with the police played through her head, and she searched for anything she'd said that could be harmful, anything that she might have given away. She'd embarrassed herself by rattling on a bit, but it was what she did, hid in the words. DC Singh had picked up Paul's sandstone figure, turning it over in her hand before she noticed Annie watching her. It hadn't felt that important at the time, but Annie had been taut with nerves, and it seemed an odd thing to do now. Was it possible that Paul actually had noticed it missing and reported the break-in? She pushed the thought away. If he had, wouldn't Singh have asked her about it?

She thought about the policewoman's careful recording of her answers. She was the cool foil to Miller's enthusiasm for the truth. Her carefully pinned-up hair and immaculate suit spoke of efficiency. Singh had definitely not wanted to be there. There was something odd about the way she'd reacted to Annie's answers, as if she was impatient to lead the questions. But Annie was grateful that she could at least say she'd spoken to the police. She'd tried to do the right thing.

The child climbed up the rungs to the top of the slide and

stood there waiting for her mother to watch. Annie messaged Lauren.

I spoke to the police. Told them I'd seen nothing. All fine.

That's good, Annie.

Annie wanted to tell her that Paul suspected someone, possibly her, had broken into his flat, but it would take too long to explain that it had in fact been her. Not broken in exactly, she'd used a key, but Annie kept her secret to herself. Sooner or later she'd stretch Lauren's friendship too much. She had to be careful. Anyway, she'd return the figurine as soon as she could, and he'd assume he'd just imagined it all.

The sandwich and the fresh air revived her a little, and she picked up an Americano to take back to her desk. Jenna was waiting for her.

'Your local paper's only gone and announced a £20,000 reward for anyone providing information that leads to an arrest.' Her face was flushed with excitement. 'D'you think you'll get it?'

Annie pulled up the website on her phone and read the announcement. The paper's online comment section was one of the most active, with many local people claiming to know the family or their friends and everyone expressing an opinion about them. This story must be an absolute bonanza for them, Annie thought. Her heart leapt at the thought of the money. If she had twenty-thousand pounds, she could afford to look for another job if Paul fired her and still keep her house. But, the truth was that she hadn't actually provided any real information. There was no way what she'd told the police would help them find Chloe, even if she would ever consider going to the papers.

Jenna was hopping from foot to foot, waiting for a response.

Annie took a deep breath, as if she was considering Jenna's question carefully. 'I guess they have to find Chloe Hills first?'

Jenna nodded seriously. 'You know, there's a rumour that Chloe was getting into a lot of trouble at school. Her parents couldn't control her.' She shook her head. 'Probably met some paedo on the internet. My mum says —'

'Sorry, Jenna, I've got to get on.' Annie knew where this kind of discussion ended up. The angry mobs might be sticking to fighting it out online at the moment, but when they moved into the real world, then people got hurt. Jenna flushed, and Annie knew she'd been unkind, but this kind of salacious gossiping and amateur pop-psychology escalated quickly. She hadn't meant to add fuel to it when she'd told the office her news that morning, and she felt shame spreading through her. She kept her eyes on her screen for the rest of the afternoon, picking up her phone if anyone looked like they might approach. Once or twice she caught Paul watching her.

Paul had sounded pretty convinced that someone had been in his flat, but how did he think they got in without breaking the lock? Annie knew where his spare key was because she'd overheard him boasting about where he kept it that time when Adrian had got locked out of his house. Paul had joined in the laughter as Adrian described taking the rubbish out in his pyjamas and having to pay a locksmith to let him back in. Lots of them would know where he kept his keys. Annie was unsettled that he'd mentioned his suspicions to her. Plus, he'd never noticed before.

Her thoughts were still scrambled on the way home, so she turned straight to the crossword and puzzles in the evening paper. She knew she'd been thinking about Chloe's case too much. It was like an obsession. Her interest was unhealthy, and the reaction of her colleagues had been like looking in a mirror. Ticking off the clues as she filled them in felt like a small return to normal, a little respite from the news about Chloe Hills.

Stepping off the train on to the platform at Westhurst was like sinking back into a bad dream. The yellow ribbons were everywhere, and she tucked the paper under her arm to read later. The cold air was a shock after the smelly warmth of the train, and her eyes were drawn to the glowing windows of the pub. Her heart faltered as she made out Sam and Alex sitting at a table in the window, both laughing at something. Sam's face was open and relaxed, and Annie remembered the way he'd told her she should talk to the police, his tone sympathetic. He'd been prepared to see the good intention inside her. This was her chance to let him know he was right, and that she had spoken to DS Miller.

She smoothed down her hair and walked into the pub. For a moment, the noise made her catch her breath. It felt as though she'd stepped into another, slightly unreal world away from the hard reality of the missing girl. She bought herself a drink, trying to strike up a little conversation with the girl behind the bar to look casual.

'Oh, it looks like all the interest in Chloe Hills has done wonders for your business.'

The girl muttered something about clean glasses and walked to the other end of the bar, so Annie was left standing alone. She hoped that Sam would notice her and call her over. When he didn't, she made a show of checking her phone and then wandered around the bar as though she was looking for someone.

As she passed Sam and Alex, she cried out, 'Oh, fancy seeing you two here. How are you?'

Sam smiled up at her and sat a little straighter, though Alex looked bored to see her. Sam didn't pull out the spare chair for her, but that was okay, he was probably wary of awkwardness between Annie and Alex. That would be just like him. Alex was likely used to most people coming over to see Sam rather than him, though, Annie told herself. She bet that happened to Alex a lot. It was Sam she wanted to speak to anyway.

'Oh hey, Annie, how are you?' He glanced towards Alex. 'Look, I hope there are no hard feelings about the other night.'

'Oh gosh no, you were quite right to encourage me to speak to the police. I was hoping we'd find her when we were searching, because my information didn't seem that important. But you were right, and I'm so glad you said it.'

Annie glanced around the pub, as if there might be an audience again, judging her as they had on Sunday. No one seemed to be paying any attention. She let out the breath she hadn't realised she'd been holding. Neither Sam nor Alex replied, and Annie felt her face colouring.

'I'm meeting some friends. But when I saw you, I just thought I'd tell Sam that I did speak to the police.' She could feel the disbelief radiating from Alex. 'Anyway, I just wanted to say thank you for encouraging me.' She focused on Sam and his friendly face. 'I was a little afraid, of course, because, well, it's the police, and everyone feels guilty when they talk to the police, don't they? Ha ha. Anyway, they were lovely, really interested. I mean, they came to my home.'

'That's great, Annie. Let's hope it helps.' Sam nodded at her.

'Anything to do with the *Herald* announcing their reward?' Alex had an expression on his face Annie couldn't decipher. 'Or are you here on their behalf?'

Annie felt as if she'd been hit, as if Alex had actually stood up and slapped her. 'But they only announced that today. I spoke to the police yesterday, actually.'

Alex sat back in his chair and folded his arms. Did he really believe that she'd only come forward for the reward? It was a terrible thing to suggest. She looked at Sam.

'So, was it your information that led to the arrest?' Sam asked.

Annie's jaw dropped. It seemed as though the sound of chatting faded, and the tables nearby seemed to be watching them. She wished she'd checked the news on the way home.

'What arrest?' Annie could feel her insides tense. It wasn't possible anything she'd said could lead to an arrest.

Alex put his elbows on the table. 'All they've said is that they have someone in custody.' He raised his eyebrows. 'So, is there a chance it was something you told them?'

Annie tried to remember if she'd given DS Miller any details that could have identified a real person. Maybe she had seen something important. The image of Chloe's hair flying from her face came to Annie, shadowy figures in the background. Footsteps. She was torn between wanting to think she might have said something useful and the knowledge that she hadn't remembered anything at all.

'Have they found Chloe then?' she looked to Sam, his blue eyes cool and steady. 'Is she all right?'

'Alas, no,' Alex said. 'Let's hope they're not barking up the wrong tree while someone completely different has the girl.'

Annie felt her heart sink. Could she have done that? She looked to Sam for encouragement, but he was staring into his beer.

'They must think making the arrest will help, though.' Annie smiled back at the top of Sam's head. All she wanted now was for Sam to see how much she longed to help. 'I mean they're not fools, are they? The police. They'd check everything.' She could hear the uncertainty in her voice, and Alex raised an eyebrow.

'And yet, Chloe still hasn't been found.' Alex stared at Annie. 'What if this person has nothing to do with it? What a waste of time it would be.' But Annie hadn't seen anyone, so she couldn't have described them. Alex was still talking, the words spilling out. 'Chloe'd be in more danger, wouldn't she?'

Annie felt the dark hole in her stomach stretching and tugging her down. Alex didn't know what she'd told the police, couldn't know that she hadn't really seen anything and hadn't claimed to. Not really. But could she have held up their investigation?

'Stop it, Alex,' Sam said, and Annie felt a rush of gratitude. But Alex pushed his chair back and stalked up to the bar. Then she realised that they were all treating it as an abduction now. How quickly they'd moved on from wondering if she'd run away. 'He's just fed up with talking about Chloe all the time. But Westhurst's suddenly full of snoopers and reporters, and it's impossible to think of anything else.'

Annie looked after Alex. She could relate to that. She could even understand the force of Alex's anger, though it hurt that it was directed at her. She really did care. Were people pausing their conversations more than usual when he passed? She didn't really know what it was normally like. The pub had always looked so appealing, but she'd never had anyone to go in with before.

'Look, I don't think the arrest is down to something I said.' She put her glass down so she could twist her hair behind her ears.

Sam shifted uncomfortably.

'Have they said who they've arrested?'

Sam shook his head. He looked miserable, and Annie wished she could say something to cheer him up. 'No, nothing. Look, I don't want to keep you from your friends, and I should go and help Alex with the drinks.'

Annie nodded. She walked through the crowd at the bar to the back of the pub, hoping they wouldn't see that she was on her own after all, and tried to stop her disappointment melting into tears. As she finished her drink, she heard Chloe's name over and over again.

'They'll never find her now — this bloke must have her well-hidden.'

'She's probably just bunking off school. I heard she had a bit of an attitude.'

'Yes, someone who knows a boy at her school said she'd got into trouble and was running away.'

'What if it was that Internet grooming?'

Annie left her glass and pushed her way back through the crowd, ostentatiously holding her phone to her ear and trying not to look across to where Alex and Sam were sitting. As she pulled the door back, she caught Alex watching her. His expression was unsmiling.

Sam was talking, his right hand waving as he emphasised a point, oblivious to her.

15

TUESDAY EVENING

Annie felt like she was drowning. The beech leaves of the hedge shuddered in the rain around her, and the road was slick with water that bubbled into the drains. She knew she shouldn't have got involved, but she had called the missing person's number because she wanted to help. It was Sam who'd encouraged her. Sam and Paul and Lauren had all said it was the right thing to do, even though her own instincts tugged her back the other way. But the opinions of the others had overwhelmed her, like the tide against Canute.

She thought of her mother. Her mother would pull her back, but Annie didn't want to ask her. She would have to tell her everything, and her mother would be so disappointed. *'No more lies between us, Annie.'* She'd told her that a long time ago. *'We won't survive if we're not at least truthful with each other.'*

Drops of rain rolled off her coat onto her legs, and she clutched her bag to her front, trying to protect it. It was stupid to think she might have impressed Sam, never mind actually been useful. The wind whistled through the dry leaves, Sam,

Sam, Sam, mocking her, and she broke into a run. Her steps created waves that broke around her feet.

She'd been in the car park when Chloe was there, the CCTV of her car proved it, and Annie hadn't even seen her. She would have pulled Chloe out of danger, she told herself. She would never have left her there if she'd known. Never. She felt hot tracks mingle with the cold rain on her cheeks and swiped at her eyes in surprise. It was no use being sorry; she had to stop it happening. She stood before her own front door, and, for a moment, she didn't know where she was.

* * *

Her father takes her by both shoulders and squats down so that his face is right in front of hers. The fine lines that crinkle when he smiles are white in his tanned face.

'You have to tell us the truth, sweetheart. This isn't you.' Behind him, her Mum stands, wringing her hands, the mascara streaked down her face. 'You have to tell them,' he says.

Lottie carefully crosses her fingers behind her back. 'I told you already. It must have been the Piskies.'

Her mother snorts. 'I told you she's hiding something. She's been hanging around with that Bronnen and Gwen. There's always talk about those two. They're a bad influence.'

'Susan, just ... leave it for now.' Lottie's father doesn't take his eyes off Lottie's face. 'Look, I don't think little Pisky hands could've pulled that stiff bolt on the gate and let those ponies out onto the road, do you? It might seem like a funny prank, Lottie, but they could've got badly hurt. You just have to tell me the truth, and we can work out how to fix this.'

Lottie shrugs. 'Piskies are magic. They can do anything.'

Her mother swears. 'I need to get to work. You filled her head with this Cornish nonsense, you sort it out.' She pulls a tissue out of her pocket and scrubs at the dirty streaks on her cheeks in front of the hall mirror. 'What am I going to say to the Hancocks?' She walks back into the kitchen and looks at them both. Lottie wants to tell her that there's still a smear of black on her cheek. 'We need to clamp down on whatever's going on with that child before it gets worse. You do know that, don't you? You're far too soft. Where will it end?' And her mother is gone. The sound of the back door rings in both their ears.

Her father sighs. 'Lottie, Tegen's already told her mum that she saw you open the gate. I don't understand why you would do a thing like that.' Her father's fingers dig into her arms. 'Just tell me what happened. It's the lying that makes me most disappointed. I really hate that.'

Lottie blinks at her Dad. He never stays angry for long, she just has to be strong. 'She's the one lying! She's always following me around. I hate her!'

Her dad sighs. He stands up and sweeps the hair back that's fallen over his face. Lottie holds her breath. It's hard keeping this promise, especially as it's making her parents more unhappy right now, but she knows it's important, and it'll all be worth it when it works.

For now, if she wants to join the Pisky Society, she has to go through The Trials.

'Lottie, I don't know what to think.' Her father shakes his head as he looks at her, and she says nothing. 'I just can't believe you would do anything so wicked.'

* * *

Annie woke at the little table in the lounge with an uneaten bowl of pasta in front of her. Her blood ran cold when she saw them lined up on the table watching her. Their little faces were contorted into grins that stretched up to their long ears.

So long they could hear the deepest wishes of humans. Some of the figurines sat cross-legged and others had their knees drawn up to their chins, pointy boots on feet. Others sat on toadstools, but all faced her. Annie cried out when she saw the sandstone baby in the middle of the circle, and she swept the lot from the table with such force that her chair fell away from beneath her. They rolled across the carpet, and Annie watched them carefully while her breathing came back under control.

She fetched a tea towel and gathered them up inside, carefully pocketing the baby so she could feel its solid shape against her body, and took them upstairs. Her suitcase lay open on the floor. She tipped the figures inside in a cascade of tin and bronze and snapped the lid down, sitting on it while she dialled the combination randomly.

Annie pulled out the baby and held it in the palm of her hand. She had to return it to Paul's flat before he noticed but, for now, she would keep it on her. Its soft, grainy edges soothed her as she sat on the case. She wanted to call him and explain why she'd given it to him, so that it all made sense, but none of it did. Perhaps he'd already told the police he suspected her. She was sure Singh had known that Annie was hiding something. She put the case at the very back of the cupboard where it was hidden by her hanging clothes.

She remembered the arrest and went back down to pick up her tablet. The #BringChloeHome pages were full of speculation. *He was her teacher. He was a sex offender. He was a neighbour.* There was no mention from the police that it was information from the public that had led to the arrest. Still, she felt uncomfortable that it might have been something she'd said.

It was probably just paranoia. Waking up to the little figures like that had just unbalanced her, that was all.

DS Miller's card was still on the table where she'd left it, so she put it on top of her handbag. In the morning, she would call him and explain that she was sure she hadn't seen anyone, just in case they'd misunderstood. She had to make them understand that they shouldn't rely on her information for any arrest. She laughed. If only they knew how unreliable she was. Sadness overwhelmed her, and she knew she had to make sure it didn't happen again. There was nothing Annie could do to help Chloe or the police other than take herself out of the way.

The girl had already been gone nearly a week, and Annie could see it was looking less likely that she'd just run off or that her friends were covering for her. She was far too young to hide herself for that long, wasn't she? It would have to be some extraordinary family argument that kept a twelve-year-old away from home in the face of a nationwide appeal. It just didn't seem realistic. Annie thought that it was still possible that her friends knew where she was, though. That was definitely still possible.

The phone rang, and Annie picked it up.

'I've been beside myself; you're not returning my calls.'

'I'm fine.' Annie considered being honest with her mother. Would she know what to do? Her mother saw truth in shades of necessity. Would she think Annie should confess that she'd been in Paul's flat and that she'd been too drunk to drive? So drunk and upset, in fact, that she hadn't seen a real, living girl walk in front of her? She would probably want Annie to pack and leave, and Annie hadn't entirely discounted that. She thought of her suitcase at the back of the cupboard.

'I know what you're like, Annie, and I just want you to stay safe. Don't get carried away by this business with the missing girl. It's not good for you.'

It's not good for you, Mum, Annie thought. She could imagine her mum checking her own suitcases, working out how quickly she could get her house packed up. Annie hadn't visited this latest house yet, so her mother had no excuse for moving. None of the neighbours would recognise Annie. But still, maybe her mother didn't want to move again. Annie looked around her lounge. It wasn't much, but it was hers, and she felt safe. She just had to extricate herself from Chloe's case and keep her fingers crossed that Paul wasn't really going to tell the police his suspicions about her. In the meantime, she had to work out how to get the little baby back into the flat.

'Sure, Mum, I promise. I'm not even interested, really.'

16

WEDNESDAY MORNING

Annie woke early, a broken night's sleep filled with the susurration of tiny waves across sand and the distant calling of gulls. She fetched DS Miller's card. All she had to do was make him understand that she hadn't seen Chloe or anyone else on Thursday. His number went directly to voicemail, so Annie left him a message.

'I just wanted to tell you I really didn't see anything on Thursday night. I'm sure the arrest you made had nothing to do with me, but I'm calling to make sure you understood that.'

She felt a little calmer when she'd done it and had time to sit at the window while she drank her tea, watching the drips from the rain that had fallen steadily overnight rolling down the pane of glass. She tried not to look at the news, but she couldn't help herself. It would set her mind at rest if Chloe was back home now. Until then, Annie couldn't face the walk past the yellow ribbons and the posters without knowing.

The police had given no further information about the arrest or Chloe. Annie struggled to remember what she'd told Miller and Singh; her panic always affected her memory. It was like the effort of answering questions erased the whole conversation almost immediately.

The press was full of speculation that the man in custody was a registered sex offender. A journalist stood in front of the parade of shops by the station holding an umbrella in one hand and a microphone, which was pointed at an elderly couple, in the other. 'Do you know anything about the person in custody?' The man scowled and pulled the woman away before she could answer. 'Would you be surprised to learn there was a registered sex offender living in Westhurst?' The reporter called after them and then turned back to camera. 'Locals are keeping their thoughts to themselves while the community digests what this arrest could mean.'

In the comments section online, Annie could see the anger of the righteous swelling and boiling.

We didn't know.
How could they let people like that live here?
How do we protect ourselves?
Who is responsible?
Think of the children.

The news cut back to the studio where the anchor referred to something on his desk to reel off those missing children's cases where the abductor had already been on the sex offenders register. Those families could be watching now, Annie thought, forced to revisit their trauma again for the sake of an audience of strangers hungry for detail and conjecture.

We should be told if there's a nonce living nearby.

Everyone always looked for reasons why it couldn't

happen to them. It was fear that drove them to unpick everything, fear that made them grasp at the thing that made the victim different.

Ah, well, that wouldn't happen to us. We'd never let our child do that.

If they couldn't do that, they needed to find someone evil to blame. *It's always a predator,* screamed the forums. No, it's not, Annie thought, not always.

There was no comment from the Hills or the #BringChloeHome campaign. She had been missing for nearly a week now, and Annie couldn't imagine how thinly skinned her family must feel. It was a long time to be holding your breath waiting for a call or a knock on the door. The only other person who could be anywhere nearly as stretched to the limits would be the person who knew where Chloe was. Would they start to make mistakes now? There was no way to avoid reading or hearing about Chloe, no respite even for those who didn't know her. It was like a match being continuously struck.

Annie felt the strain, too. She tried again to think back to the car park, but no single piece of information could unlock her memory.

Local celebrities had changed their Twitter banners to display yellow ribbons. A private investigator involved in the case of another child abduction was being interviewed about what he would do next if it was his case. 'What do we know?' everyone was asking. Forums of amateur investigators were ripe with ideas, swapping more and more outlandish theories. They read meaning into the colour of Mrs Hills' clothes, the sports Chloe had played, Berman's new car. Annie didn't have enough time to read it all. *We all want to know how to help,* Annie thought. *How can there not be a way to help?*

The walk to the train station gave her a short break from it, but then she found herself buying a local paper from the newsagent. Inside it, there were more photographs of West-hurst, a group of teenagers in the park, the road the Hills lived on, the yellow ribbons blowing from lamp posts and gates. She glanced towards the block of flats where Paul lived, just behind the shops. The little baby was in her coat pocket, but Paul would be at home now, so she couldn't risk checking whether his spare key was still in the exhaust pipe of his car. Maybe later, if she waited until it was properly dark, she could slip into the car park unseen. There wouldn't be too many people around then, and nobody would know for sure who should be there or not in that block with its high turnover of residents. She put her hand into her pocket and grasped the sandstone.

The train wasn't too busy, so she was able to read the rest of the newspaper while casting an eye around the carriage, noticing who'd got on with her. She noted their descriptions so that she could recall them later, who was on the train, which way they went at Waterloo. The story about the reward money had been given a double-page spread. The accompanying article suggested that the police had been slow to react, and that it would have to be the power of the press that picked up the slack. It was a provocative piece for a regional press, designed to spread fear and hysteria throughout the community.

She thought of speaking to Alex and Sam the night before. How could they have thought she'd cynically called the police to claim the reward? If he only knew, that even if she had wanted the money or been eligible for it, there was no way she would risk the publicity. Not with every journalist and every reader turned amateur detective focusing on Westhurst right now. It served her right for inflating her involvement. There was a man being questioned in custody who might be completely innocent, and now the public were calling for his blood. Annie had to focus on not making things worse for Chloe, and that meant not sending the police in the wrong direction. She dropped her head into her hands. She never slept well, but now she felt at the very edges of her capacity to function.

'Excuse me, are you getting off?'

Annie hadn't even noticed that the train had arrived at Waterloo. She gathered her paper and bag and walked on to the concourse and into the stream of commuters. She cut across at the last minute, down the steps and under the arches towards the river, away from the crowd. As she looked down towards Blackfriars Bridge, the salty, easterly breeze stung her skin and whipped strands of hair into her eyes. Above her on the bridge, a steady flow of people crossed to the north side, like a column of soldiers, completely unaware of her as she watched from below.

Eventually, she climbed up the stone steps to the bridge and slotted back into the crowd, carried across the river as if she had no will of her own, like a piece of flotsam tugged along by the current.

Jenna and the others stopped to chat with Annie as they arrived, and she allowed herself to be pulled in by their goodwill. She felt herself warm up and was able to slough off the disturbed night and the feelings of futility she'd felt on the bridge, until the conversation turned to Chloe Hills.

Annie tried her best to keep it light and play down any part she might have had in the arrest, but she could tell her tone was off by their reactions. Their disappointment hung in the air. The others melted away, exchanging looks that told Annie that they were just waiting for her to revert to uninteresting, awkward Annie. She kept her head down, focusing on directing the sales leads to the right team and updating the database. It was tedious, repetitive work, but Annie found it soothing.

Paul stopped by her desk, and she froze. The sandstone baby was in her handbag on the floor. She held the bag shut with her foot and waited for him to speak. He reached for a file from her in-tray and then pointed at the pad in front of her.

'Cave or existential hole of despair?'

Her pen was poised over a scrawling tangle of caverns in a cliff fringed by jagged waves. Annie snapped the pad shut. *He doesn't know*, she told herself, *he doesn't know*.

'Relax! I'm just after the sales figures for Germany.' He handed the folder he'd picked up back to her.

Annie swallowed and nodded, but her hand shook as she pulled the right file out of the drawer. Paul had an unnerving ability to see right through her. But he couldn't see everything, she reminded herself. No one could see everything

'What did I say?' Paul looked at her hands, and she hid them under the desk quickly. 'You don't seem at all well.' He sat on the edge of her desk, and Annie had to resist every impulse to shove him off and run. 'You've been acting unusually odd, ever since the drinks last Thursday.' For a moment, she was fooled into thinking he was genuinely concerned. 'Something on your mind?' He tipped his head to one side, studying her reaction.

He knew about the sandstone baby. She kept her foot pressed hard against her bag, though there was no way it could roll out. It was wrapped up in tissue and right at the bottom. He'd like to see her off sick though, she thought. Then, he could start building a case to dismiss her.

'I'm fine. Just worried about Chloe Hills.' She picked up her pen and then put it down again so she didn't have to open the pad up. 'I can't believe you live in Westhurst and don't seem to care at all!'

Jenna looked up from her desk, and Annie realised she'd raised her voice.

'Honestly, I'm sure the police are doing everything they can.' Annie could feel his breath on her ear. 'I have my own worries, to be honest. I'm far more concerned about whoever it is who keeps getting into my flat.' He looked at her for just a beat too long.

She kept her face still. 'Well, I don't know anything about that.'

Paul watched her for a moment and then sighed.

The photocopier whirred into life behind him, making her jump. Annie's nerves were tight and brittle, as if she might snap into a thousand strands at any minute. It took up all her energy to hold herself upright in the chair. Adrian appeared and hovered near Annie's desk to catch Paul's eye. Paul gave her one last long look and walked off to talk to Adrian. How on earth could Paul possibly have figured out that she was the person in his flat? It didn't make sense.

17

WEDNESDAY AFTERNOON

The afternoon went slowly, and Annie kept up a constant scan between the door to Paul's office and her own phone. Until Miller confirmed that he'd heard her message, she couldn't relax.

It was a relief to know she would be seeing Lauren later. Lauren had messaged earlier to ask about the Chloe case, and Annie had said she couldn't talk in the office. The time crept on slowly, and her tiredness deepened. She just had to hang on to see Lauren, who was always defiantly positive in all circumstances. It was one of the reasons that Annie valued her friendship. She was a little pool of joy, and the one relationship she'd do anything to protect.

'Hey, Annie, have you heard?' She looked up to see Jenna waving her mobile at her. 'They've only released that bloke! Must have been a dead end.'

Annie felt relief bubbling up. DS Miller had got her message. Jenna showed her the screen.

Police confirm the thirty-eight-year-old man arrested yesterday has now been eliminated from their enquiries. They appeal to members of the public who might have any further information about Chloe to come forward.

Annie's phone pinged as the notifications built up.

We know he's a nonce now. Better not be coming back to this village.
Eliminated from the enquiry, or they just couldn't make anything stick?
Perhaps a few of us should go around and have a word with him.

Annie looked for a statement from the family, but only the image of the man in the waxed jacket popped up. Jason Berman had been caught on camera in the estate agency office. The recording was from an odd angle, as though the phone had been held out of sight, but his voice was clear.

'If that man's harmed her but the police can't prove it, we're going to have to sort it ourselves.'

His sleeves were rolled up, and his face red and puffy. He looked nothing like the calm supportive friend he presented when he was around the Hills. Annie didn't think he knew he was being filmed. The village must be full of journalists and crime tourists armed with phones, secretly recording every encounter. Annie shivered. She needed to keep an eye out for them; they could be anywhere. She would need to be on her guard.

There was a short quote from Det Supt Thomas.

We strongly advise that members of the public report any information directly to the police and do not take matters into their own hands.

Annie felt her head spinning with her own fear and the outpouring of anger and grief that she read. Here and there was also a hint of something she recognised. That little spark of hope that, now, there was something people could actually do. It was human nature to want to take action rather than to sit back and wait; it was a way to ignore the fear. She knew very well how a week's worth of frustration and speculation and media hysteria could build up.

The girl's parents didn't get on.
She had a secret boyfriend that her friends didn't approve of.
She was such a nice child, but in the last six months her behaviour had been out of control.
How was it possible that she could just disappear into thin air?

Annie put her phone away. Speculation and the gossip was as unsatisfying as it was addictive. She tried to clear her head and concentrate on the spreadsheet open on her screen. As the day wore on, it began to look like she didn't need to be on her guard for a call from Miller. At five o'clock, she almost knocked Paul over in her rush to leave the office.

'Half-day is it, Annie?' Paul raised an eyebrow as she left. She ignored the jibe; he was only staying later to attend one of those client meetings that always ended up in some badly lit club until the early hours.

She took a wide loop round Lincoln's Inn Fields, where a

game of netball was just starting, down to Fleet St and along past the Royal Courts of Justice and St Clement Danes before carrying on down to The Strand and up into Covent Garden. There was something reassuring about being able to put her head down and pace through the streets unseen and unquestioned while her thoughts calmed.

For once, Lauren was waiting for her at the bar with a bottle of wine. Annie poured herself a glass and drank deeply.

Lauren smiled widely at Annie. 'Well, go on then, tell me all about it.' She put a hand on Annie's arm, and Annie could feel her skin warming under her friend's touch, steadying her. She thought of her Dad hoisting her on his shoulders, of walking to the play park with her little friend's hot hand in hers. Annie took a breath. As a teenager, the best part of her day had been sitting shoulder to shoulder on the playground wall, flicking through the pages of *Seventeen*. It was good to talk to someone she'd known for so long.

Annie described her interview with the police. 'Of course, I didn't get that bloke arrested. It's standard practice to question known sex offenders in the local area. So, it's nothing to do with me at all.'

They walked over to an empty table and sat down. 'I'd have thought you'd be hoping you had helped them make an arrest. What makes you think you'd given them bad information?' Lauren asked.

'I just can't really remember much about getting home at all, but the police were really pushing me for answers. I got completely muddled up.'

Lauren rolled her eyes. 'Everyone gets nervous talking to police officers but not so much they tell them things they don't know.' She laughed and patted Annie's hand. 'Of course, you wouldn't have done that.'

Annie could almost see her secrets hanging in the air between them. This was an opportunity to tell Lauren who she was, but, when she looked up at Lauren's broad smile, she couldn't face it.

'I saw those two guys from the search party in the pub. You know, Sam, the nice one who'd encouraged me to call, and the other one, Alex, who was a bit rude actually. Said I'd probably just called to get the reward. I wish I could bump into Sam without Alex. He's so lovely, and he seemed interested in knowing more about me when we were on the search.' Annie couldn't see how she and Sam would have a chance of being friends though, if Alex was always there like a shadow.

'Oh Lord, Annie, you should just forget about him. Sounds like another Paul.'

Ignoring her friend, Annie decided she would try and talk to Sam alone if she had the chance. Lauren had dismissed her interest in Paul, too, but it was just her way of letting Annie know that she thought they weren't good enough for Annie.

Lauren had already forgotten about Sam. 'But what if you did say something useful to the police? And they've just released him to see where he goes. Perhaps, they're waiting to see if he'll lead them to Chloe. Tell me again what they asked?'

It was sweet of Lauren to be so interested in her, but Annie wished she could share her real fears. She couldn't tell Lauren what she was actually afraid of, because she was so ashamed, and she couldn't bear to see Lauren disappointed in her. Annie was nothing if not an expert at keeping secrets. Annie couldn't share her demons with anyone, and that was fine, because they were too awful. Perhaps she deserved to be alone.

She spun a bar mat around with her middle finger. 'Honestly, I've told you everything. They asked about Thursday evening and my journey home, but I didn't have anything useful to say, Lauren, because I have no memory of it at all. That's the killer. My car is on the CCTV image with the lights on, but I have no memory of sitting in it. Or even getting home for that matter. I was far too drunk.'

'Then why did you call them? When you said you couldn't remember, I thought you'd just not seen Chloe being taken. Not been completely oblivious.'

Annie thought Lauren's tone was a little tart, but it was nothing she didn't deserve.

'And I drove home, Lauren. I was too drunk to remember seeing anything, and then I went and drove home. What if they find out?' Annie shook her head. 'If I tell them I was too drunk to remember anything, they'll know I drove over the limit. And I didn't see anything either. I said I did, I thought there were other people who got off my train. But I'm not even really sure about that. And what if they ask Paul, and he tells them I was so drunk he sent me home?' Annie pushed the bar mat away with force. 'What if I lose my driving licence?'

Lauren looked confused and shocked at the same time. 'Look, arguably, you've wasted a bit of their time when they could have been speaking to someone else, but I've read they had over a thousand calls in the last week and, let's be honest, not all of those people can have seen anything useful either.' Lauren put the beer mat neatly back on the pile. 'Or she'd have been found by now.'

Annie moaned. 'I really wanted to help. If only I had seen something. If only I had been paying attention.'

Lauren took her hand off Annie's and rolled her eyes. 'Come on, Annie, you're overreacting. If you didn't see anything useful, they're not going to speak to you again, and, quite honestly, they've got more important things to worry about right now than you driving half a mile pissed. Of course there were other people getting off the last train. They'll have that on their precious CCTV too, won't they? In fact, they've probably been speaking to them, too — suggests none of them saw anything useful either, doesn't it?'

Annie allowed Lauren, and the wine, to talk her round, but Lauren's point about the CCTV scratched away at the back of her mind. She'd have to think about that properly later. This was the power of Lauren, Annie thought. She was beginning to relax for the first time in days. She was lucky to have managed to hold onto her, despite her mother trying to move away for the sixth form. It had been the one time Annie had managed to get her own way. Her mum had wanted to pack up and move once again to some random part of the country where no one knew them. It was the only occasion when she'd really dug her heels in. Annie had told her mother she was going to use her own name, find her dad, and move in with him. She was calling her mother's bluff, but her mother finally agreed.

'This reminds me of what you were like when that little boy went missing in Reading.' Lauren's voice brought her back to the moment. 'Do you remember? You followed the news obsessively about that, too. Never understood why. The one where it turned out to be a custody battle in the end, and the kid was absolutely fine.'

Annie could remember.

'Must be something about them being so close to home, I guess?'

Annie nodded, not able to speak.

'Mind you, once you start paying attention you can't get away from hearing about it either. It's in your face all the time, isn't it?'

Annie sighed and drank her wine. If you pay attention, people go missing all the time. Old people, young people, married people. By now, Annie could tell the stories that would be taken up by the press, the particular set of attributes needed to strike a chord with the general public. She was aware of all of them. If someone wanted to choose a victim that no one would miss, it would be pretty easy to work out whose loss wouldn't be noted.

18

WEDNESDAY EVENING

Annie sat on the bench opposite the ticket office, waiting until the other passengers had left the station car park. The wine that she and Lauren had drunk was still warm inside her, and she didn't want to go home yet. There was something soft and inky about the sky after the days of cloud and rain, and Annie sat back and watched lacy streaks floating across the moon. A faint smell of garlic drifted from Tandoori Villa, and, nearby, Annie could hear someone putting out their rubbish.

It had barely been a week since she'd sat in her car, in this car park, and failed to notice a twelve-year-old-girl disappear. Since she'd let herself into Paul's flat and left in such a hurry that she'd run out with the little figurine. She felt the soft contours of the baby in her pocket.

The alleyway through to the little private car park for the apartment block was poorly lit, but it seemed empty. Annie had ten minutes before another train arrived, so she took a good look around and then ran softly down the alley and found Paul's car.

She counted to ten in her head, in case there was someone else standing silently in the car park, and then went around to the boot. She crouched down and peered into the exhaust pipe using the torch on her phone. It was impossible to get the angle right, so she pulled her sleeve up and reached in. After a few minutes, she gave up. Paul must have moved the keys, which meant he was sure that's how she'd got in. Unless he'd given them to the woman with the fur hood. *Claire*. Annie felt a stab of pointless jealousy.

She wouldn't be able to place the figurine back in his flat tonight. She rested against the wall for a moment. The opportunity to make Paul think he'd just lost it and then found it again was narrowing. She stood up and wiped her hand with a tissue from her bag and started back across the car park to the alley, when she heard voices.

A memory stirred. Had she heard voices when she went into Paul's flat? It wouldn't have been so remarkable if she had.

She dropped into the shadows behind a motorbike. If anyone looked closely, they would see her, but it was the best she could do. She held her breath as they came closer.

'Shh, lower your voice.'

A girl's voice, or a child at least, Annie thought. She pulled herself up a little, so she could peer over the wheel.

'I don't want to do this anymore. My parents are going to lose it if they find out.'

Another girl. Annie stayed absolutely still as they walked past the motorbike. She could just make out the features of Megan, Chloe's friend, but the other girl's face was in the shadows. It could have been Hannah, but Annie wasn't certain.

'Shut up, Megan, let's do it quickly and then get back. That way they won't find out, will they?'

Annie's bag slipped off her shoulder, and the strap clanked against the metal body of the bike. The girls stood very still.

'What was that?' The second girl's voice.

Annie shrank as far into the shadows as she could.

'I don't know. Please, Hannah, let's just go.'

But they ran towards the entrance to the block of flats, and then Hannah stopped and stood with her back to the door, peering back into the car park as Megan struggled with the lock. She held a full shopping bag. Annie's knees ached. Megan pushed the door open, and both girls ran in, slamming the door hard behind them.

Annie took a long rasping breath and checked her watch. She could make out the sound of another train pulling into the station and pulled herself off the ground. She ran out the long way to the road, so that she wouldn't come face to face with anyone using the alleyway, but nearly sent a woman in high heels flying as she rounded the corner to Station Parade.

'Watch out!' The voice carried after her as she ran.

'Sorry,' she called back automatically, hoping it was enough to make her look less suspicious. When she reached the traffic lights, she had to stop running, her side splitting and her heart racing. The alcohol pumping around her system.

What on earth were Hannah and Megan doing at Paul's block of flats? She knew where Hannah lived, because her house was marked on all the maps showing Chloe Hills' last movements. It was Hannah's house she'd been to on the night she went missing. Maybe Megan lived in the flats. After all, she had the key. But there was something about their conversation that made it unlikely. What had they been saying?

Annie's breathing settled, and she became aware that she was standing exposed under a streetlight. She started walking. It had sounded like they'd sneaked out of Megan's house to visit the apartments. Twelve-year-olds wouldn't be sneaking out to meet boyfriends, would they?

Annie certainly hadn't done that but, then again, she hadn't been friends with the sort of girls who might have. If she had, maybe she'd know how to get the figurine back into Paul's flat. The walk was sobering her up just enough to realise how reckless she'd been. He could have turned up at any moment. It could have been him she ran into on the way out.

She should just throw the figure away. Paul couldn't prove she'd taken it unless it was found on her or with her, and, anyway, he hadn't said anything was missing. She pulled it out of her pocket. The sandstone felt soft and hard and fit perfectly in the palm of her hand. The figure's eyes were closed, and there was a gentle smile on its wide face. It could have been a boy or a girl. Their knees were drawn up under the chin, and their arms wrapped around the legs. She ran her finger over it, marvelling that so few marks could make such an effective image. She closed her fingers around it.

Annie had bought the little figure from a charity shop not long after she moved into Westhurst. There was something content and confident about its rounded shape and smooth face that she found calming. It sat alone on her mantelpiece for six months and brought her joy, and when she drew Paul in the Secret Santa, she'd thought he might love it, too. He'd given her that job when she'd had very few options and always made an effort to check in on how she was coping. She saw him doing that with everybody, a few words in the morning, a smile when the work piled up, a squeeze of a shoulder, but, with her, she just felt there was something more personal. The way the little figurine made her feel mirrored her pleasure when Paul noticed her.

* * *

'But I already gave you the money from my Mum's purse, and I let the ponies out, and I got into a lot of trouble, and I never said why. Please!' Lottie holds her hands above her eyes to stop the sun dazzling her. Gwen and Bronnen are sitting on the swings while Lottie stands in front of them, hopping from foot to foot. Gwen scuffs the toes of her shoes along the ground as the swing moves.

Bronnen has thrown the other seats over the bar of the frame so that Lottie can't reach them. They aren't letting her on the swings, and they aren't letting her join the Pisky Society. They'd made it sound so wonderful, and she knows she has to do what they say, but it's taking so long.

'Can't I be a member of the Pisky Society now?'

Bronnen jumps off the swing and lands right in front of Lottie with her hands on her hips. 'But you haven't completed the final challenge.' She tips her head to one side, so that her curls bounce like flames, and stares at Lottie until she blinks. 'I don't know if you're ready yet.'

Lottie's heart sinks. She doesn't usually get into trouble at home, but after the missing five pounds and the ponies, things are different. She can't take anything else. She keeps catching her parents watching her with a funny look in their eyes all the time, as if she might suddenly explode or something.

Gwen jumps off her swing, too, and stands beside Bronnen. She hasn't noticed that her skirt has rucked up at the side, and Lottie doesn't feel brave enough to tell her.

'You have brought us a Tribute of money, which is Challenge One, and you have demonstrated Obedience in the freeing of the wild animals, which is Challenge Two,' Gwen nods as Bronnen speaks, 'but now you must face the third and final challenge.'

'Yes, the final challenge,' Gwen agrees.

Lottie clasps her hands. Ah, this is it. 'And then will you show me the Pisky cave?'

Bronnen nods her head solemnly. 'We will.' Gwen nudges her,

and the two link arms. 'We, the Keepers of the Pisky Society Secrets, will show you the Pisky cave.'

Lottie claps her hands with excitement. 'What's the third challenge?'

Bronnen smiles broadly. 'Sacrifice.'

19

THURSDAY MORNING

Annie skimmed the news on the way to work. There were several articles in the national press arguing against the reward offered by the *Herald*. A journalist claimed that they had access to someone on the investigation team who'd told them they were now overwhelmed with calls to the incident room, many of them from time wasters hoping for the payment. There were editorials from former police officers describing the complex balance between offering potential witnesses an incentive to come forward and the risk that those witnesses could be undermined at trial if they were motivated by the reward money.

Annie hadn't thought about a trial. That seemed like something that had nothing to do with the immediate urgency of finding Chloe. Now, the threat of it hung over her as she watched the fields and houses turn to office buildings. The idea that she might have to stand up in front of a courtroom full of people and have her testimony challenged was terrifying. She had to make sure Miller knew she hadn't seen anything at all. There was no way she could face any scrutiny in court.

At least she wouldn't have to testify about the man they'd just released. Her mind wandered, and she imagined what it would feel like to be the person that sent another to jail. She couldn't think of the names of key witnesses in other high-profile cases, but the families and friends of the victims would surely remember them, probably even be grateful to them. She wondered if they would meet after the trial, maybe become friends. If the victim's family didn't forget though, Annie thought, then neither would the family of the convicted. It was all a risk.

When she arrived at work, she was astonished to see that Paul was already in. He beckoned her into his office and waited while she shut the door. She used to feel a lift when Paul called her in. He always asked about her house and whether she was happy with her work. It gave Annie a warm feeling to know that he cared. He was the only person who'd shown any interest in her life outside work, apart from Lauren.

'The police rang me yesterday.'

Annie bit her tongue. About Chloe? About his flat? She studied his face for clues. He looked tired, fine lines around his eyes and bloodshot eyes. His usual confidence was absent. Annie wanted to reach across the desk and pat his hand and ask about how he was. She wondered if she should, but there was something in his tone that felt like a warning.

'Oh?' she said. She sat down so that she didn't have to keep holding herself upright.

'They asked me to confirm what time you left the conference drinks last Thursday.'

Annie tried to look unsurprised. DC Singh *had* asked if anyone could corroborate her story. She searched his face for the signs of anger she'd seen that night when he'd pushed her into the taxi. Singh would definitely have asked him how much she'd drunk and written it down in that little notepad of hers. She pulled her mind back to what Paul was saying. She needed to concentrate, work out how she needed to react. She said nothing.

'Actually, they asked me quite a lot of questions. How much did you drink? What sort of mood were you in? Do you have any close friends? How were you the next day? Have you been acting in any way different to usual? And so on.'

Annie felt her pulse slow right down, like a pause button on reality. Why would they ask all those questions? Was it normal to investigate witnesses like that? Witnesses who hadn't actually seen anything.

'It was almost as if they were investigating you.'

They even had the same thought process!

He raised his eyebrows waiting for her to respond. 'What exactly was it you saw on Thursday night?'

She shook her head, the tears gathering so she couldn't speak without revealing her panic. What had she said? There was nothing; she'd been able to tell them nothing.

Paul leaned across the desk. He sighed. 'What should I have said, Annie? That you were drunk and angry? That you left the conference early enough to have been sitting in your car for nearly an hour before Chloe walked in front of it?'

Annie was shocked by the sharpness in Paul's voice, but maybe he'd stumbled on the answer: she'd fallen asleep in the car. She was just so sure that she hadn't.

'That you seem to be obsessed with Chloe Hills and the investigation?'

'I'm sorry, Paul.' Annie didn't want him to see that he'd shaken her. 'What did you say?'

He shook his head. 'D'you know what they *didn't* ask me?'

She stared at him. 'They didn't ask me whether I really thought you'd gone straight home from the station or whether you might have gone somewhere else first. I know it was you in my flat, Annie.' He put the name badge she'd been given at the conference on the desk. 'I found it on the sink in my bathroom. I was hoping you'd be honest with me.'

Annie could feel the blood draining down through her body, leeching away. He absolutely had known. She put her hand into her pocket and closed it around the sandstone baby. She'd wanted to return it to him, hadn't she? Maybe she could just apologise and hope he wouldn't take it any further. She blinked away the tears and pulled the figure out of her pocket and placed it on his desk facing towards him.

'I'm sorry. I was drunk and angry. I didn't know what I was doing. I didn't mean any harm to you.' She pushed the figurine across to him. 'I know how it looks, but I heard a noise, and it was in my hand, and I just left without thinking. It was so wrong of me; I won't do it again.'

She didn't dare look at him. He'd suggested that he'd already told the police someone had been in his flat. If that was true, he had his proof. If he wanted to call the police, he could do it right now.

The only response she'd have would be to tell them that he'd had the figure in his office all along. It was the only way she could think of surviving it. His word against hers. He can't prove she left the name badge there, it could have been on her desk. So, he tells them a colleague has broken into his flat, with a key, and the only thing taken is a small sandstone baby. She could say he was claiming she'd broken in to his flat in retaliation for refusing to have a relationship with him. It was a dirty move, but she was desperate.

She'd been awake for most of the night working it all out. If they believed Paul, the police might think she was trying to give herself an alibi by saying she'd seen Chloe. But then there was the image of her car in the CCTV with the lights on. It would show her in a bad light to Miller, though, her own boss claiming she'd broken into his flat. Would he wonder what else she'd been up to? That she was hiding something about Chloe?

The humiliation had folded her down on herself, and she made herself sit up straighter to look Paul in the eye. He hadn't moved, just stared at her. Then he reached across the desk, picked up the sandstone figure, and dropped it in a drawer.

'Please leave,' he said.

20

THURSDAY AFTERNOON

Annie watched Paul through the glass panel of his office door all day. Every time he picked up the phone, she assumed he was calling the police, and she could only stare at her screen, unable to concentrate on her work. At one point, Jenna had come up behind Annie with a cup of tea, and she shouted out in fright. The whole office turned to see what was going on.

'Woah, are you all right, Annie?' Jenna looked hurt.

Annie waved Jenna away feeling guilty but unable to find the right words. A couple of people exchanged looks, and Annie dreaded the thought that Paul would tell them what she'd done.

'Sorry! Headache.'

If they didn't speak to her again, she hadn't lost anything, she told herself. She'd have to leave the job now anyway, fired or not, so what did it matter? There was no way Paul would let her stay. It had been no more than a nice moment in her life. Like the way she'd felt searching for Chloe Hills.

The hours dragged by and the police didn't arrive, nor did Paul speak to Annie again. She'd spent most of the day correcting her own mistakes in the sales database and had failed to make the slightest inroads to her workload. Annie made herself go up to his office door to ask him if he'd spoken to the police again before she left but found she didn't have the courage to knock.

Her tension eased a little out of the office, but she felt jostled and shoved as she walked through the crowded streets. She hugged her bag close and kept an eye on everyone around her, her senses prickling with danger.

All the way home, she expected a tap on the shoulder at any minute or a whisper in her ear. There were ribbons and posters along Annie's road now, creeping along like fingers reaching out from Westhurst station. By the time she sat in front of the TV to watch the news, her whole body was taut and sore.

'Chloe's friends have organised a vigil to be held at 8pm tomorrow night. They ask that you wear yellow ribbons ...'

Annie switched off the television. Since Chloe went missing, the whole of Westhurst was changed, and now her own way of life, small as it was, hung in the balance, too.

She didn't trust Hannah and Megan; there was something about the way they didn't seem too anxious about Chloe ... and what were they up to at Paul's apartment block the other night? Maybe they weren't real friends, just the sort that hang out with you for their own kicks, or maybe, they knew where Chloe really was. Had she told Miller about them, or had she been too absorbed in working out how to protect herself? She wished she could say something about what she'd overheard in the car park of Paul's apartment block last night, but it would confirm that she'd at least been hanging around his place.

She curled into the sofa cushions and checked out their Facebook pages. Annie had never used Facebook. Partly she had never made enough friends to need it, but mostly because she had nothing to say. She skimmed through Hannah and Megan's accounts and found nothing remarkable, until Chloe disappeared. Already, their timelines were filling up with people committing to come to the vigil, and Annie recognised Sam among the responses. She searched for a notification from Alex, but couldn't see anyone who might be him. Sam's message was warm and caring like his manner with the search party while they'd been out. She thought of the way he'd encouraged her to talk to the police, trusted that her input would be valuable.

If she went to the vigil, she might bump into Sam, and he would see that she really did care about Chloe, too. The thought was like a little pool of hope after the stress of the day. She wondered what it would be like to be one of Sam's friends. It would be hard to feel alone with a friend like him. She supposed that's why Alex clung to him. The thought of him sent her mind skittering back over the things he'd said to her. Alex wouldn't expect Annie to go to the vigil. So, she knew she had to be there to prove that her concern was genuine in the face of Alex's suspicions. Then perhaps he wouldn't constantly put her down in front of Sam. Or would they think it was even more suspicious that she kept involved when she didn't know Chloe or her family? Her head ached again. She couldn't keep all her thoughts straight.

She wished she had someone to talk to. Lauren had been interested in the investigation, hadn't she? She rang Lauren.

'There's going to be a vigil here tomorrow for Chloe. Will you come with me?'

'Oh, hello, Annie. How are you?'

Annie sighed. Lauren was in one of those moods.

Annie could hear Lauren whispering to somebody in the background. 'I mean, couldn't you have asked me in the morning?'

'Please, Lauren, please say you'll come.'

'Just don't go if it'll worry you, Annie.' The frustration in Lauren's voice was sharp, and Annie checked the time: twelve thirty in the morning. Had she really been sitting online for so long? She couldn't remember if she'd eaten.

'I have to go, because they'll probably be watching me. Everyone'll be watching me. Don't make me go on my own, Lauren. I'm always on my own. Please.'

'Annie, do you really have no one else?'

Annie took a deep breath. 'No.'

She could hear Lauren trying to work out what to do. 'Sure, why not.' She sighed heavily down the phone. 'Talk to me tomorrow.'

She'd have to remind Lauren in the morning, but Annie felt the panic subsiding. She'd go to bed just as soon as her heart rate dropped to normal.

She opened up her laptop again. A still from Hannah and Megan's appeal was on the front page of all her news feeds. She scrolled down, reading the comments. There were so many different ideas about what might have happened to Chloe and what the police should do that it was like a whirlwind of rumour. But not many of them suggested that Megan and Hannah knew anything about it.

Annie wondered if anyone was watching the girls to make sure. They'd stuck in her mind the first time she saw them hanging up the posters. Then, they'd been hiding from Jason Berman at the reconstruction, even though he was a close family friend of the Hills. And now, they'd turned up at, sneaked into, actually, Paul's apartment block. Annie made a mental note to consider mentioning it, if she spoke to the police again. She tried to remember what Kieran had said about them and Berman.

There was not one comment online from anyone about the girls. The majority were aimed at Chloe's parents. Suggesting that she and her parents had a difficult relationship, that Chloe might have run away, that her friends said she'd been acting out of character for ages, that they were covering up a terrible accident. Even more amateur sleuths had popped up, sharing ideas and questions, some from the other side of the world. Someone who claimed to be a body language expert had analysed the Hills' appeal and identified three key points that showed they'd lied. Annie considered these possibilities.

All she was certain of was that Chloe's friends knew more than they were saying. Everybody always assumes it's a man, Annie thought. They never, ever investigate little girls.

2 1

* * *

'We have made our own sacrifices already,' Bronnen said. 'You need to choose yours.'

'And no one's actually going to get hurt?' Lottie whispers.

Gwen smiles and her eyes dart back towards Bronnen.

Bronnen ignores Gwen. 'Course not! They get to live an enchanted life with the Piskies, and we'll get to choose treasure from the Pisky cave.'

Lottie feels uneasy, but she is desperate to complete the challenges now. They've described a cave that is full of treasures that only deserving members of the Pisky Society can see. If Lottie completes her challenges, she will become a member and be permitted to enter the cave.

She has a tiny but growing doubt about the Piskies and why they would pick Bronnen and Gwen. She really hopes they won't turn out to be like the tooth fairy. Lottie pushes her tongue into the gap where her first tooth has been lost. She'd wrapped the tooth in a tissue and placed it under her pillow and tried to stay awake. But the only person who came into her room was Mum, and she felt around under Lottie's pillow while Lottie pretended to sleep. When Lottie checked for her tooth, she found a shiny fifty pence piece.

'Who do you choose, Lottie? You must show yourself worthy and complete the third challenge to join our society.' Bronnen makes her voice formal and doomy.

Lottie looks across to where Tegen sits on her tricycle with Paddington, a melting ice lolly in one chubby fist. Tegen told everyone that she'd seen Lottie letting the ponies out, and, even though Lottie has denied it completely, her father had still gone to apologise to Mrs Harris, and Lottie hadn't got a comic that week.

'What about her family when they notice she's gone?' Lottie doesn't want Tegen to be taken away by the Piskies, not really, but she doesn't really think Bronnen and Gwen mean it. If there's just the tiniest chance they will find some treasure, Lottie must try, so she can make things up to her parents. She crosses her fingers in her skirt pocket.

Bronnen shrugs. 'The Piskies will probably leave a changeling.'

'Won't they notice?' The babies the Piskies leave behind are usually sickly and weak. Everyone knows that.

Gwen shrugs. 'Has anyone you know ever noticed they got a changeling?'

Lottie looks at both of them. 'But it's just a game really, isn't it?'

Bronnen doesn't bother answering Lottie, but Gwen leans forward and whispers in her ear.

'Of course, silly, it's just a game.'

22

FRIDAY AFTERNOON

Annie went to meet Lauren at her offices so they could travel to the vigil together. Lauren had been sending her regular messages all day, saying she thought it was a really bad idea for Annie to go. Annie had to keep reminding Lauren that she very rarely asked her only real friend to do more than stop by for a quick drink.

The foyer stretched across the front of the building, tiled floors and bare walls, so that every sound was amplified. Annie's heels rang out on the stone floor as she crossed to the seating area. She sank into a sofa that was just too low, out of proportion with the high ceiling, and wondered what kind of person thought this would make visitors feel welcome.

She'd arrived early because she was half expecting that Lauren might try and sneak out to find something more interesting to do. The last reminders she'd been sending Lauren had been met with silence, and she was beginning to panic.

Paul had still said nothing about whether he intended to speak to the police. It had been a long day as she tried to avoid him but also secretly hoped to bump into him, just so she could get a sense of what he'd done. He had sent her three emails, strictly about work, and each time she saw his name pop up she'd had to steel herself to read them, holding her breath so much she felt dizzy.

A security guard wandered over to the reception desk and chatted to the women sitting behind it. Annie checked her phone for the millionth time in case Chloe had been found and the vigil cancelled. In fact, there was no new information at all, other than a steady stream of images of Westhurst getting ready. It looked like a macabre street party with ribbons and candles everywhere.

Annie twisted her gloves as she waited, watching the fabric stretch and wrinkle in her hands. Eventually, when she'd nearly given up, she heard Lauren's heels, her confident step recognisable even before she walked around the corner from the lifts. Annie stood up, ready to grab her and hold on tight until they were at Westhurst.

'Look, I really don't think you should do this.' Lauren stopped in front of Annie and raised an eyebrow. 'It's weird.'

'I told you, I have to be there. If I don't go, everyone will think I don't really care.' She grabbed Lauren's hand. 'Besides, it might jog my memory.'

Lauren rolled her eyes. 'Everyone? Half a dozen people who've probably forgotten you exist. Anyway, if they are suspicious of you, won't this make it worse?'

Annie felt herself wobble.

'Joke!' Lauren said quickly, 'Jesus, Annie, what's going on with you?'

Annie put her arm through Lauren's and steered her through the large revolving doors so that they were at least out of that suffocating tank before she replied.

'They already doubt me, Lauren. What if they do think I took Chloe? You know, because I was in the car park when

Chloe was. Who's going to believe I didn't see anything and no one else was there?'

'They're probably not even thinking about you at all.' Lauren's phone rung. 'Shit, sorry I need to get this. Keep walking, and we can talk on the train.'

There was something about walking alongside a person who was on the phone that felt even more lonely to Annie than walking on her own. She resisted the temptation to get out her own phone and pretend to be listening to messages. She kept half an ear open to Lauren's call though, in case there was any suggestion that Lauren might need to back out of the vigil.

The pavements were full of commuters hurrying to get out of the cold, and Annie had to jink and hop to avoid getting knocked over. When they reached Waterloo, they had to squeeze through the crowds to reach the platform. They ran onto the waiting train, but it was so packed that they didn't get to stand close together. Lauren stood staring into a reality that Annie couldn't reach. She looked more and more uncomfortable the further they got from civilisation, as Lauren put it. Finally, the train pulled to a halt at Westhurst, and Annie pushed her way onto the platform, clearing space for Lauren behind her. This at least was her territory. Lauren sniffed at the air as they walked along.

'What is that?'

'Fresh air,' Annie said. Lauren snorted. There were quite a few people getting off the train, and the station car park was already starting to fill.

'So, is there time for a drink first? You can't make me stand outside in this weather unfortified.'

Annie didn't want to risk not being able to get Lauren out of the pub for the vigil, but it was too cold to wait in the open air. Lauren turned and waved at the car park when they reached the top of the steps.

'Funny old place for so much drama.'

Annie ordered them a bowl of chips and asked for it to come quickly. She listened gratefully as Lauren talked about her day, about Tony, the problems of getting a table at the latest restaurants. Annie tuned out slightly, enjoying the warmth and Lauren's company. Eventually, Lauren cocked her head and said.

'Well, out with it. What's going on?'

Annie looked around to check the nearby tables weren't listening in. 'The thing is,' Annie said, 'you know I was in the car park at the same time as Chloe? What if no one else comes forward, and they think that *I* did something to her?'

'Why on earth would anybody think that?' Lauren frowned. 'And who are we talking about now? The police?' Lauren looked puzzled. Annie knew she was assessing whether Annie was just being paranoid or whether there really was anything to it. It was an expression that Annie was familiar with, and she knew she had to be careful. Lauren's patience only lasted so long.

Their chips arrived, and Lauren tipped ketchup in a wobbling blob in the middle so they could dip. Annie checked her watch. They'd have to be quick.

'But why didn't I see anything? Won't they assume I'm covering something up?'

'Jesus!' Lauren's drink spilled as a group of lads shoved passed, and she jumped up before the pool spread to the edge of the table. Annie only just moved out of the way of the drips, her hands shaking as she moved her own glass.

'Hey, don't mind us!' Lauren shouted at their backs and pushed her way to the bar for a cloth and another drink.

'Well, you could just tell them the truth.'

Annie's breath snagged. How did Lauren know about Paul's flat?

'You were totally plastered!' Lauren wiped the table and sat down.

Annie felt the shame of it, of the fact that she had gone to Paul's flat and the fact that she couldn't help find Chloe and the fact she was caught up in all these little lies and omissions.

'Is that why we're here? Because you think it will affect whether the police consider you a suspect or not?' Lauren sucked her teeth. 'That's as mad as thinking it will impress whichever unsuitable boy you've developed a crush on this time.'

Annie just wanted it all to be over now. 'We should get to the vigil, Lauren.'

The cold was like a slap in the face when they left the pub, but they followed the crowd down into the car park. There was now a large group of people gathered near the ticket office, some holding candles or phone torches and others with photographs of Chloe. Annie searched for Sam in the crowd but couldn't see him. Near the steps to the ticket office were Chloe's parents, their friend Berman, and a vicar, his collar visible in the open neck of his parka. Behind them, standing in the shadows, were DS Miller and DC Singh.

Annie could see that the trickle of commuters still emerging from the station were being stopped and questioned by two uniformed police officers. Near the top of the steps were several cameras and journalists.

'So,' Lauren said, stamping her feet, 'what do we do now? Can't say I spend a lot of time at these sorts of things.'

Annie looked around at the crowd pressing close around them. In the dark, everyone seemed unfamiliar, faces distorted by the flickers of fake candles and the lights from the cameras that panned across the crowd. Lauren was restless beside her, but Annie felt rooted to the ground, trapped by so many still bodies on every side. The air was ripe with curls of breath, the sound of feet shuffling, and the rustle of whispering voices.

'We are gathered here together ...' Lauren murmured, and Annie elbowed her in the ribs.

DS Miller led the vicar to the front of the crowd. Annie shrank behind Lauren. Lauren looked from Annie to DS Miller.

'Is that the guy you've been speaking to?'

Annie shushed her just as DS Miller glanced towards them. He continued to look in Annie's direction as the vicar began to speak, and she felt her pulse quicken.

'Chloe's parents would like to thank the local community for their support and especially Chloe's friends, who have been working tirelessly running the campaigns online to find her.' The vicar looked around, and Annie could see Megan and Hannah standing off to one side, their arms around each other and heads bent. The crowd hummed, reluctant to clap.

'Tonight, we have gathered to pray for Chloe's safe return. Wherever you are, Chloe, we are thinking of you and hoping that you will be back with us soon.'

'You know what,' Lauren whispered, 'I bet at least one of those cameras is filming the crowd to spot anyone who looks dodgy. And us, of course, looking beautiful.'

Annie shifted uncomfortably and fell further back behind Lauren.

The vicar finished speaking and someone stepped forward with an iPhone and played a message from one of Chloe's idols, and the crowd joined in to sing her favourite song. At the end, edges of the crowd split off and broke away. Annie drew Lauren to the back of the crowd, away from the journalists and their cameras, who were now trying to record the reactions of the crowd.

'Right,' Lauren said and turned around with such force that she nearly fell over. Annie laughed and went to steady her, only noticing Sam as he appeared on her other side.

'Oh, hello.' Annie felt her cheeks colour. 'Nice to see you, Sam. Well, obviously not here. Wish it wasn't here, because that means Chloe's still missing, and that's really not nice. It's dreadful, of course.'

Lauren looked between them and coughed pointedly. She was taller than Sam in her heels, and Annie noticed that it took him a moment to realise that Lauren was with Annie. She felt a flash of pleasure that he would meet her friend.

'This is my best friend, Lauren.' She nudged Lauren. 'This is Sam. From the search party.' Lauren looked Sam up and down. He recovered enough to extend his hand.

'Right, hello, Lauren. And Annie.'

'Someone's trying to attract your attention.' Lauren nodded behind Sam, and Annie saw that it was Alex. He didn't look keen to come over, but Lauren was hard to ignore; her massive hair and entirely inappropriate clothing for cold weather, meant she was attracting more attention than Annie had anticipated. Alex reached Sam's elbow, and Sam introduced him.

'One more from the search party?' Lauren directed her question to Annie without taking her eyes off Alex.

'Anyway, I guess we just leave now,' Annie said, waving at the dispersing crowds. 'That's it?'

'What else were you expecting?' Alex's tone was off, and Lauren looked surprised.

Lauren stepped a little closer to Alex. 'Rude,' she said.

Annie was more concerned about the journalist who was

heading towards them with a cameraman in tow. She hadn't thought how distinctive Lauren was.

'Let's go, Lauren. We can warm up in the pub before your train.' She ignored Alex. 'Would you like to come with us, Sam? I mean, no pressure, just might be nice.' She took Lauren's arm to pull her through the crowd.

'Well,' Alex said, 'if you think I'm going to risk saying anything in front of the press.' He turned and stalked away.

Sam looked a little embarrassed, his hands shoved down into his pockets. 'Everyone's a little upset.' Sam kicked his feet. 'A journalist pretended to be one of Chloe's relatives the other day. She convinced a few of the pupils at Chloe's school to share their memories of her, and they were quoted saying some pretty unpleasant things. It's been humiliating for them and for Chloe's family. No one wants to make the same mistake again.'

'Well, I can assure you that neither of us are journalists. I mean, look at her.' Lauren rolled her eyes and headed for the steps up towards the pub.

'Night,' Annie mumbled and followed after her. She felt her stomach contract. Had they really thought she was a journalist? She wondered if Sam would feel differently now that he knew she wasn't. She didn't think so, and her stomach contracted.

23

FRIDAY EVENING

The pub was heaving, but they managed to squeeze onto a long table at the back. Lauren kicked off her shoes.

'What? You try standing on these all day.' Someone in the group at the other end of the table laughed. Annie turned to look but couldn't see if it was directed at Lauren.

'So, why on earth does Alex think you're a journalist?'

'I guess I asked too many questions? They must really hate reporters.'

Lauren looked confused. 'He's got that wrong then, hasn't he?' Annie nodded. 'Well, cheer up then, that's not so bad.'

'Lauren, what if the police think I had something to do with Chloe going missing?' Annie felt miserable.

Lauren sat back and folded her arms. 'Why would they be suspicious of you?'

Annie sighed. 'It's just that they know I was there when Chloe went missing, but I don't remember seeing her. And the police said they haven't spoken to anyone else who was there at the same time, even though I said there were other people there. So, either I'm lying, or there's some reason the others haven't come forward.'

'Have they interviewed you as a suspect?'

'No.'

'Have they searched your house?'

'No.'

'Well, they can't be taking it that seriously then.'

'Someone not taking you seriously, Annie?'

Annie jumped as Paul appeared beside her. To bump into him twice in Westhurst in such a short time, now that she'd actually prefer to avoid him, was the worst sort of luck. He'd probably come to gloat about calling the police about his flat. She looked past Paul to see if there was a police officer with him, but there was no one there. Lauren raised her eyebrows.

'Um, this is Paul. From work.' Annie waved at him and then back at Lauren. 'This is my friend, Lauren.'

Paul nodded to Lauren. 'Would you excuse us a minute please, Lauren?'

Lauren leant over and whispered in Annie's ear. 'The Paul?'

Annie nodded, and Lauren pushed her chair back and took her glass of wine to the bar. Annie watched her lean over and strike up a conversation with the barman.

Paul took Lauren's seat. Annie braced herself to hear that he'd reported her to the police and was firing her. He took a little while to speak, his eyes flicking towards Lauren. 'Look, when I saw you in here, I thought it was a good opportunity to chat away from the office.'

Annie's heart flipped, as the tiniest hope surfaced that Paul might be interested in her after all, but flattened when she saw that Paul was frowning. She was a problem he was dealing with, not an opportunity.

She sighed. 'You called the police. Of course you did. You definitely should have.' Annie studied the whorls in the grain of the wood in the table. She kept her hands on her lap, where he wouldn't be able to see them shaking, and tried to put her shoulders back. 'I didn't mean to take anything — that was an accident. I didn't mean to scare you either.' She could barely look him in the eye. 'I don't know what I was thinking. I just wanted to talk to you and, I don't know. I got it wrong. Sorry. I don't know what else to say.'

'I did call the police,' Paul shifted in his seat, and Annie looked up, her forehead tensing with confusion. 'Initially, straight after it happened, but I've called them back and told them I made a mistake.'

Why would he have done that? She wasn't worth black-mailing, unless he was going to make her resign. If she resigned, he wouldn't have to go through the disciplinary process before firing her. He was waiting for her to respond. But at least she wouldn't have to speak to the police. Or tell them she was drunk when she drove home. Or make them look too closely at the fact she was in the car park when Chloe went missing.

'Thank you. I won't do it again. I mean I can't ...' She bit her lip before she told him that she'd already checked for his spare keys. 'I'm not used to drinking so much, and I just got upset about ...' she spread her hands out, 'things.' She couldn't read his expression.

Paul pulled the sandstone figure out of his pocket and placed it on the table in front of her.

'Annie, just stop.' He'd been waiting for her to finish, but now held up his hands. She sat up straighter, ready for him. 'I called the police and told them I was mistaken about the break-in,' he laughed awkwardly, 'because, I mean, they've got better things to do, and it's fairly trivial. Although, the idea that someone was creeping into my home gave me the chills for a while, still does actually, so I'd be grateful if you gave it up now.'

He was trying to make a joke of it. Annie couldn't quite take it all in.

He pushed the figurine over to her. 'I think you gave this to me, and it probably means more to you than it does to me.'

The pain sank into her as she felt her whole body accept the reality that Paul was never going to be anything more than her manager. Well, of course he wasn't now.

'Oh, okay,' she said. 'Thank you.' She felt small, as small as the sandstone baby now enclosed tightly in her fist. 'Do you want me to resign? I mean, I will, but I really need another job to pay rent. I'll start looking for something else straight away. I know you don't have to help me, but I'd be really grateful.' She couldn't believe that she was actually begging.

'No, Annie, you don't need to resign, but maybe you do need some time off? You look unwell, and I really think you should see a doctor, maybe talk to somebody.'

Ah, he was going to make sure she owed him, and then he'd gradually push her out of her job. He was probably already laying the foundations at work, telling people that she couldn't cope. She'd need to be careful what she said then.

'Why don't you take a few days off. All this,' he waved around the pub, 'seems to have affected you.' He gave every impression of real concern. 'I mean the ribbons and posters, and now this vigil. To be honest, it's freaking me out a little, and I'm not ...' He stopped himself, but Annie could fill in the blank. *I'm not the one who's crazy*, he was going to say.

Annie felt tiredness wash over her. If Paul was being honest, she didn't need to worry about the police arresting her for breaking into his flat. A few days off did sound appealing. She could catch up on her missed sleep. It was so much easier for her to sleep in the daylight than in the dark when she was this tired. But she couldn't give Paul any ammunition if she wanted to keep her job until she found another. She couldn't relax her vigilance one bit.

'I'm fine, Paul.'

'I think you should consider it, Annie. Maybe get away from here for a while, if it's all stressing you out. You've plenty of untaken holiday.'

Annie never really took leave except for the dentist or shopping. She already spent enough time on her own. Paul looked around the pub and shifted awkwardly. The atmosphere was odd, everyone half listening to other people's conversations.

Lauren reappeared with two more glasses of wine and stood beside Paul pointedly. Paul sighed and got up. Lauren took the seat.

'Think about what I said, Annie. You can let me know over the weekend.' Paul turned to Lauren. 'Look after her.'

Annie watched Paul leave, trying to make sense of it.

'Wow, did he just tell me to look after you?' Lauren shook her head extravagantly. 'I mean, okay, that's sweet, but is that really the man you said has been so awful?'

Annie felt a flash of anger with Lauren. She was so dismissive of Annie's feelings. Behind her, Annie could see Paul pick his way through the tables to sit down with the woman she'd seen him with before, Claire.

Lauren followed her gaze. 'Ah, he's got someone. Give it up, Annie.'

Annie dropped her head into her hands.

'All right,' Lauren said, reaching across to pull Annie's hands away, 'what else is going on?'

Annie stared through the crowded pub to where Paul was sitting, trying to avoid the steel in Lauren's eyes. She looked soft and girly in her fluffy jumpers and her big earrings, but

Annie knew there was a spine of iron in there. Not like her; she was shaky inside and out.

'You know I told you I didn't go round to see Paul last Thursday night?'

Lauren stared at Annie and blew her breath out through her teeth. 'You did see him? Why didn't you tell me?'

Annie shook her head. 'He wasn't there, but I know where he keeps, kept, his spare key.' She looked at her hands. The intensity of Lauren's stare was unbearable. Annie waited a moment for her to say something, but she'd pursed her lips in a mammoth effort to let Annie finish. 'Well, I went into his flat. I didn't do anything, not deliberately! But I heard a noise and left in a hurry. The next day, I realised I'd picked up an ornament and put it in my pocket, just a keepsake I'd given him, nothing important. I took it home by accident.'

'Sorry. You did *what?*'

Annie flinched away from the storm of disgust blowing over Lauren's face.

'And he knows?' Lauren was sat right back in her chair, as far from Annie as she could be. 'I don't believe this.'

Annie twisted her fingers back and forth. 'He was furious and reported it as a break-in to the police. I've been expecting to be arrested at any minute. My nerves are wrecked.'

Lauren was rarely speechless.

Annie took a deep breath. 'I've already apologised and returned the ornament. He was just telling me he's called the police to say he made a mistake and wasn't burgled after all.'

'He did that for you?' Lauren frowned. 'Again, doesn't sound much like the Paul you've described lately.'

Annie felt the shame wash over her. Of course, Paul wasn't all bad, not really. He'd been truly kind to her from the start. That's why she'd thought there might be something there between them.

She took a jagged breath. 'He suggested I take some time off. I think he's probably trying to push me out of my job. I mean, why wouldn't he? He's probably building a case against me, and I've just made it really easy for him. I'll have to find a new job. I don't know what to do.' She couldn't bear to admit that maybe she'd got Paul wrong.

Lauren seemed to gather her breath. 'So, let me get this straight. You *broke into* a man's house, took something, and, when he tells you he's made it good with the police for you and won't accept your resignation, all you can think is that he's trying to get you sacked?'

Annie had never seen Lauren so angry. It did sound bad when she put it like that. Annie's judgement was never to be trusted. She knew that, and yet she kept getting things wrong. It would always be like this.

'You don't understand, Lauren.' Exhaustion and despair hit Annie, and she couldn't marshal a single thing that might make sense of what she'd done.

Lauren snorted. 'I mean it's not even funny, Annie. This isn't a rom-com. What you did was so wrong. It's illegal.'

'I didn't do any damage. I just looked at his stuff. It's not that interesting actually, ha ha. So, you know, I haven't really done any harm.' Lauren said nothing. 'He probably should take advantage of it to make me leave though.'

Lauren remained silent for a moment. 'You didn't do any harm? That's no excuse, Annie.' She sucked her teeth. 'You've always been a bit odd, but I don't even know who you are.'

No, you don't, Annie thought sadly.

Lauren looked at her watch. 'You know what, I need to go.' She stood up. 'I really can't believe you did that. That's fucked up, Annie. I don't think I can keep being the only person you dump this stuff on; it's too much. You're too much.' She picked up her bag and put it over her shoulder.

'Don't go, Lauren, please!' This was why Annie hadn't told her anything in the first place, but the reality of Lauren's reaction cut her to shreds.

Lauren stepped away from Annie. 'I've had enough, Annie. I'm done.'

'Lauren, please!'

'You know what, maybe I should go to the police. If you're capable of that, who's to say you're not capable of abducting a young girl?'

And then Lauren was gone.

* * *

Bronnen and Gwen have collected oxeye daisies and indigo sheep's-bits and woven them together, so that the four children are wearing floral crowns. They pick their way through the sea carrot that hangs into the path and exclaim at the gulls diving from above their heads to land on the mobile water of the estuary below. Lottie's stomach is doing excited somersaults, and she chatters to Tegen, whose hot little hand is firmly held in her own.

They reach a rickety bench by the path, and Bronnen pushes the grass to one side, so they can see that there's a way down over the rocks to the beach. Bronnen goes ahead, and Gwen steps back to let Lottie and Tegen pass. Lottie shows Tegen how to go down on her bum and then hands her to Bronnen to jump her down the last few feet. Lottie lands on the sand and looks along the beach. It's a golden horseshoe and empty apart from the odd gull walking through the seaweed. A large bird watches her with one eye and then reaches down to pick up a dead crab. She feels the crunch of the crab's shell in her bones.

Tegen shrieks, and Lottie looks up to see that she's run down to the water's edge and is jumping over the tiny waves that are retreating from the beach. The tide is now too far out for any sight-

seers to reach by boat. Behind Lottie, Gwen shouts, too, and then cartwheels to where Tegen is playing. She chases Tegen, and their laughter echoes around the rocky cliffs.

Lottie looks for Bronnen. She is walking purposefully towards a pile of rocks at one end of the beach. Lottie covers her eyes to block the sun and makes out the dark opening to a cave. She jumps up and down with excitement. This must be the Pisky cave! She shouts to Bronnen to wait and nearly stumbles as she hares off after her.

Bronnen turns and pauses with her hands on her hips. Lottie skids to a standstill and sprays sand over Bronnen's bare feet. She kicks off her own shoes high into the air and laughs as they fall at odd angles either side of her.

'Well, you'll have to go back and get those two now.' Bronnen points towards where Tegen and Gwen are running in a wide circle through the shallows, glittering droplets rising around them. Lottie sighs and turns back, calling out their names as she leaps across the sand.

When they return, Bronnen has reached the mouth of the cave and is sitting cross-legged on a patch of sand where the sun has been filtered through the leafy trees overhanging the cliffs. She leans forward and draws in the sand, and the other three gather around to look.

'Before we go in and start the ceremony, we need to prepare.'

'What's a cemery?' Tegen looks at Lottie.

'Shh,' she replies, 'you'll find out.' Lottie's head is buzzing with excitement. Finally, she will be admitted to the Pisky Society and be able to enter the Pisky cave. She is dying to look inside, can already imagine that the sun glimmering on the water is a reflection of the gold and gemstones they're bound to find there. She pinches herself hard, because she knows there is no point rushing Bronnen.

'What's the plan then, Bron?' Gwen points at the markings that Bronnen has made in the sand.

Bronnen raises her arms on either side of her head, so that she is *the shape of a tulip and closes her eyes. Tegen looks up at Lottie, and Lottie puts her finger to her lips and then pulls Tegen's little hand into her lap.*

'First, we need to make sure we have everything we need.' Gwen nods and pulls out a skein of green twine and a small penknife and places them in one of the circles she's drawn in the sand.

24

SATURDAY AFTERNOON

Annie took down the pad from the fridge and sat down to write her list for the day. She watched the jagged writing fill the page and then tore it up to start again. She couldn't seem to get it quite right. There was an item missing or the order was wrong or she couldn't remember how to spell something. L A U N D R Y. What a funny word. It didn't look like lawn or yawn. Didn't sound like quandary. This wasn't a quandary she wanted to be in.

She gave up and rested her head on the table. Her eyes were gritty from the hours she'd spent walking the house during the night. Doors locked. Windows closed. Fire extinguishers in date. At least she didn't have to worry about the police arresting her for the break-in at Paul's flat. She held the thought at the front of her mind, ignoring the memory of Lauren's expression of disgust, and made herself get up.

The tea was still scalding hot when she gulped it down. The pain cleared her foggy head a little. She scribbled down her list again and got started. The messiness of it made her feel uneasy, and she had to keep checking what she'd done, but, each time she checked an item off, she felt a little calmer. Eventually, each task she completed brought her more peace, until she felt able to leave the house. A walk was what she really needed to blow away this hovering sense of dread.

Annie considered phoning her mother. Lauren was out of the question, and there wasn't anyone else. She couldn't imagine what her mother would say, even whether she'd believe that Annie couldn't remember seeing Chloe, but she knew she'd be disappointed. Annie didn't think she could bear to hear her mother say that. She couldn't bear to hear her mother question what she'd done. Although, Annie was beginning to wonder herself what she had done.

It was late when she cleared the final item from her list. The house was clean and tidy, the laundry drying, the shopping put away, and her dinner laid out in the kitchen. There was nothing else she needed to do. She'd had to keep rewriting the list and repeating some of the tasks and missing others out and her head was on fire but it was done at last.

Annie decided to walk up to the village and pick up some books from the library before it shut. If she could get immersed in something, she wouldn't have to keep thinking about the loathing in Lauren's eyes.

The dark sky was clear of clouds, so there were a few scattered stars. Annie knew some of them were actually planets, but she'd never learned which ones. Maybe she'd pick up a book on astronomy, perhaps a child's one, and wrap herself up warm to sit in the garden tonight. She couldn't imagine why she hadn't thought of that before. A perfect solitary pastime, she'd pick up a new notebook, too, so she could record what she saw. It would be far better than scrolling through the news and the comments about Chloe. There was nothing she could do about Paul or Lauren until her head was clear.

It was shocking how much the yellow ribbons felt a normal

part of the fabric of Westhurst now. In the library, the volunteer librarian spoke in hushed tones to an older man checking out a stack of books about military history. Annie didn't need to hear what they were saying to know that they were discussing Chloe. When the man had gone, the librarian asked Annie if she'd finished choosing her books.

'I've asked my son to pick me up, so I don't have to walk home on my own.' The woman looked out into the dark street.

Yes, with Chloe missing for more than a week, there probably was something or someone to be worried about out there. Annie felt a tingling on the back of her neck, as if a thousand eyes were staring at her. She made her choice quickly and put the books into the canvas bag that she'd rolled up in her pocket. She wasn't the only person who was frightened. She wished she could reassure this woman.

'Shall I wait with you until your son turns up? I mean I'm sure there's nothing to worry about, really. Not that you can be sure that I'm not just waiting for everyone to leave before I pounce. Ha ha!' Annie curled her fingers like claws.

The woman went pale and stepped back away from Annie. 'No!' She took a breath and said more steadily, 'you go, and I'll lock up behind you. My son's probably sitting in the car watching for me now.'

Annie realised her mistake and felt herself flush with embarrassment. She ran from the library, the eyes of the librarian hot on her back.

It was the quiet time between shops closing and people coming out for dinner. A train pulled up at the station, and passengers alighted with shopping bags that were now illustrated with stars and holly leaves. It felt clear and cold enough for snow, too, Annie thought, and she pushed her hands a little further into her pockets. A group of three men crossed the car park, and Annie recognised Jason Berman and Kieran. She looked around for somewhere she could hide before they saw her. The shadows of an office doorway hid her as she waited for them to pass, but they stopped just by the alleyway.

'So, are we going to do it or not?' Kieran's voice was spiked with frustration.

'How can we be sure we've got the right person?' The third man's earring glinted in the gloom, but his face was indistinct, blurry. 'What if he hasn't got Chloe?'

Kieran shifted, and Annie could make out Berman, bulky in that waxed jacket, pull his hands out of his pockets. He put an arm around the man who'd spoken.

'Look, mate, even if he hasn't got Chloe, he's still a paedo, and we don't want him round here. How old's your daughter, Kev? Ten, eleven? I need to be 100% sure he's not hiding her, or any other kids.' Berman took his arm back and jabbed the man in the chest. 'That girl's important to me.' Annie could hear the catch in his voice. 'I mean, the family is.'

Annie wondered who they were talking about. Why hadn't they told the police if they thought they knew who had Chloe?

Kieran bounced from foot to foot like a boxer. 'I agree. It's a win-win.'

Did they mean the man the police had already released? Annie had seen the comments about him being a registered sex offender, but was that speculation or had it been confirmed? Berman had his back to her, and she could see his thin hair curling over the collar of his jacket. She was almost near enough to smell the musty odour of it.

''Course, but I mean how can you be sure you've got the right address?' Kev looked to Kieran for support, but Kieran shrugged and looked back to Berman.

Annie wanted to walk away and not listen to this, but, if she moved now, it would be obvious that she'd overheard them. She stepped back further into the doorway and knocked against the wall.

'What was that?'

Annie froze, holding her breath. She couldn't see the group now, but it sounded like they were standing still, too, listening. Someone walked out from the shadows of the alley, and Kieran appeared on the pavement and looked around. Annie could feel her muscles straining to move so that she considered stepping out as if it was perfectly normal for her to be there, but, before she could, Kieran shouted back to the others.

'It's nothing.' He raised his arms and turned in a slow circle. 'Just us. Everyone else is hiding at home.'

'Perhaps we should discuss this over a drink back at mine.' Berman appeared with an arm around Kev's shoulder, and the three walked up towards Christchurch Road

It took Annie a few minutes to gather enough courage to step out of the dark and walk across the car park to the steps up to the road. She wasn't sure what she'd just heard, but it had set her insides churning again. She glanced back towards where the three men had gone but they were long out of sight.

25

SATURDAY EVENING

I t was a clear dry night, the sky flat as a cinema screen, and the silhouettes of the bare trees spiked the darkness above her as she walked home. The faintest stars pricked the sky so far away that Annie felt as though she was shrinking, diminishing into a tiny speck of herself compared to the world around her. She pulled her coat tighter, wondering about Berman and where he thought Chloe was. The men's conversation had made her feel more uneasy, but she couldn't work out what to do. If only she could ask Lauren, but she knew Lauren would be suspicious of anything she said now.

As she came around the bend at the bottom of the hill, she saw a car parked outside her house and stopped where she was, muscles tense and ready to run. There was something familiar about the figure standing beside it, and when he turned towards her, she could just make out the relaxed features of DS Miller leaning against the car. He raised his hand to make it clear that he was waiting for Annie.

Had he driven past and seen her listening in on Berman? It couldn't be that. Berman couldn't possibly have done anything in the time it took her to get home. She started walking again. She'd already left a message to say that she hadn't seen where Chloe went after the car park. Hadn't he received it?

'I didn't know you were coming.' It was the last thing Annie needed; her head had been all over the place from the moment she woke. 'I'd have thought you'd be busy with all the calls coming in for the reward. The papers say you've been absolutely inundated. You must have plenty of other people to talk to.' Annie thought of Berman and Kieran and wondered if she should say something. All she'd really heard was them talking about looking for Chloe. There was something about the tone Berman had used when he'd talked about her, but Annie knew she couldn't explain that. She was already too involved, and for no good reason. 'You're bound to find someone who knows something, aren't you?'

'We want to ask you a few more questions about the night Chloe went missing. May we come in?'

The other officer, Singh, got out of the car, and Annie unlocked her front door. She walked straight through to the kitchen and put the kettle on. Exhaustion wound its way through her body, and the headache that had been blooming all day hammered when the kettle hissed to a boil.

'We don't need tea, thank you,' Singh said. Annie heard her through a fog and nodded her head.

'I do. I'm freezing and my head hurts.' Should she tell them about Berman? What did she actually know though? She'd wasted enough of their time already.

Miller tried to make small talk while Annie got out a mug and tea bag. 'Actually, we have a team answering all the calls to the helpline.' He stepped back out of the way as she took the milk from the fridge. 'Most people say they're not interested in the reward. What about you?'

'Apparently that's all I'm interested in,' Annie muttered. 'That and digging up a story.'

'What was that?'

Annie shook her head and tried to tune him out. She wondered who the man with the earring was, Kev. He'd sounded less keen on Berman's plans. Maybe he would talk them both round and no harm would be done.

'I left you a message,' she said, once the tea was made. 'I only rang because I wanted to be sure that I'd told you I didn't see anything — you needn't have come here. I don't remember seeing Chloe at all. So, I can't have seen anyone with her. I mean, obviously the CCTV shows I was there, but I just don't remember. That's all I wanted to say. You could have rung.'

She walked through to the lounge and sat down on the sofa, holding the steaming cup in her hands. Ordinarily, Annie might have taken pride in the fact that someone was seeing her home, neat and tidy after the efforts of the day, but not today. Miller pulled a chair out from the table and sat very close to her, so near she could have kicked him if she wanted to. Singh went to stand in front of the fireplace. Annie noticed her stop to look at the little sandstone figurine and watched to see what she would do with it. Now that Paul had actually given it to her, she didn't need to hide it.

Miller cleared his throat to attract her attention and leant forward.

'We want to ask you a few more questions about that night.' He checked his watch. 'It won't take long. Singh here is on a hot date later.' He smirked over his shoulder to his colleague, but she ignored him. 'What time did your train arrive at Westhurst, Annie?'

She tried to remember what she'd told them already. 'I don't know, before ten I think.'

Singh wrote something down in her notebook. She didn't look overly excited about her date, Annie thought.

Miller nodded. 'Yes, that's what you said. And Mr Brand confirms that you left the conference drinks before 9pm. So that all fits, doesn't it?' He shook his head. 'The thing is, though, I would have expected you to have left the station car park before Chloe was even there, and yet …' He tapped the CCTV still that he pulled out of the folder on his lap and narrowed his eyes. It wasn't a question, so Annie didn't answer.

Singh shifted position.

'Oh, that's right,' he glanced back at Singh, 'you were finishing the crossword?'

Annie knew he didn't believe her. 'I didn't see Chloe. I didn't see anyone else. I didn't see anything.'

Miller sighed and twisted round to set the folder on the table. He rested his elbows on his knees and brought his gaze back towards Annie. A hint of coffee and cheap deodorant reached her, and Annie recoiled. 'Now, I'm finding that very hard to believe, given you seemed so keen to help us when you rang.' He smiled and pushed his hair back, and, for a moment, the gesture reminded her of Paul.

She stiffened. His knees were almost touching hers.

'Has someone told you not to speak to us?'

Annie saw something that might have been concern in his eyes and felt herself soften. She shook her head.

'Because if anyone has warned you not to speak to us, you know, threatened you, we can help.'

She thought of her mother. Her mother had warned her not to get involved. She stifled a giggle; would they protect her from her mother? Miller frowned.

'Oh, no, nobody has told me not to speak to you.' She pulled her face under control. 'Quite the reverse, actually. I shouldn't have wasted your time, just wanted to put my hand up to say, "that's me in the car, so you needn't waste time looking for me," and to tell you I didn't see a thing. Not one useful thing.' The thought that someone might threaten her sank in suddenly, and she sobered up. 'Why would anyone want to stop me telling you that?'

Miller said nothing.

'Oh. Do you think someone saw me when they took Chloe, and now they might want to keep me quiet?' If only they knew the truth. Annie thought of the threatening tone of Berman, but they were talking about visiting a 'him', not a 'her'.

Miller stood up and moved the curtain aside to look out the window. Annie had to stop herself from following. 'Is someone there?'

He turned around on his heel and smiled. 'No, but you are worried?'

Annie hadn't been. The thought that someone might be kidnapping people from Westhurst was scary, but she'd tried to push it to the back of her mind. That was a normal reaction, wasn't it? She shook her head.

'You're not? Well, that's good. Although, I'd understand if you were.' Miller sat back down slowly and watched her for what felt like minutes. 'Okay, well, now I'm going to ask you to go over your movements again once you'd left those conference drinks.' He looked up at her, a small tight smile of false apology.

Annie glanced at Singh, but she maintained her inscrutable expression and stared at her notebook. Annie could feel her headache spreading to her shoulders.

'You said you thought other passengers alighted at West-hurst with you?'

'Yes.'

'Can you describe them?'

Annie closed her eyes and tried to think back to the Wednesday night. So many evenings stepping off a train into the darkness that they all merged. 'I can't. I don't know how many people or what they looked like. It's not as though I was trying to remember them or anything. I'm sure I'd have noticed if I was on my own, though. That's all I meant.' Would she really? She was always on her own. She smiled at them both. 'So, that's it I'm afraid.' She was so tired, and the whole conversation felt unreal and meaningless.

'When you reached the car park, do you remember seeing anyone else? Perhaps a car leaving or a pedestrian near the shops?'

Annie thought of the arcade and the alleyway through to Paul's apartment block. She frowned. All she could think about was Berman, Kieran, and Kev hiding in the dark there earlier.

'No.' She tried to appear calm, but her heart was racing.

'So, that would make you the only person in that car park when Chloe was last seen? You don't seem certain.'

Did they really suspect her? Annie felt the guilt coil and writhe in her stomach. She was the last person to see Chloe; that's all they had. They didn't need to know what she'd done. She tried to focus her attention on Miller.

'Well, I guess somebody could have come off the platform at the unlit end of it.' She thought of Berman skulking in the alley. 'Or maybe be waiting in that alley beside Tandoori Villa.'

DS Miller looked up. 'Yes, that's right, you didn't have full view of the car park.'

Annie nodded, and he smiled. They were just checking after all. Of course, they had to do that. She smiled back.

'So, you just have a sense that there were other people around?'

'Yes.' Annie looked at Miller. 'But I was tired. I just wanted to get home.'

Miller nodded again, and Annie took a breath. He was just doing his job. Should Annie tell him about overhearing the conversation between Berman and Kieran? She couldn't really be sure what she had heard. It would be another coincidence, too, that she was the one who'd been there to see them. The last thing Annie, and Chloe, needed was for her to be drawn in further.

'The thing is, Annie,' DC Singh broke in, 'at the moment, we haven't found anyone else who says they were there. So, it's interesting to us that none of these people have come forward. Yet.' Her eyes held Annie's, and Annie sensed that Singh wanted to say more.

The skin on Annie's neck prickled. 'So, do you think that one of the people who got off the train with me took Chloe?'

'We certainly need to speak to them.' Annie felt Miller's eyes searching her face. 'That's why it's so important that you tell us everything you know ...'

'... As the only person who claims they were there when Chloe was on the CCTV,' Singh finished.

Annie wondered why Singh emphasised 'claims' despite the photographic evidence. Singh's face was carefully blank compared to the encouraging smiles of Miller. Did Singh think Annie was lying?

'So, you're sure Chloe's been abducted?' Nearly ten days missing. It was rare for a missing persons case to have a good outcome after that length of time. There was the girl whose mother had faked an abduction, a few teenagers and young women who'd escaped their captors after years of abuse, but mostly it was bodies or nothing at all. Annie closed her eyes and tried really hard to think about that Thursday night, but all she could remember was the desolation she'd felt in Paul's flat and hearing a voice outside his door.

'We are keeping all lines of investigation open.'

'But I can't have been the only person there then.' Annie looked at DS Miller. 'What about the man you arrested?'

He was still smiling, but a flicker of muscle moved in his jaw. If they believed Chloe had been abducted, and Annie was the only other person there, did they think she was the abductor? She should never have called, never have pretended she might be important. What had she been thinking? If Miller or Singh found out who she was, they would never believe she wasn't involved.

'Do you think I had something to do with it?'

A black hole opened, and Annie felt her mind spiralling away. It wasn't fair. It was her fault, though. She could never break free of it, never relax.

* * *

The tide is almost completely out, and the sea water that has collected in the sand ridges sparkles as the sun bounces off it. Lottie wants to run and play through the little pools, but Bronnen is intent on her final challenge. Tegen squirms in the shallow hole they've dug out of the sand and keeps asking to go home. Lottie fishes out the last biscuit from her bag and hands it over.

'It's time,' Bronnen says, and she and Gwen stand up. 'Now, we can enter the Pisky cave.'

Lottie feels a surge of excitement and leaps to her feet. 'Come on, Tegen, let's look for the treasure.'

Bronnen and Gwen laugh, but then Bronnen puts her hand up. 'You must follow me and not touch anything, unless I say.'

The rocks by the entrance to the cave are slippery with the fine sand that has been scattered across them when the tide left. A ragged line of seaweed makes a visual barrier between the golden beach and the shade of the cave. Lottie feels the loss of warmth on her back with a shiver as she follows Bronnen and Gwen into the darkness. She has to tug at Tegen's hand to make her come, and the little girl whimpers in complaint.

Gwen pulls two torches out of her own backpack and passes one to Bronnen. They switch them on and shine them around the cave in arcs so that Lottie can't really see more than slick black walls and jumbled stones. The floor is dry, but there's a faint smell of salt and cigarette butts. Lottie wrinkles her nose, and Tegen almost slips out of her grasp as she trips on a plastic bag. Empty cans scrape inside it.

'Where is the Pisky bit?' Lottie asks. These are not the gem-studded walls she expected, and there are no chests overflowing with gold or jewellery.

'Oh, well, we haven't finished the final challenge yet.' Bronnen shines the torch into her own face, and it bleaches the colour from her skin, so that just her head is visible in the darkness. Tegen screams and Lottie squeezes her hand. This isn't what she's been expecting at all. Her stomach turns over, and she feels a little nauseous. Probably hunger, her mother would say, but the skin on the back of her neck prickles, and the sounds of the sea and the gulls seem very faint in the distance.

* * *

When Singh took the mug from her hands, Annie realised she was standing in the middle of the room. She could see scalding tea was over her hands, and she stared at them waiting to feel the pain.

'I'll get a wet cloth,' Singh said and left the room. Miller led Annie back to the sofa and sat down beside her.

'What's just a coincidence?' DS Miller asked. 'Why do you say that?'

Annie looked at the skin on her fingers turning pink. She must have been shouting, but she had no idea what she'd said.

'Come on, Annie. I know you want to do the right thing. I felt that as soon as we met you.'

Annie shook her head. She just wanted it all to stop now.

'But what about the CCTV? Can't you just check that?'

Miller sighed. 'We both know that only covers the area just outside the ticket office. Not the other exit off the platform.' He leant forward. 'But you would have noticed someone there, wouldn't you? Let's see if we can jog your memory?'

Annie stared at the pink skin on her hands and brought them up to her cheek. 'Okay.' Her hands were burning, but everything else felt numb.

Singh came back and wrapped a damp tea towel around Annie's hands. It dripped through her skirt, the stain spreading across her legs. The pain shot through her head and expanded so much that her vision blurred.

'Great.' Miller smiled. 'Take your time.'

Singh glared at Miller. Annie wondered why she looked so angry with him. It wasn't her hand blistering or her head being poked and jabbed.

'It was dark, but I'm pretty sure there was someone else.' She couldn't let them believe she was the only one there. 'In the car park,' she just wanted them to go now, 'so they must have got off the train.' She remembered footsteps in the alley. Had she heard people talking? She thought so, but where exactly?

'Good, Annie, good. Let's try something. I'll ask you some questions and you answer them as quickly as you can.'

Like a game, Annie thought, concentration or word association maybe. Fine.

'Man or woman?'

Annie almost laughed. 'Man.'

'What height would you say?'

She sighed. 'I didn't notice.'

'Taller than me?'

Annie nodded, Miller wasn't tall. Singh wrote in her notebook.

'White? Black? Asian?'

'Too dark to see.'

'Coat? Jacket? Suit?' He looked at her expectantly.

Annie's vision swam. 'Jacket.' Her hands were throbbing, and she looked to the door again. As long as she didn't say anything distinctive.

Not smoking. No beard. Dark hair. Thinning.

She wondered if Berman had already told the police about his suspicions. Was that why he wanted Kieran and that other man to go with him, because the police hadn't listened to him either? She could picture his bulky shoulders and the way his face jutted forward when he spoke.

'Anything else?'

Annie shook her head.

'Last question, I promise: did you notice the type of jacket? Denim, padded, waxed?'

'Waxed.'

'Great, I think we've got what we need. You've been very helpful.'

DC Singh glared at Miller again.

'Oh, did you have any questions?' he asked her.

'When you got off the train, did you go anywhere else before you drove home?'

Ah, this was it. Paul had lied to her; he hadn't called them back. She should just admit it, tell them it was her. She could stick to her plan and claim that Paul was trying to set her up out of spite. It probably wasn't really important to Chloe's case anyway.

'Where would I go?' She stalled while she tried to work it all through. Tell them the truth and hope they'd see it as a trivial thing compared to a missing child. Hope they'd accept that it was a mistake. But it was a risk. What if they decided they should investigate her further?

'I'm just wondering why you would be sitting in your car right in front of Chloe Hills and not be able to remember seeing her? Is it possible you'd gone somewhere else?'

Miller coughed, but Singh ignored him. He looked furious, as though he didn't agree with Singh's question. Had Singh read Paul's initial break-in report and suspected Annie? Annie remembered her picking up the sandstone figure on their first visit. She took a breath.

'The headlights are on in the photo. So, I must be in the car.' This was her last chance to tell them what she'd done before they could accuse her of deliberately misleading them. She thought of Lauren's reaction and felt her insides squirm. If you were guilty of the one thing, everyone expected you to be guilty of others. 'I'm sorry I can't give you enough to identify anyone. Besides, whoever was there has probably got nothing to do with it. No more than if I'd seen her friends hanging around there.'

'What's that?' Singh looked up.

Annie wondered if she should mention her suspicions of Megan and Hannah again, but she needed to concentrate on protecting herself, and her hands were in agony. It wasn't that night anyway, Annie remembered. She'd heard the one voice that night, but that was from outside Paul's flat. And she couldn't tell them that. She shook her head.

'Sorry, look, I'm tired and getting confused.' She lifted her hands. 'I really need to see to these.'

Singh closed her notebook. 'I won't ask you to sign this

now. Perhaps you can come into the station sometime?' She waited until Annie nodded before standing.

Miller opened the door. 'Don't go anywhere, will you?' He smiled, but his tone made it clear that he wasn't asking a question.

Annie held her hands in the sink, watching the ice cubes she'd tipped into the water bob and twist. The cold water was helping her hands, but somehow made her head throb more and more. Her brain was full of the pain on her hands, the skin bright and angry, and she had to fight against the urge to scream. Always, she had to fight against that urge.

'You should get a doctor to look at that,' DC Singh had said when they left, 'in case of infection.' She'd hovered in the doorway while Miller got in the car, as if she wanted to say something else. Annie started to shut the door firmly, and Singh stepped back out of the way. The buzzing in her head made it impossible for her to think about what she'd said to them. Miller's questions felt ambiguous. Was she a witness or a suspect? She tried to work out what reason they had to suspect her. It was just because she'd been in the car park — but didn't the fact that she contacted them count for something? Also, almost all child abductions were carried out by men not women. Almost all.

There'd also been an undercurrent of something between Singh and Miller that Annie hadn't understood, but it made her feel fearful. Did they disagree on whether she was suspect or witness? But why wouldn't they have searched her house then? It didn't make any sense at all. And then Singh had noticed the sandstone baby again. She wished she'd asked Paul if he'd reported it missing when he first went to the police. It wasn't impossible that they might both have one, but it would be another 'coincidence'.

She took a couple of painkillers, washing them down with the now cold tea, and sat down to eat. She switched on the television, more for company than because she felt like watching. She quite often had it on in the background, like having other people there with her. The noise calmed her and the ibuprofen had started to work, numbing everything.

When the news came on, her heart skipped a beat. She recognised the Hills being interviewed on their doorstep. The mother read from a sheet she held out in front of her like a shield. Mr Hills had his arm tightly wrapped around her shoulders. In the hallway behind them, she could just make out their friend Berman. He was always around it seemed. That must be amazing, Annie thought, to have a friend that was always there.

Annie noticed that Mrs Hills had scraped her hair back neatly and wore no make-up.

'We love you, Chloe, and we aren't angry. Please, come back home. We all miss you.'

Mr Hills didn't speak. It seemed unfair that he didn't, but Annie wasn't sure if it was more unfair to him or Mrs Hills. Annie could hear the clicking of camera shutters as she spoke.

'If anyone is holding Chloe against her will, we beg you to return her to us or tell someone where she is. You can call anonymously and just tell us where she is. All we want is for Chloe to come home.'

The image cut to a series of photographs of Chloe at a

birthday party, sitting on the swings, in school uniform with Hannah and Megan. In the last photo, the Hills were pictured with Berman and a woman and child who might have been Berman's family. Berman stood next to Chloe, who was standing close to her mother. Through the gap between Berman and Chloe, Annie could see a swing and climbing frame in the garden.

Annie switched it off and curled up where she was.

* * *

'I wanna go home now, Lottie. I'm hungry.'

Lottie's tummy is rumbling, too, and she wishes she'd brought more biscuits. Bronnen and Gwen have taken it in turns to issue challenges and dares to Lottie, and, each time she fails, they wrap the twine around Tegen and Paddington a little tighter.

'The next dare is to stay here until midnight; that's when the Piskies come out!'

Lottie looks into the dark innards of the cave. They are sitting just inside where the sun still lights up the rock and sand around them.

'Don't want to,' Tegen cries. 'I want Mummy!'

'It's okay, Tegen,' Lottie says, 'it's just a game, isn't it?' She looks at Bronnen and Gwen, because it hasn't been feeling much fun so far, and there was no sign of the Piskies or their treasure.

Gwen glances at Bronnen.

'It's a challenge, silly, it's not supposed to be easy.' Bronnen crosses her arms. 'Don't you want to join The Pisky Society after all? Don't you want the Pisky treasure?'

Lottie looks at Tegen, who is wiggling in the sand, her pale face bent down towards Paddington's grubby hat. Lottie's head has started hurting, and she doesn't like the expression on Bronnen's face, but she really, really wants to stay and get the treasure. If they only had a little more money, her parents wouldn't fight so much.

'Are you sure there'll be gold?'

'Of course there will be, stupid. How can you not believe this is the Pisky cave?' Gwen snorts. 'Okay, your challenge now is to name all the kids in your class who take lunch money to school, or you'll have to arm wrestle with Bronnen.'

Lottie can't look at Tegen now. She wishes they'd never come. The shadows creep across the beach, bending over the rocks and reaching towards the entrance of the cave. Lottie takes a deep breath and tries to push her chest out.

'I'm going to take Tegen home now.' She starts to unwind the wool, but Bronnen pushes her away, and she falls, cutting her hand on the barnacles that speckle the rocks.

Tegen is sobbing now. 'I want Mummy.'

Gwen puts her hand on Bronnen's arm. 'I told you all along she wouldn't pass the test, Bronn. Let them go. They're no good to us.'

Bronnen shakes her off. 'Oh no, you can't leave now without a forfeit, Lottie. Who do you think you are?'

Lottie's legs are shaking, but she stands up. She waits for the next impossible challenge, but Bronnen shoves her towards the light.

'You forfeit Tegen!'

Tegen screams for Lottie, and Lottie looks at her and then at the flushed face of Bronnen. 'Run away, coward!' Bronnen screams in Lottie's face. 'But don't you dare tell anyone where we are, because if you do, we'll hurt her bad, and then we'll come for you.'

They won't hurt her, Lottie tells herself. They're her friends. Aren't they?

Lottie looks at Gwen. 'Please, let me take her.'

But Gwen is staring at Bronnen and doesn't answer. Lottie tries to reach Tegen, but Bronnen shoves her away. Lottie's stomach is full of eels and worms, and the slight tang of low tide drifting through the cave makes her feel dizzy and nauseated. Gwen pushes her out, and the sudden glare of sunlight blinds her.

'Please. You will bring her back, won't you?'

Gwen nods at Lottie.

'Promise?'

Gwen glances back at Bronnen who is saying something softly to Tegen. Gwen's face is pale and sick looking, and she leans closer to Lottie. 'You'd better go while you can.'

26

SUNDAY MORNING

The skin on her right hand had blistered, and it hurt to move her fingers. Annie made tea with her left hand, spilling brown fluid across the worktop as she took the bag out. Another time, she would learn to use her left hand, too. It was a life skill everyone thought they'd get around to learning but never did.

There was still no news about Chloe. The appeal of looking online for information was wearing thin, and she found herself wandering around the house taking stock of the things she cared about. In an emergency, she could probably pack up her most important possessions in less than hour.

Her dreams had been full of menace and fear again. She couldn't avoid coming back to the conclusion that DS Miller suspected her of being involved. It gnawed at her, worrying at all her thoughts. If she hadn't told them it was her car that had been captured on CCTV with Chloe, they would never have considered she might be involved. The irony of the fact that she'd called the police to avoid coming under suspicion didn't escape her. It had only ever been partly about impressing Paul and Sam.

Miller's visit had knocked her even further off her usual weekend timetable. This was the second disrupted weekend, and it made her feel untethered and nauseated. It took her longer to iron with her left hand, but, as she worked, she went over and over the options open to her. The ultimate choice was always to pack up and leave.

First, she wanted to explain things to Lauren. She owed her that at least. Since Friday night, Annie had left her five messages, but Lauren hadn't replied. She was always busy at the weekends, but Annie knew it was more than that this time. It was just that she couldn't accept it. Deep down, she under-stood Lauren only ever really tolerated her — that's why Annie had been so careful not to push too hard. As that knowledge solidified in her stomach like stones, Annie realised this was something she'd always known. She'd created a semblance of friendship, nurtured the outward appearance but not the beating heart.

She took her suitcase out of her wardrobe. It was dusty and made her cough as she wiped it clean. Inside, the little figurines had rolled together at one end. She left the case open to air and ignored them. While she collected her clean clothes and stacked them up nearby, she was conscious of their little grinning faces tumbled together. She pulled a few of her more precious possessions off shelves and out of drawers and piled them near her clothes. If she had to leave in a hurry, she would at least be ready.

* * *

It's so hot already and her face is burning from the sun. She's tired and hungry and just wants to go home. Why don't they leave her alone? The room is too bright and everyone is shouting. Their voices bounce off the walls, and Lottie sits very still, twisting the hem of her school dress through her fingers. Something very bad has happened, but she's so confused, and she can't work it out. Why doesn't her mother say something? Why doesn't she just take her home?

* * *

When the phone rang, she found that she'd drifted off and was still sitting beside her suitcase. Her heart leapt at the thought that it might be Lauren.

'Thank God I've got hold of you! I've been worried sick.' It was just her mother. 'You're all over the news!'

Her voice was high pitched and anxious. Annie rested against the wall and readied herself.

'Are you there, Annie? You promised me you'd stay away from this Chloe business, and there you were at the bloody vigil. I saw Lauren first and couldn't believe my eyes. What were you thinking!'

Annie sighed.

'It's fine, Mum, it's a small place. It would have looked odd if I didn't go.'

She could hear her mother take a long drag on her cigarette.

'I hope you're keeping far away from the police, young lady, because you're doing a very poor job of keeping away from the TV cameras. Jesus, do you want that braying crowd to find you out? Do you know what would happen to you? Twenty-odd years of my life I've spent trying to keep you safe, and I'm not the one who did anything wrong. Do you want all that effort to be for nothing?' There was an unusual wobble in her mother's voice, and Annie felt a pang of guilt.

'Sorry, Mum.' She found she didn't have any fight left. Her

mother was right. She shouldn't have got involved at all. She hadn't seen anything, and there'd been no reason to call the police, just pride. It was all her own fault.

There was silence at the other end of the phone. Annie could hear the sound of the radio in the background and suddenly felt nostalgic for the little house they'd lived in before everything that happened. She remembered dancing with her mum in the kitchen while they waited for her dad to get home. They hadn't had much, but there had been fun, too. She knew that her parents were unhappy, she could see that now, and no amount of money would have changed that. The knowledge hit her like the breaking of a dam.

'What happened to Dad?' She heard her mother sigh. 'He hated me, didn't he?'

They never discussed it. Annie didn't remember much but the bear hug when he'd left, his tears wetting her hair, the crush of his arms, and then he was gone.

Her mother sighed. 'That's not true.'

Annie looked at the case on the floor and shoved it under her bed. She was as capable of running as her mother, that was true. But, if she didn't want to run, was she capable of doing what it would take to stay still?

'Annie, he didn't hate you. He just wanted an easier life. Look, you need to get yourself packed and keep out of sight. I'll get something sorted. I'll find you somewhere to stay for now and let you know.' She hung up, but her voice seemed to reverberate around the room.

Her mother had kept her out of sight, that was true. Annie tried to imagine what would happen if people found out who she was. It was all such a long time ago; she'd been so young, and the case hardly ever came up in the news. Someone local might know about it, she thought, but not here, so near to the big city where there was something going on all the time.

Even though, in Westhurst, there didn't seem to be any news other than the search for Chloe, people would soon move on.

She sat with her back against the radiator and searched for The Babes in the Cave case on her phone. There was a tiny image of her, cut out from a class photo. She found a mirror and held the screen up beside her face. There was no way anyone would recognise Annie as the child in the article. She read the text, realising that she'd never done that before. Of all the many cases of missing children that she'd inadvertently committed to memory over the years, the details of this one were as alien to her as they were real. There were photographs of the other three girls, too. Two girls dead and two run away. Annie didn't know that she wasn't the only one to run. It didn't make her feel better. Thinking about it never made her feel better.

She threw the phone down and grabbed her coat. She needed to get out of this house. Clear her head.

27

SUNDAY AFTERNOON

The sky was grey and the ground still damp, but Annie was already running by the time she left the drive. Her feet slammed into the pavement as she raced up the hill under the spreading fingers of the oaks, feeling the heat raw in her calves. Her breath punched out in clouds into the cold air, and the blood pumping around her system made her feel more awake than she'd felt in weeks. How far could she keep running?

She went straight over the crossroads towards Chloe Hills' house without thinking. The yellow ribbons stretched without break along the side of the road. A banner with the words #BringChloeHome hung from the footpath bridge, and water dripped from it onto Annie as she ran underneath. Annie had been running for five minutes when she realised her face was wet with tears not rain.

Her heart thudded, the glorious pain spreading across her chest as she sucked in the cold air. The sound of feet slapping on the wet ground numbed the thoughts that crept into her mind. Had anyone ever been missing for this long and been found alive? Her head was bursting and another headache brewed. She cursed herself for coming out without water and circled back to the shop on Christchurch Road.

Annie bent over outside to catch her breath and became aware of a small crowd gathered near Berman and Hills Estate Agents. There was a police car parked outside.

'Are they talking to Mr Hills? I hope they're bringing him good news.' Hushed voices threw out questions and conjecture around her.

She could just see the silhouettes of three people inside, but she couldn't make out anyone's features. Another couple wandered over to look. A few people were filming on their phones.

DS Miller came out, followed by Jason Berman and DC Singh. Singh put a hand on Berman's head as she guided him into the back seat of the car.

'Is he under arrest then?' A woman behind Annie called out, and Miller looked up. He stared directly at her. She felt her cheeks burn with embarrassment at being caught watching. The car door crunched shut, and then Singh took the driver's seat. Miller nodded at Annie before getting into the car, too.

'Did he just nod at you?' The woman filming asked, swinging her camera round to look at Annie.

'No!' Annie stepped back. She heard the engine start and pushed her way through the little crowd that had gathered and away from the woman.

'Who was that then?' The usually quiet Christchurch Road throbbed with questions as word got around that Jason Berman had been seen leaving with the police officers investigating Chloe's case. Annie listened to the chatter until someone put a hand on her arm. She froze.

'That copper seemed to know you. What's going on?'

Annie shook her head. 'I don't know. You must be thinking of someone else.'

Others in the crowd turned to get a look at Annie. Her heart hammered as she caught a glimpse of Kieran joining the crowd.

'Nope, it was definitely you.'

Annie pulled her arm away, flinching as the burnt skin on her hand connected with a man's sleeve. She shook her head. 'Just out for a walk,' she said and moved off quickly, trying to look as innocuous as possible. She didn't dare glance behind her, but she could feel eyes watching her.

It did look like Berman had been arrested. Why else would they have put him in the car like that? The sickness rolled in her stomach as she realised she'd told DS Miller that the person she'd seen the night Chloe went missing wore a waxed jacket. If the other arrest was just the standard routine for registered sex offenders, this one was definitely down to her. She felt the blood drain from her head. She'd hadn't told Miller about Berman's conversation with Kieran and the man with an earring, but somehow his description had leaked out anyway.

Annie ran home as fast as she could and flung herself inside, bolting the front door behind her. She found her phone and checked the news.

The police have announced that they have a suspect in custody. No further details have been provided, but we understand from witnesses to the arrest that it is forty-five-year-old Jason Berman, the partner of Mr Hills. Mr Berman was seen leaving the Berman and Hills Estate Agents offices in the company of officers working on the Chloe Hills case. No announcement has been made about the whereabouts of Chloe.

The screen showed a picture of Jason Berman standing next to Mr and Mrs Hills at the first televised appeal. His sparse hair curled over the collar of his jacket, and he kept an anxious eye on Mr Hills while Mrs Hills spoke. Annie felt her insides shift and slide. Kieran and Berman had been talking about confronting somebody in the alley the previous evening. Maybe they had done something terrible and Berman was being arrested for that? She couldn't find any reference to an attack or the discovery of Chloe anywhere in the news or the chat sites. But that didn't mean it hadn't happened. She should have said something to Miller about what she'd heard, not what she hadn't seen.

Why couldn't she get anything right?

She called Lauren before considering that Lauren wouldn't answer, but she did.

'The police came back and they kept asking me and asking me if I'd seen anyone and if I could describe them. They went on and on, short or tall, long hair or curly, and I couldn't think straight. I just wanted to help, so I just answered. I don't even know what I answered really, but I know I did. I just wanted them to go.' Annie spoke as fast as possible before Lauren could hang up.

'What? Look, have you told them about Paul's flat yet?'

What did that have to do with it? At least Lauren had answered the phone. That must mean something.

Annie didn't respond.

'Don't you think you should do that? I mean, aren't your lies all tangled up now? Don't you want to put things straight?' Annie could hear the distaste in Lauren's voice.

'Right,' she said, 'sorry. I shouldn't have rung.' She didn't hang up though, and, when Lauren didn't either, she decided to take a chance.

'Lauren, I don't know what to do.' Annie took a deep breath. 'You're my only friend.'

She heard something like a snort at Lauren's end. 'Annie, I really can't help you.'

'I think I accidentally described a real person.'

'For fuck's sake, Annie. You broke into Paul's flat. You made up a description when a young girl's life could be at stake. You don't even tell me the truth! Look, I've got to go.'

'No, I didn't. I didn't mean to,' Annie plead. 'I didn't realise. I just picked answers at random.'

Lauren hung up.

Annie should leave. All she had to do was get in her car and drive. Her mother would sort things out; she always did. Annie thought about how much money she had and knew it wasn't enough to survive on until she could find a new job. She might even have to go back and live with her mother. She would ruin both their lives in one go. Again. What would her father do? She often wondered where he was. He would have said she should tell the truth, but he wasn't there now. Her mother told her he'd left for the States, couldn't bear the hiding. Or the lying. Annie knew he'd been unhappy leaving Trehaven. He'd gradually started fading out of their plans, until one day he'd disappeared altogether. Annie wondered what it would have been like if he'd stayed. Or if they'd never left.

She checked her phone again. Most of the coverage was about the arrest interspersed with images of Berman standing with the crowd as it sang at the vigil. Journalists were standing outside the Hills' home waiting for them to comment, but they hadn't appeared yet.

It's always the ones nearest, isn't it?
The police are pulling at straws now.

If he's got her, why hasn't anyone noticed? Where could she be?

I had a drink with him once. Full of himself he was.

Chloe used to have go into the estate agents to get her house keys after school. She hated it if her dad wasn't there, said she found Berman creepy.

The police have really gone mad now, completely useless.

She thought about what Lauren said. If she was honest about why she hadn't seen Chloe on Thursday night, perhaps the police would stop using her information. She had to tell them she was so drunk that she'd gone into Paul's flat, and that she was the one who took the figurine. She didn't think Singh would be surprised. If it hadn't been for the headlights on her car being on, she could have said she was in his flat when Chloe passed by, but at least it would prove they couldn't take her account seriously. Annie tried to calm the panic rising in her throat. What if they arrested her? Drink-driving, breaking and entering. She deserved it though, and Chloe and the Hills needed her to get out of the way now. She was just dead weight.

The lying had started with Paul's flat. Could Annie start by putting that right and unravel it all from there?

She found a piece of paper and listed her options with pros and cons. She would need Paul to tell the police that someone had broken into his flat after all. But why would he do that for her? She'd risk losing her driving licence, too. And her fastest means of escape. It was the price of her mistake.

Her mother was right, too, that she risked the police finding out her history. The more time Annie spent with the police, the harder it would be to stay hidden. Hiding was such a reflex that she barely spent any time thinking about why it was so important. It was all such a long time ago now. She wondered, not for the first time, what would have happened if her family hadn't run before the police had finished their investigation.

Would she still have to move on again and find a new job? She felt a pang as she thought about losing Lauren, but the reality was that Lauren, or the Lauren that Annie had wanted her to be, had never really been there.

However Annie looked at it, Chloe was still missing and in more and more danger as each day went by. Each time the police were diverted down a wrong path, her time was running out. Annie didn't think she could cope with the guilt if something happened because of her; she was already at bursting point with remorse. She had to retract what she'd said, had to get it right this time, whatever the risk.

Annie would have to ask Paul to back her up. He had no reason to help her, though, and he'd already retracted his statement about the break-in. Annie didn't want to risk making him any angrier than he already was, but if she had to leave suddenly, she'd be looking for a new job anyway. Maybe he would understand. Maybe he would see she needed to do it for Chloe. She pulled out her phone and selected Paul's number. It rang until his voicemail picked up.

'Hey, Paul, it's me, Annie.' She took a breath. 'Look, I have a favour to ask you. I need you to tell the police I was in your flat the night Chloe was taken after all. I have to tell them the truth. They keep trying to twist what I say, and I can't keep the lies straight, so I have to be honest. Please, Paul, I wouldn't ask if it wasn't important.'

28
* * *

Lottie sits under the cherry tree watching for Tegen. Her arms are stinging with sunburn from playing on the beach, and she feels shivery, like the cold of the cave has settled right inside her bones. It's getting cooler now, and she gently hugs her bare arms to warm them up. Tegen's house looks empty. Lottie hopes that maybe Tegen came home when Lottie had gone in to see her mum, and they're just all in the garden. Inside her, though, is a sick feeling, and she knows she doesn't believe that.

She cranes her neck to look down the road. She really needs to talk to her dad now; she wants to persuade him to go to the cave beach, but he's running late, and her mother is cross again.

'Come and have a sandwich, Lottie,' her mum calls out from the front window. Lottie shakes her head. If she moves, she won't see when Tegen gets home. Besides, her tummy hurts, so she isn't really hungry anyhow. She taps the little twig swing back and forth. The wool has started to fade in the sun.

There's a whirr of bicycle wheels, and Bronnen and Gwen pull up to the kerb. Bronnen's face is glittery with excitement. Lottie feels a rush of relief. They are bringing Tegen home safe. She looks passed them to see if Tegen is running down the road, but she's not there. Maybe they cycled too fast for her to keep up. They didn't take their bikes to the beach, a little voice tells her.

'Where's Tegen?' Lottie whispers.

'Oh, she's away with the Piskies.' Bronnen laughs. 'Probably sitting in a big pile of treasure, right now. You'd love that, eh, running off with the Piskies?' Lottie doesn't like the tone of Bronnen's voice. 'Maybe you'll be next.'

She looks to Gwen, who is silent, picking at the rubber on the handlebars. Bronnen nudges Gwen, who jumps off her bike and lets it clatter to the ground. She crouches in front of Lottie. 'You'd better not say anything about it though, because you're one of us now. The Pisky Society secrets are sacred.' Gwen glances back up at Bronnen. Lottie notices that there are scratches on Gwen's arm, and she feels weak with fear. Gwen catches Lottie looking. 'If you tell, we're going to hurt all of you.' She gestures towards Lottie's house.

'Yeah, keep your mouth shut, Charlotte-Anne, or it's off to the Piskies with you, too.' Bronnen draws her finger across her neck and lets her head fall to one side, her tongue sticking out.

'But you're bringing her back, aren't you?' Lottie reaches out to Gwen, but she's already back on her bike watching Bronnen carefully. 'Aren't you?'

Bronnen laughs. 'Remember, if you tell, and something bad happens to Tegen, it'll be all your fault. It already is your fault, actually,' she says and shrugs. 'You wanted to catch a Pisky. You failed the test and now they're angry.'

Gwen puts her foot on the pedal and looks back at Lottie and, for a moment, Lottie thinks she's going to say something, but she just frowns.

And then they're flying away down the road, and Lottie is on her own again.

29

MONDAY MORNING

Annie slept in parts and woke when the sky was still slate. She'd thought about driving straight to the police station, but she wanted to plan exactly what she would say. She had to have it clear in her head because, once she stepped into the station, as soon as she did, all the old panic and fear would come rushing back, and she wouldn't be able to keep it together. She found the card DS Miller had left her propped up against the kettle where she'd put it the night before.

She pulled out the sheet of paper with the notes she'd prepared: she'd had too much to drink and ended up in Paul's flat. All she had to do was just tell them she'd really wanted to help, but she didn't want to tell them about the flat because she was ashamed. She'd only answered Miller's questions about the description to make him leave her alone.

Annie had to leave straight away, before she changed her mind, and before they looked too closely at her. Her mother's words ran through her head, a stream of reasons why she should run and hide. At six in the morning, the drive to the station was fast, the rest of the world still sleeping. The dark clung to the sky, and the lights of the car blurred in the drizzle.

She parked in a side street and sat in her car, practising her words over and over until it felt impossible that she could make a mistake. When she saw the blue lantern hanging over the door, her insides churned, and she had to stop for a moment. As she put out a hand to steady herself against the wall, the door burst open, and two young police officers in uniform walked out, deep in conversation. They stopped when they saw her.

'Are you all right?'

Annie nodded and pointed to the door, not trusting herself to explain why she was there. She grabbed the handle and slipped into the station before they could ask anything else. Inside, the light was harsh and clinical, a few posters with Victim Support numbers curling up at the corners on the wall. She walked up to the counter and waited until the woman behind it finished with whatever she was writing.

Finally, she looked up at Annie.

'Can I help you?'

'I've come about the Chloe Hills case. I need to speak to DS Miller.' Annie twisted round as if she'd heard someone marching down the corridor towards her. There was no one else there; the echo of footsteps seemed to be coming from the floor beneath them.

'Are you a witness?'

'Yes. No. Well, yes. Is he here?'

'I'll phone up to the incident room. What's your name?'

For a moment, Annie forgot her name in the cool gaze of the woman. Had she been taught to spot guilt in body language? The blood rushed in her ears, and she had to hold onto the counter. The woman frowned at her.

'Um, it's Annie. Annie Marwood.' Annie fished out DS

Miller's card from her pocket and put it on the counter. 'He told me to call if I remembered anything else.'

'Take a seat.' The woman nodded at a row of metal chairs fixed to the wall opposite. Annie put the card back into her pocket and sat down. She pulled her coat tight across her front and closed her eyes. Somewhere, someone was pushing a mop across the floor in soft, stabbing movements, and the water in the bucket splashed gently. The smell of the disinfectant filled Annie's nostrils, triggering a memory that stopped her breath and made her head fill with pain.

'Sorry, excuse me.'

Annie opened her eyes to see the woman behind the counter covering the mouthpiece of the phone.

'What did you say your name was?'

'Charl—' Annie sat up, shaking herself awake. 'Sorry, Annie. It's Annie Marwood.' She stood up and grabbed her bag. 'If he's not there, I'll call later.'

'Wait!' the woman called as Annie walked to the doors. 'Someone's coming down now.'

Annie paused, her head throbbing, and then she could hear footsteps clattering down the stairs at pace. It was a female PC that Annie hadn't seen before.

'Come through,' she said and held open a door with a security buzzer. Annie felt trapped. She looked to the woman at the counter for help. 'Is DS Miller not here? Or DC Singh?'

The PC held the door with a foot and reached for Annie's arm. 'He'll join us when he can. Let's go and talk somewhere comfortable.'

The little room they entered was stark. A table, a couple of chairs, and a recording device. Annie noted the panic strip around the walls and wondered how fast the others would come if she just reached over and pressed. Whether the alarm would sound in the room or only out in the corridor. She couldn't remember.

The PC waited for Annie to sit down before pulling out her own chair. She took out a pen and pad and then sat back.

'So, you have information for us regarding the Chloe Hills case?'

Annie looked at the woman. 'The thing is, it's about what I said to DS Miller. I really need to speak to him, because he already knows what I've said. It won't make sense otherwise.' She tugged at her hair.

'Well, he's not here. I'm PC Hayward. I'm in his team, so you can talk to me, and I can fill him in when he arrives.'

Annie didn't know where to start. 'I was in the station car park the night Chloe went missing.'

The woman said nothing.

'But I didn't see Jason Berman. I think DS Miller might have thought that I did. I got muddled. I think I sort of gave a description, but I didn't mean it.' Annie shifted in her seat and nodded at the recording device. 'Is that on?'

The woman smiled and shook her head.

'But they're listening outside?'

PC Hayward looked surprised and turned around, as if she could see through the door. She shook her head and frowned. Annie plucked at the seam of the blouse.

'You didn't mean it?' Hayward asked.

'Look, I just don't want you to be wasting your time on Berman because of what I said. It wasn't quite right. I was a bit tired at the time, and …' Annie took a deep breath and tried to bring up an image of the words she'd prepared on the paper. 'I kind of gave a description, which I didn't mean to, and it does sound a bit like Berman, but it wasn't. I mean, it wasn't him.'

'Okay, so you need to add something to the description of the person you did see?' The PC picked up her pen.

ALL YOUR LITTLE LIES

'No, I didn't see him.'

The woman looked confused. 'You didn't see Berman?'

'No. But you arrested him anyway. And you still haven't found Chloe, have you? So, that proves you've got the wrong person, doesn't it? You should release him. I didn't see anything.'

'Has someone told you to change your description?'

Annie sighed. 'No, this is all me.'

'But now you're saying you gave a description of a man you didn't see? How do you know Jason Berman was there, if you didn't see him?'

Annie shook her head. 'No, it wasn't him.'

'So, you described the wrong person?'

'No! I didn't say I'd seen anyone. I just gave a description, because it's possible there was someone who looked like that!' Annie looked around as if searching for someone who could help her. 'DS Miller got me muddled. But I didn't see him.'

'You didn't see this person, and you definitely know he wasn't there?'

'Well, because I didn't see anybody.'

'Okay, okay, so you were the only person there?'

'No! I just didn't see anyone! You're putting words in my mouth again. Look, I'd had a few drinks, and I don't really remember anything. I just wanted to help. I thought, if I got in touch, I might remember something!' Annie tugged at the loose thread and pulled the seam undone.

Hayward looked at Annie with more interest.

'I really just need to speak to DS Miller.'

'So, do you know something that could help us find Chloe? If you were there?'

'No, no. Where is DS Miller?' Annie jumped up and backed away from the table, stopping only just in time before she triggered the alarm.

'Sit down, Annie. Look, are you all right? You're not making a lot of sense.'

'I just want to talk to DS Miller; he knows he pushed me.'

The policewoman leant across the table. 'Are you saying DS Miller pushed you to say something that wasn't true? That's a serious allegation. If you know something, you need to tell us. Even something that seems unimportant could be the thing that helps us find her.'

'This is pointless. I have to go now. I won't say anything else.' Annie stood up.

By the time the PC opened the door to the front lobby, Annie was gasping for air. She flew through the doors, the posters on the wall rustling in her wake. When she got to her car, she turned the engine and pulled away, still tugging the seatbelt across her. She checked in the mirror that no one was following her and then drove to a different station to get the train to work. Perhaps Hayward wouldn't even mention her visit to Miller.

* * *

'I'm just going to take this over to Mrs Hancock. She must be in bits.'

Lottie's mother wraps a tea towel around the pan of chicken soup. It smells sweet and cloying against the bitter tang of her father's coffee. She's already poured him out a bowl, and it steams untouched on the place mat in front of him.

Her father nods at Lottie's corn flakes, his eyes red and puffy with fatigue, and pulls a facsimile of a smile.

'Eat up and then get yourself ready for school, will you?'

Lottie stirs the milk in her bowl, watching the orange flakes disintegrate as they swirl.

'Have they searched the beaches, Daddy?' Lottie whispers.

Her father rubs at his forehead and sighs. 'No, love. Tegen

ALL YOUR LITTLE LIES

wouldn't go that far from home on her own, darling. She won't be there.'

Lottie worries at her bottom lip. 'But has anyone asked Bronnen or Gwen? They were around here yesterday when Tegen was out playing.' Lottie feels something twist deep in her stomach. They wouldn't have left Tegen there; they said they wouldn't. If only she knew for sure.

'I'm sure everyone's been asked that could be. Don't you worry, I'm sure she'll turn up safe and sound.' Lottie can see the worry etched in the lines on his forehead. 'Now go and get ready for school.'

Her father picks up his spoon and stares at the soup. He's eating dinner for breakfast because he's been out searching all night and didn't even come home for dinner. It makes everything feel topsy-turvy.

'Daddy, I think we should check the cave beach. I can take you?'

Her father shakes his head. 'She won't be there, Lottie. Besides, it was spring tide last night; it'll be covered in rubbish now.'

Lottie takes her bowl to the sink and dresses for school quickly, all the while thinking about Tegen. When she comes back down, her mother hasn't returned yet, and her father is leaning back in his chair, his eyes closed and his head hanging over to one side. Ever so quietly, Lottie fills her water bottle with Ribena and takes a packet of biscuits from the cupboard and leaves the house.

There's a group of men and women gathered outside the Hancock house, just returned or just about to leave. Lottie has watched this crowd come and go all night, peeping through the curtains of her bedroom window. Someone has set up deck chairs on the lawn, but no one uses them. On the Hancocks' drive is a police car.

Lottie strains to hear what is said, but, for such a group, they are eerily hushed, as if Tegen's life depends on their silence. Gwen's father is there with her brother. She watches as he pulls his school blazer out of a backpack and puts it on, the barest of waves to his father as he walks away towards the bus stop. She can't see Gwen or

Bronnen. The low sun breaks above the houses, and Lottie lifts her hands to shield her eyes, scanning for Bronnen's dad among the others. He isn't there either. Maybe, Bronnen and Gwen are at the beach already. Lottie wants to tell them all that it's all right, Tegen will be back soon.

No one seems to notice the six-year-old as she heads off in the direction of the school that sits among the playing fields at the top of the estate. Ahead, there is a small group of children with a couple of adults. Normally, those children would be walking on their own. Lottie doesn't follow them but turns off the pavement and climbs over the stile to the coastal path.

Behind her she hears a man's voice and the sound of boots sliding over the rocks.

'Tegen!' she tries to call out, but her voice wheezes and squeaks. 'Let's go!' She's immediately blinded as the bright sunlight gives way to the dark of the cave, and she drops to her knees, crawling through seaweed and shells. Finally, her eyes adjust, and she can make out a heap of blue denim and Paddington's red hat in the corner and shouts out. She pulls off her bag and pulls out the bottle and biscuits with trembling hands. 'Wake up, Tegen. I've got your favourites, Jammy Dodgers!'

The noises behind her coalesce into shouts, and she is shoved out of the way as a figure hurtles towards the little girl. And then, she is knocked off her feet and a weight lands on her.

'What have you done?'

Lottie looks up, but all she can see is the black silhouette of a man against the sunlight pouring through the mouth of the cave.

30

MONDAY AFTERNOON

Paul hadn't returned her call. She was sure that asking him to tell the police she had broken into his flat was the right thing to do, but her head was whirling from her conversation with PC Hayward. She checked her phone again, but there was no message from DS Miller and no news about Chloe.

It was still dark when Annie had arrived at the office. She'd been the only person there, so she made tea and threw herself into the list of emails that popped up on her screen when she'd logged in. She kept her head down when the others started arriving, too, keeping away from the morning's gossip. Like she used to, she thought. Back to invisibility and safety. She checked Paul's calendar. He was out of the office in meetings.

The monotony of her work soothed her, made her feel like the trip to the police station was part of some other life where things were painful and harsh. When Jenna had stopped at her desk to offer tea, Annie'd batted her away, waving at the piles of paper on her desk in explanation. The numbers on the screen settled into familiar patterns, and Annie updated the latest sales and revenue numbers, keeping her mind fully absorbed in the process.

At lunch time, she left the office and walked through the back streets around Covent Garden, avoiding the tourists and the shoppers. She walked until she could feel it in the balls of her feet, the tiredness of the early start seeping through her as she pounded the uneven pavements. She bought a sandwich and a coffee and headed to the Drury Lane Gardens. A couple sat on her favourite bench, heads together. Annie moved round to the shaded sided and rested against the railing while she unwrapped the sandwich awkwardly. The couple looked up at the sound of the wrapper dropping in the bin, and Annie saw them share a glance.

Self-conscious, she pulled her phone out of her bag and turned it on. The notifications burst across the top of the screen, and she opened up the Breaking News banner.

A body has been found on the Sussex coast, and there is speculation that it could be that of missing schoolgirl Chloe Hills.

The body was found was close to the location of a recent school trip. Annie's stomach turned, and she threw the sandwich away. She searched through for more information, but all she could find was that no positive identification had been made. Police had applied to hold Berman for a further twenty-four hours.

Annie felt sick. Had Berman killed her? But she knew he'd been looking for her on Saturday night, so it can't have been him. It was an elaborate double bluff, if only for Kieran and Kev's benefit, if he had. She couldn't believe it; he'd sounded genuinely desperate to find her. Oh, she'd made everything worse. What if Chloe had still been alive when they arrested Berman? Could the police have found her in time if Annie hadn't interfered? Would they have uncovered another suspect in time?

She could feel the tears start to roll down her cheeks. She never meant it to get this far. One silly phone call and now she might be responsible for yet another girl's death, when what she'd really wanted was to be the hero that saved the day. That person who stepped forward and told the truth whatever the cost to themselves.

She should have made Miller listen to her about Hannah and Megan; they knew more than they'd said. The girls had probably met someone on their school trip. Annie had heard about grooming and how easy it was for children to be lured away from home. It can't have been Berman, not with his constant supportive presence for the Hills. Annie was sure Chloe's friends knew something. It was always the friends. Something must have happened on the school trip.

She felt the coffee scalding her foot as she knocked the cup over and yelped. The couple on the bench looked at her again, wary and ready to move. The pain brought her back to herself.

It might not be Hannah and Megan. They were just kids. It was rare for kids to kill. Very rare. It was her, getting in the way; she was the problem. She wiped the worst of the coffee off with a paper napkin and walked out of the garden, straight down to the river. She walked along the embankment, staring at the grey of the water that wallowed and surged sluggishly with the tide, reflecting the dirty metal grey of the November sky.

They wouldn't notice her absence in the office unless Paul needed something, and he was out. Anyway, he'd replace her easily enough. She was no better at her job than anyone else would be, certainly not a team player, as he was always telling her. Dead weight. Lauren wouldn't have to keep propping her up either, and her mother could stop worrying about her, too. A wave of grief hit her. She'd probably already lost Lauren. On Hungerford Bridge, she hung over the side staring down into the swirls and eddies around the stanchions until an older woman came up and asked her if she was okay.

Annie shook her head and then remembered herself and forced a smile. 'I'm fine,' she said, but the woman didn't move away. So, Annie carried on through the Southbank, under the arches, and crossed round the IMAX, so she could walk up the wide steps to Waterloo. One small person in a big grey jungle, usually insignificant, Annie thought, and felt the hole in her stomach expanding, so that she was outside and inside it at the same time.

The yellow ribbons flapped and snapped around Annie like gulls' wings as she walked down the hill from the station, head bent into the wind. Westhurst had felt muted when she got off the train, paying careful attention to the other passengers alighting with her. She knew they were all thinking of Chloe and the news her family might have been given already, the shock and grief the Hills would be feeling. She wondered what it must be like to wish your child was alive when it meant someone else's was dead.

Annie felt the dark spaces around her as she passed the fields on her way home and pulled her collar tighter, concentrating on the rhythm of her feet stepping one after the other. As she came around the bend before her house, she heard a shout.

'It's her!' Light bulbs flashed, and a woman with shiny hair stepped out in front of her.

'Did you see Jason Berman the night Chloe went missing? Did you see him take her?'

Annie blinked and paused. The crowd was between her and her front door. She put up a hand in front of her face and tried to push through the bodies.

'Why did it take you so long to come forward?'

Annie kept her head down, and the journalists moved out of the way a little, still far too close for comfort, but behind them, Annie could see people she recognised from the search party and the vigil. People with pale, angry faces. Was that Kieran there, too? Just her imagination.

How could Jason Berman have got her to the coast when he's been here all the time?
She's a liar!
Better check out what she was doing the night Chloe went missing!

Annie stopped when she got to the door and turned back to the woman with shiny hair who had followed her down the drive. 'Is it Chloe? The body?' Annie whispered.

The woman didn't answer. She just pushed the microphone into Annie's face again and asked, 'Why has it taken this long for you to come forward? What are you hiding?'

Annie's cheeks burnt, and she turned her back, searching for the keys in her bag through her tears. 'Just go away!' She turned the key in the lock and shoved, a volley of light around her as the cameras tried to look into her house.

'Why won't you talk to us? We know you took part in the search party!'

Who had they spoken to? Annie felt afraid.

'We can't find anyone who really knows who you are. No one who knew you before Chloe went missing.'

Annie slammed the door shut behind her and sank onto the doormat, slipping on a pile of business cards, each with a handwritten note on the back, so that she landed on her bottom.

She pulled out her phone to check the news, but there was no confirmation that the body found was Chloe's.

As she sat there, someone shoved the evening paper through her letter box and it fell on her. There was a picture of Annie at the vigil with the headline:

Does this woman hold the key to what happened to Chloe Hills?

Annie read the article. Her heart burst with fear in her chest.

We are still waiting for formal identification of the body found on the Sussex coast and further information about the man, believed to be Jason Berman, friend of Mr and Mrs Hills, who the police have in custody. But Berman cannot have acted alone; we've spoken to people who say they were with him on the night Chloe went missing.

Did Berman have an accomplice? We received a tip that Annie Marwood, a Westhurst local, gave the police the information that led them to arrest Berman. While Marwood's background is still largely unknown, she joined the search party, appeared at the vigil, and, it seems, is now supplying the police with information.

We spoke to Alex Patterson, who was with Marwood during the search party last weekend. He said she asked many personal and distressing questions about Chloe and her family and that she made the rest of the team uncomfortable. 'At first, we thought she was a journalist, snooping around for a story, but now we're not so sure. There's something not right about her.'

Investigations thus far have found no links between Chloe Hills and Marwood, but, we will continue to investigate further.

The phone rang, and Annie let it go to voicemail.

'Annie, Annie, are you there?' Annie listened to her mother's voice. 'What have you done? You need to leave, get away before they find out about you!'

The letterbox opened again, and a voice shouted through. 'You should talk to us; we can give you a deal and keep the others away.' Another business card dropped through the door with a sum written on the back. Annie scooted away.

She picked up the phone; her mother was right. If journalists were investigating her background, she only had a short time to get away or face up to everyone knowing the truth about her. She had to throw away all hopes of a normal life in Westhurst or a friendship with Sam or any of the others.

She checked her phone to see if the story was in any of the national papers. A debate raged online about the exposing of witnesses and the potential impact on any subsequent trial. A police spokesperson refused to confirm that Annie had been spoken to in the course of the investigation and warned the press and public not to interfere with potential witnesses. Some commentators blamed the reward money. It encouraged so many to come forward with any trivial and irrelevant piece of information that the police were inundated with calls, diverting manpower and resources away from where it was needed most.

Photos and short videos of Annie walking through the crowd to her house started to appear, the comments below full of fury and wild theories.

The phone rang and she answered.

'They won't go away,' she said quietly.

'I'm calling the police.' Her mother hung up.

Annie could hear sirens in the distance. Sounded like someone had called the police already. But were they coming to protect her or arrest her? She sat in the dark, listening to the shouts outside and hugged her knees to her chest.

31

MONDAY EVENING

Flashes of blue light scattered across the windows of Annie's lounge. She peered through them and saw two uniformed police officers get out of the car. Moments later there was a knock on the door.

'Annie Marwood? It's the police.'

Annie eased the door open cautiously.

'We've had a complaint about the crowd outside your house. Are you all right?'

Over the PC's shoulder, Annie saw her neighbours at their front door watching as the other PC spoke to the crowd. The shiny-haired woman seemed to be arguing, but the PC stood her ground, arms folded.

'Yes,' Annie's voice was croaky, 'thanks. Will they come back?'

The woman shrugged. 'Probably. We've warned the media that they can't talk to any witnesses, without confirming that you are one, but there's not a lot we can do about people standing around outside. I should warn you that, if you have made a witness statement, you should not mention anything you've said to the media, and, if you take my advice, you'll say nothing at all. They'll get bored and find someone else.' Annie nodded. 'I'll just check round the back and then we'll wait outside just until people have moved off.'

Annie closed the door again and walked into the lounge in the dark. She could see that the crowd had been moved back to the pavement and were beginning to leave. She was pulling the curtains shut tight when another car arrived, and the crowd fell back further. DS Miller parked on the drive blocking her own car in.

At the sound of the car door slamming, Annie opened the front door and then returned to the lounge, waiting for him to enter. DC Singh walked in first.

'We've warned them to stay off your property, but if they choose to hang around on the street ...'

DS Miller appeared behind her and peered into the house, followed by the police officer who'd knocked at her door. 'Mind if this officer has a look around?' Miller pulled out a chair from the table. Annie waved her hand in agreement, and Singh took some gloves from a pocket and followed the first officer upstairs.

'Is it Chloe? The body?'

Miller sat back in his chair and studied Annie's face until she felt her skin burn under his gaze. His expression was unreadable. Annie heard the hatch to the loft being popped open. They were still looking for Chloe. 'It's not, is it?' She felt the weight on her easing. 'You wouldn't be searching for her here, if you knew she was dead. Unless you're just trying to throw me off balance.'

That morning, Annie had been terrified that the police might think she was involved in Chloe's disappearance, but now it didn't worry her, if it meant the girl was alive. She reached for her phone automatically to see what the news made of that, but Miller reached a hand to take it.

'May I?' He looked at it for a moment and then put it down.

'I've got nothing to hide,' Annie said.

Miller didn't reply but kept watching her. Annie could feel the words bubbling up, zipping around her head, trying to escape. Footsteps upstairs moved to her bedroom.

'Did you tell the press that I saw Jason Berman the night Chloe went missing?' She thought of the articles she'd read. 'Why would you do that?' And then it hit her what an idiot she was being. 'Oh, because you can't get a warrant to search my house, so you needed my permission to come in?' Annie felt something uncoil inside her, and she stood up. 'How dare you. You should get out.' She bit down hard on her lip to stop from saying anything else.

She felt a wave of rage rising through her like relief. She'd just been trying to help and now they'd tricked her. They needed to leave right now. She walked to the foot of the stairs and shouted up. 'You can stop that. I want you out of my house.' She turned, aware by the prickles on the back of her neck that Miller had crept up right behind her.

'If you want to see any more, you're going to have to get a warrant. Or arrest me. Go on, you haven't listened to me at all. I keep telling you I didn't see anything, and you keep putting words in my mouth. I was only trying to help.' She pulled the door open. If any of the journalists were outside, she couldn't see them, but no doubt the footage of the police visiting her house would be all over the internet by now.

DC Singh shook her head at Miller as she led the other officer down the stairs and out the door.

Miller turned to Annie. 'Don't go away. I don't think we've finished talking yet.'

Annie raced to where her phone sat on the table. There were four messages, and Annie listened to her mother's voice becoming more and more hysterical. She felt her nerves stretching and fraying with each word. This was the eye of the storm now. The crowds and the media would return, and sooner or later someone would find out what she'd done. Maybe they'd even manage to make it look like she was involved now. That was too much. She paced the house, thinking about what she should do.

It was her mother who'd pushed for them to leave Trehaven and kept going when her father couldn't take it. Annie recognised the inner strength that ran through her and the fear that drove her on, contracting their names and hiding their past from everyone. She'd kept them safe and away from the consequences of the mistake she'd made. Because Annie was the girl who should have told the truth when it mattered. But chose not to.

* * *

Her father is shouting across her, and her mother is weeping. Lottie can hear her snuffling and blowing her nose. She wants her mother to put her arms around her, but she doesn't, stays just out of reach.

'She's only a child, for God's sake. Can't you see she's scared?'

'Sir, you need to calm down.'

'Don't tell me what I need to do!'

Her mother's mascara is running over her cheeks. 'How is this possible?' she's saying. 'We're so sorry. Poor little Tegen. How will I face her mother?'

'Stop that, Susan!' Her father's voice cuts across her mother's sobs, and Lottie sees her shoot him a look full of anger. He crouches down before Lottie.

'Just tell them the truth now, kid. That's all you can do.'

Lottie is shaking. Everyone has been shouting forever, and she hopes they won't wake Tegen up. Tegen must have been fast asleep, because she was all floppy when the man picked her up.

'How did you know she was there, Charlotte-Anne? At least tell me that!'

Lottie looks at her mother and her father. She doesn't understand why they're in the police station. Tegen has been found, hasn't she? She wants to crawl under the table and curl up, but it's too bright, and now her father has his hand on her shoulder. He's shaking her gently.

'Lottie, please? For Tegen's sake. Her parents deserve to know the truth.'

Lottie frowns and rubs at her forehead. 'Didn't Tegen tell them?'

The skin on her father's face pales, and he looks towards the police officer on the other side of the table.

'She doesn't know?'

Her father picks up Lottie's hands and kneels on the floor. His voice shakes. 'Tegen's dead, Charlotte-Anne.'

Lottie doesn't understand. 'Did the Piskies do it?' *she whispers. She remembers the twine wrapped around Tegen's arms.*

'Jesus, no! Please, stop with the Piskies.'

She's aware of the dark-blue uniform of the police officer as he stands over her. Lottie had promised that she would never tell, but how could Tegen be dead? They'd promised no one would get hurt, hadn't they? She frowns. Gwen said it was just a game, and Lottie had trusted Gwen. She could see the scratches on Gwen's arms in her mind. Had she done something to Tegen?

'Gwen promised she'd bring Tegen home. They said I couldn't tell.' *Lottie thought of Tegen and started sobbing.* 'Is Tegen coming back?'

Her father dropped to his knees. 'No, Lottie. Is this true about Gwen?'

Lottie nods.

'Just Gwen?'

Lottie thought of Bronnen pulling her index finger across her throat and letting her head drop to one side like a corpse. She buries her face into her father's shoulder. 'Uh-huh.'

* * *

She looked around. The few things she'd accumulated over the years seemed incongruous in this small house that didn't belong to her. If the crowd returned, she'd be trapped inside with just her memories, and she understood her mother's urge to run. Her mother was right that she needed to get far away if she didn't want to face all of that, all of the judgement and disgust they'd been hiding from for years.

The right choice was obvious. Annie went upstairs and packed her case. Then, she took it down and put it by the front door. The pavement outside looked empty, but Annie could see the lights of a car parked further down the road and two people sitting inside. They could be police or journalists. Either way, Annie didn't want them to see her leave; she would have to wait until they'd gone.

She went to the upstairs room at the front to watch. The street was quiet, but the car was still there. She couldn't make out who was in it, but they appeared to be talking. Annie considered the possibility that they'd just pulled over to chat, but when they were still there after twenty minutes, she decided they were probably keeping watch for her.

She was trapped. Now that she'd packed up the little things that mattered to her, the house felt alien and oppressive. She stared out the window into the garden, watching for movement. The sky was slick and tarry in the night. The walls seemed to close in around her as time wore on, so Annie put a few key things in a day bag, grabbed her coat and slipped out the back door. She crept along the fence to the gate at the bottom of the garden into the allotments. The wet leaves swiped her face and hands as she pushed her way through the hedges, the sharp tips of the branches catching in her hair. Eventually, she burst through to the fields behind, sinking into the ploughed ruts, the mud flicking up onto her legs.

She followed the fence to the top, where she pulled herself up to catch her breath. The yellow glow of the streetlamps curved towards the station. She could follow their lights walking in the fields and then cut down and be on a train in an hour. The suitcase could wait until later, when things had calmed down, or she could ask her mother to collect it.

The wind whipped up the leaves and her hair, and she shut her eyes, her brain filling with the images and sounds of the yellow ribbons flapping across Westhurst. Annie wondered if the body on the beach really wasn't Chloe. Was Chloe's family still waiting to hear? And all those other people, greedy for news and information and ready to judge, reaching for their phones as soon as they wake to see if anything's happened overnight.

How could a twelve-year-old disappear?
Who would do such a thing?

Now some of them were waiting to see what part Annie had played in the story, too. It was surely only a matter of time before some sharp journalist worked out who she was. Then it wouldn't be long before some would start to assume that she was in some way responsible for Chloe's disappearance. Annie didn't want to be trapped in her house when that happened.

Annie knew her father would still be asking her to tell the truth. He'd never run away from anything in his life before they left Trehaven. That's what he'd said to Annie's mother when she was packing. He said that it was done, and that it couldn't be changed, but that Annie was young and most people would forget about it in time. It would be stupid to run, he'd said. That would make everyone believe they'd something to hide after all. The police had asked them not to go anywhere while they investigated, but they hadn't actually done any more than talk to her.

It wasn't until that brick came through the window that he changed his mind. And then he'd kept running, until eventually, he'd even run away from Annie.

She turned it over in her mind. If Chloe was already dead, then Annie couldn't do any more harm, the damage was already done. But Annie knew she'd sent the police in the wrong direction, and she didn't think she could bear the guilt of that. She was full up to the brim with guilt. If only she'd never made that call in the first place. It had led to the opposite of what she wanted; she'd got in the way, and Sam and the others weren't fooled at all.

The moon popped out from the clouds streaming across the sky, and Annie rubbed her hands to get some life back into them.

Why had the police wanted to search her home, though? She still didn't fit the profile of most kidnappers.

She pulled out her phone and saw a message from Lauren. Her heart did a little skip, but she took a deep breath before she read it. Even her friendship with Lauren wasn't true, not really. It was the longest she'd had any kind of relationship with anybody, but it wasn't based on truth. They weren't even really alike; they didn't enjoy the same things. It was a sham. Lauren just had a lot of room for other people in her life, and Annie had managed to cling on. When she took the whole thing out and looked at it, their friendship was just a mirage. It was a cover for the fact that Annie wasn't normal, didn't have normal relationships. The reality was that half of it made her feel less alone, and the other half threw her isolation into stark relief.

Lauren had probably seen the crowd at her house and wanted to know what was going on. She read the message.

Are you okay? I think you should go to your mum's.

Lauren was always trying to point Annie in someone else's direction. Annie could see that now. She took a deep breath and rang Lauren back.

'There's something I want to tell you about, Lauren, before it's all over the news. Worse than Paul's flat. Please, don't say anything. I just need you to listen to me all the way through. If you don't want to speak to me after that, I understand.'

Annie shut her eyes as she spoke, trying not to imagine Lauren's reaction. But once she'd started telling Lauren about Trehaven, she found the words poured out. 'I'm so ashamed, Lauren, and I know you'll hate me. That's why I was too afraid to tell you before.' When she'd finished, there was silence at the other end of the phone, and Annie found herself holding her breath.

'I don't know what to say.'

'It's okay, Lauren, you don't have to say anything. I've got to go now.' Annie hung up.

The lights of Westhurst winked at the rise of the hill. Through the wind, she could hear the sounds of the night, mice or hedgehogs pattering, a fox calling across the fields, a lorry on the distant ring road. She wondered how long she could sit there before anyone found her. Sooner or later in the day, her mother would ring with plans and instructions. Paul or Jenna would notice her absence, too, but would Paul assume she'd taken his advice to take some time off? She checked her phone to see if he'd replied to her message. Nothing.

She did feel a little lighter though. She was scared that she'd never hear from Lauren again, but now that the worst had happened, she could breathe a little. It was one less burden to carry.

Now, she had to tell Miller the truth. She could decide where to go after that. At the least, her mother would have a plan. If she left, as her mother wanted, she could just start again like last time. The first place they'd moved to, Annie had forgotten her new name, and one day they walked back from school to find a journalist on the front doorstep. They moved that night, discarding all but the bare essentials, and, after that, Annie kept her mouth shut. It was exhausting and lonely, but she was good at it now. Annie didn't want to leave her little house, but she knew it would only be a matter of time before her past caught up with her. She could run from it, or she could face it.

In the meantime, she had to make Miller understand that she hadn't seen Berman. The crowd outside her house had scared her, but they would be worse outside Berman's. She knew what those sorts of emotions did to people, how they could lose control. She tried to remember what Kieran had said about Berman's family. He had a wife and child, but she'd left. Annie hoped she was far away and the papers left her alone. It was Annie's fault that he was still in custody, that he'd been made the object of public outrage and disgust. It was her fault that the Hills had lost their friend at the moment when it looked like they'd need him the most. The rumour mill was going mad online, and now even Chloe's friends were saying Berman had been harassing her. They were saying Chloe had complained that her parents wouldn't listen when she'd told them. Hannah and Megan's images came to mind, but Annie pushed them away. Of course she would suspect Chloe's two friends. It was ridiculous.

And the crowd was just looking for justice. *If there isn't someone to blame*, Annie thought, *then they'll find an angle anyway*. She knew what happened when people took things into their own hands.

The sky lightened in the distance, and she knew she had to get home quickly if she didn't want to be seen. She wanted to speak to DS Miller on her own terms.

She sent Paul a text to say she wouldn't be going into work.

32

TUESDAY MORNING

The wind dropped suddenly as she crept through the garden, and Annie kept to the fence where the shadows fell. She listened out for sounds of the crowd returning and, once inside, she left the lights off and felt her way through to the lounge. There were now two cars parked outside. Not directly in front of the drive, so she could leave if she chose to, but she would certainly be seen. Neither cars nor occupants looked like police, but she couldn't be sure.

Miller's phone went straight to voicemail. Annie didn't want to leave a message. Instead, she pulled out a notepad and started writing. Her memories were dream-like and difficult to untangle. She had spent so much time trying to ignore them, she wasn't clear anymore what was true.

She pulled out her tablet and searched for The Babes in the Cave case again. Little Tegen's face smiled back at her, and Annie could smell cut grass and marmalade and then the stench of seaweed and rotting crabs on the beach. The bile rose in her throat.

She clicked through the articles, passed her own photograph, and pieced together the story. She knew about Tegen. Still had nightmares of being trapped in the cave with her in the dark as the tide bubbles and spits across the sand towards the rocks at the entrance, the ropes tight around Tegen's little arms as she begs Annie to take her home. *'Please, Lottie, help me.'* And running back in the morning to see the debris of the springtide higher on the beach. Seaweed and wood and broken shells high up inside the cave. Annie could still feel how her relief at finding Tegen had turned to confusion when the little girl hadn't answered. She could still hear the cries of the men when they found her and feel the pain in her own arms as she was dragged into the blinding sunlight.

Annie didn't realise what had happened until later, when the adults had become increasingly angry around her. She thought the Piskies had taken Tegen and would bring her back. Her own father, his face red and sweaty, had told her that Tegen was never coming home. Annie had loved Tegen. She'd been angry and scared, and she wanted the little girl back as Gwen had promised. Lottie was scared of Bronnen, but it was Gwen who'd lied.

Annie stood and looked out the window. The two cars were still there. She went to change and called Miller again. There was still no answer, and she wished she knew how to get hold of Singh. Singh knew she hadn't seen Chloe. Singh had noticed the sandstone figurine, too. Annie fetched it from her bag. She pulled out her little brass Piskies and the wooden mouse and lined them up with the stone baby.

Her phone lit up, and she grabbed it, but it was just Paul telling her to take the week off, if she wanted.

I need you to tell the police I was in your flat. Please.

Her finger hovered over the phone, and then she deleted

the text. It wasn't up to Paul to save her from this. Instead, she rang her mother. It was time she told her what was going on.

'I don't think it's Chloe, the body they've found,' her mother said.

'No?' Annie asked. 'How do you know? You haven't been following it all!' Her mother had always seemed impervious when these other cases happened.

She heard her mother sigh. 'Of course, I have, Annie.'

Annie didn't reply. She brought up the latest news on her tablet. There was no announcement, just more speculation and rumours and images of flowers piling up outside West-hurst station.

'I saw what happened last night. Please, tell me you've left?'

Annie sat back. 'I can't. Besides, I'll never be able to get away from it wherever I go. Not really.'

She heard her mother light a cigarette. 'Well, you're old enough to decide for yourself what to do.' Her mother's voice was tired, and there was an uncharacteristic wobble. 'You're involved in this Chloe business somehow, aren't you?'

Annie had been waiting for that, but it hurt all the same. Her own mother thought the worst of her. And yet she was right, too.

'The photo of Chloe in the paper, the one from the CCTV, shows my car in the background. I was there when she walked across the front of the station, but I don't remember anything. I keep telling them.' It all flooded out, Paul's flat, the pub, the phone call to the police, and the interviews with Miller. Her guilt. She collapsed on the sofa, waiting for her mother to react, waiting for her to ask if she'd hurt Chloe. It had been her father who spoke up for her before, but he wasn't here now, hadn't been for a long time.

'Sounds like you've got yourself in a bit of a state,' her mother said. 'What do the police know about you?'

Annie took a breath. 'I don't know. Maybe nothing.' This was where her mother would insist they leave, run away. Annie didn't have the energy anymore. It was more than that, too; she wanted to be done with it. Done with hiding and lying about who she was. It seemed Bronnen had moved away, too, but it hadn't taken Annie long online to find out where she was. Bronnen had never given an interview, never admitted anything, and yet she lived not far from Trehaven. Running this far away had just made Annie look more guilty.

'I didn't mean to keep hiding, you know, Annie. We always intended to go back when things had settled, but your father blamed me for what happened to Gwen and blamed himself for not warning them. We kept going, hoping it would get better, and then, after he left, it felt too late.' She paused a moment. 'Besides, I'm kind of good at it.'

Annie told her mother what she was planning to do and tried Miller again. There was still no answer, but her phone suddenly lit up with notifications. Police confirmed that the body found in Sussex was not Chloe Hills, but they were releasing no further details. Annie sat on her sofa to read the news. The frustration of the public could be seen in the speed the comments were being uploaded under the announcements. A single reporter stood in front of the station, interviewing an older couple.

'Police incompetence, isn't it? Looking in the wrong place. She'll have been taken out of the country by now, one of those grooming gangs, I expect.'

'There'll be hell to pay when this is over.'

'A forty-two-year-old man is still being held in custody and police have declined to comment further. Earlier, we were outside the Hills' house, when we believe they were given the news that the body discovered on the beach in Sussex was not in fact that of their daughter. There's been no sign of the Hills today and no comment made by them or close friends regarding the arrest of, who sources tell us, is their friend Jason Berman.'

Annie felt a rush of urgency. Chloe could still be alive, so it was more important than ever that she make Miller understand that she hadn't seen Berman. Should she tell them about the conversation she'd overheard him having with Kieran? She rang Miller again and this time she left a message.

Outside, one of the cars pulled away, and Annie decided to chance driving to the police station. If the silver Golf that remained followed her, they wouldn't be able to do anything there. She pulled on her coat and grabbed her car keys. As she opened her car door, a young man got out of the Golf and started walking down her drive. The passenger door opened, and a woman with a camera got out and started taking photographs. Not police, then.

'Annie!' the man called as she slid into the seat. 'Talk to us! We know who you are. Everybody's going to know soon.'

She cursed Miller. She needed to tell him before he heard it from some journalist. Her heart twisted as she thought of Paul reading about it online, of the pleasure Alex would take in showing it to Sam. What had she been thinking? There was no way somebody like her could ever have helped do something like find Chloe.

'We can take you to a hotel, keep you safe, if you talk to us.' The man was right beside her car now, and the woman stood in front taking photographs through Annie's windscreen. She revved the engine, but the black car returned and pulled in, slightly blocking the drive. A flash of anger nearly drove her

ALL YOUR LITTLE LIES

to put her foot down, but she thought of her mother and that she might be watching. She knew it wouldn't be right to leave her alone to face the consequences. She cut the engine and slammed her door open so that the young man jumped back a bit. It gave her just enough time to open the front door before he was right there, his aftershave enveloping her. She slipped in and slammed the door.

She could sense the man still standing outside and a hurried conversation going on between him and the woman with the camera. The older man in the other car had got out and lit a cigarette. He walked down to join the others. Were they allowed on her drive?

A message flashed up on the screen.

Stay at home. I'll be in touch later. DS Miller.

Annie threw the phone across the room, and it span on the carpet where it landed, little rainbow sparks of light flying from it.

* * *

Splintering glass scatters through the lounge and dances in the air as Lottie sits on the sofa, waiting for her parents to stop shouting in the kitchen.

'We can't stay here, Arthur. The whole village is out for blood!' The brick lands in front of the fireplace, and now Lottie can hear the words the men are using. 'Freak, killer, evil.' She can't move.

Her mother screams, and her father picks her up, handing her over to her mother who runs upstairs with her. She tips out drawers and cupboards and yells words at Lottie that Lottie can't make out. Her ears are full of the things the crowd are shouting, and she drifts to the window, matching the words to the moving lips and the angry faces. Some of the men were in Tegen's search party. Some of the women are the mothers of her school friends.

She hears her father on the phone, and then he is taking the stairs at a run and pulling Lottie away from the window. He sees the packing and wipes a hand across his eyes. Lottie sees tears. The only time her dad left Trehaven Sands was the holiday to Spain where he met her mother. He tells everybody that once he'd found the only thing the outside world could offer him and brought her back, he never needed to leave again. Her mother would smile a tight little smile as he crushed her hand in his.

A police car pulls up outside, and the noise reduces. Lottie's mother peers out the window.

'We need to leave as soon as they've gone.'

Her father sighs, but he nods and carries the suitcases down to the hall. Lottie can hear him speaking quietly with the officer who knocks at the door. Her mother leans out the window and shouts down.

'I don't know why you're all here. If you want answers, it's Gwen Hammett you need to speak to!'

Something thuds against the wall near the window, and then a shout goes up. Lottie creeps over to stand beside her mother. There's arguing amongst the group, and then the police officer turns to say something, and they start to move away.

'What have you done?' Her father is upstairs again, and he is shaking her mother by the shoulders so that her head wobbles.

Her mother pushes him away. 'They're going, aren't they? Help me pack what we can and let's get out of here!'

Lottie finds her Piskies and the wooden mouse and puts them in her pocket. She stands at the window looking down across the rooftops and the streetlights to the dark sea. She shudders at the thought of the currents under the surface and the shipwrecks hidden on the rocks below. There's an angry mermaid in there, her father had told her, that lures sailors to their deaths. She wipes a big fat tear from her eye, and then runs downstairs when her mother calls.

* * *

Annie waited. For Miller, for Lauren, anybody. Eventually, she rang her mother back.

'I've been told to wait here, but there are journalists outside.' She flicked the Piskies off the table one by one. 'They say everyone knows who I am.'

'I'll come over, Annie.'

Annie thought of those years when it had just been the two of them. 'No, it's —'

'Wait a moment, Annie, something's happening. Switch on your TV.'

Annie clicked it on. Outside the windows, she was aware of the journalists looking at their phones. The black car pulled away, and the woman with the camera shouted after it.

'Police have been called to an incident in Drayton Drive, Westhurst today. A single man was taken from the scene by ambulance. Neighbours say they believe he was an early suspect in the Chloe Hills case and a registered sex offender. There have been no arrests, and a spokesman has appealed to the public to stay calm.'

A small crowd was gathering outside the house, and Annie could see the two police officers there struggling to keep everyone behind the cordon.

'I don't like the look of that crowd, Annie. Maybe it's better that you come here. Can you get your car out now?'

Annie walked to the front window. 'One of the cars is still

here. If I'm quick, maybe.' She walked back to pick up her bag. 'The police have told me to stay here, though.' She sat down.

'Okay, I'm coming to you.' Her mother cursed. 'Where is that bloody girl?'

Annie scanned the news and finally found her own name with a picture of her standing at the vigil. It had been taken as she'd tried to step back out of sight and made her look particularly shifty. It reminded her of Chloe's friends stepping back into the crowd when Berman neared and the way it had triggered her suspicions. There was a photograph of Tegen, too, toothy smile and stained Paddington Bear. Annie wondered how long it would be before the story was picked up by other channels. She went back to the window and the young man, who was leaning against the front wall, waved his phone at her and pointed at the screen and then his watch. Annie pulled the curtains shut.

She put the news back on. The mob was still outside the house in Drayton Drive, and it was growing. A second police car had arrived. Her stomach turned over with fear. Those people wouldn't be satisfied until they'd taken some action. She squinted as the camera panned across their faces. Kieran and Kev, the man with the earring, were there. Kieran's face was red, and he was shouting at the police officer who stood in front of him.

As long as the crowd was there, though, they weren't outside her own house. She checked the time and cursed. What did Miller mean to stay here? She tried his number again. It would be another half hour before her mother arrived. It was crazy of her to come, but Annie felt a tiny curl of gratitude that she wouldn't be alone. Maybe Miller would come soon, too, and they'd be able to explain things to him and leave.

* * *

'Where are you going, Arthur?' Annie's mother sinks down into her seat. She glances back and pulls the blanket further over Lottie's head, but if Lottie looks up, she can see the sky. The car turns to the right, and then her father slams on the brakes. Lottie is knocked into the car door.

'Jesus Christ, is that the Hammetts' house?' Her mother's voice is raw, and Lottie can hear the fear in it. Her father's door clicks open, but her mother hisses at him. *'Don't, Arthur, Lottie's in the car. They mustn't find her.'*

Lottie shuffles up on her bum, so she can peer out the window behind her mother's seat. There's a group of people in front of one of the houses further down the road. Their shouts reach the car. Someone leans out of one of the upstairs windows waving the crowd away, but the shouting continues. A few of the neighbours are standing in their front gardens watching, and others wander over to join the mob. Lottie recognises some of the men and women who'd been standing in her own front garden earlier. Her limbs are getting stiff, and the bruises on the top of her arms still ache from the hands that had pulled her roughly from the cave.

'Is that Alice in the window?' Lottie's mum asks. *'Where's Pete? Where are the children?'*

Lottie's dad curses. *'What did you do, Susan?'* Her father slams his hands onto the wheel so that the car shakes. Neither of them notice Lottie sitting up now so she can see better.

There's a whoop from the crowd as someone sets light to something and hurls it towards the house. It bounces off the bricks and lands in the front garden, sputtering out in the grass. Something else is thrown and this time hits a window, shattering the glass.

'We need to leave, Arthur,' Lottie's mum leans across and whispers to her father. *'We can call the police from the phone box by The*

. She glances back and swats Lottie down again, but Lottie
 help but keep looking.

Another missile, this time spitting sparks, is thrown, and the
figure pulls back from the window as it spins through. The crowd is
silent, and then there is a roar as the curtains catch, and flames
shoot up the side of the window.

'What if they're all in the house, Susan?'

Her mum swears. 'They won't let them get hurt, will they?' She
waves at the neighbouring houses. The crowd is still shouting, but
Lottie can see the odd individual stepping back, looking around at
the others. A tall man in a baseball cap looks straight at her, and she
whimpers as she sinks down. The sharp smell of burning curls into
the car through the ventilators, and Lottie finds herself gagging with
fear. She doesn't know if it's screaming she can hear or the sound of
the building burning in the hot night.

A horn sounds behind them, and a battered van turns into the
road at speed.

'That's Pete Hammett's van,' her dad says. 'Oh god.' And he falls
silent as the van accelerates and bumps off the pavement towards
the mob.

'Arthur!' her mum shouts, and her father turns the engine on and
throws the car into reverse, stopping at the corner to swing around
onto the road out of town. He has barely straightened up when a
police car with its siren blaring passes them, and then the car picks
up speed, and Lottie is pulled down into the footwell as her father
careers around the bend on to the road to Bodmin.

33

TUESDAY AFTERNOON

Annie monitored the press as her story was taken up by other websites. It was like watching an incoming tide, wave after wave breaking over the rocks. She should be running far away, but an unfamiliar feeling of calm spread through her. Her identity had finally been revealed, and now she'll find out the consequences after so many years of anticipation.

A loud rapping on the front door caused her to jump, and she ran to see if it was her mother just as a business card was pushed through the letter box. Someone shouted after it.

'Like I said, we can get you away in return for an exclusive story. You could leave right now before my colleagues from the other outlets get here. Or any of those angry locals.'

She paused for a moment, stunned by the figure written on the card, and then pushed it back out through the brushes of the letter box without answering and returned to the window. He was right that she should leave, but it was too late. She had to wait for her mother now, and Miller had told her to stay.

It wasn't long before a journalist had found someone to

talk about her. She cringed as an image of Jan and Moira appeared on her screen.

> 'Well, we knew there was something off about her from the start, didn't we? The whole group did.'

Annie couldn't see Sam mentioned anywhere, but it didn't matter. Sam, Paul, they'd just been castles in the air like her friendship with Lauren. Even the name she used was a trick.

On a whim, she rose and turned the TV from the news channel to the radio, so that she wasn't so alert to every sound from outside, and went into the kitchen to see what there was to eat. Her last meal had been lunch the day before, and she suddenly felt sick with hunger.

A car pulled into the drive and stopped with the characteristic hard slam of brakes that announced her mother. Annie cracked open the door. Her mother harangued a small group that had gathered in front of the house and then stomped inside, and Annie felt a fierce punch of love and gratitude. She was glad she hadn't known so many people were there.

'Nearly got one as I pulled in.' Her mother had a slightly wild expression in her eyes. Annie made them both sandwiches, and they sat at the table in the lounge to eat them.

'Right,' her mother said. 'I think it's time we talked about your options. Let's see what you've got.'

* * *

Lottie sits on the bed in the motel room watching the TV with her dad. Mum has gone to get some sandwiches from the petrol station and has told them they have to stay inside, out of sight. There's a hole in the sheet that Lottie puts her finger through and worries at. Her father starts snoring beside her. They drove through the night,

Lottie only just aware of the lights on the motorway blinking past the windows. She pulls the Piskies out of her pocket and stares at their little grinning faces.

The news comes on, and Lottie looks for the remote control to change the channel. The door clicks as her mother unlocks it, and Lottie decides not to mess with it.

'This morning, Trehaven Sands is mourning the second casualty of The Babes in the Cave case.'

The image on the TV shows a house with blackened smudges around the upstairs windows and a grey van abandoned across the front garden.

'Arthur!' Her mum's voice is angry, and she grabs for the remote and turns it off. Her dad moans in his sleep. Lottie looks at her mum. She doesn't understand what the reporter meant by a second casualty, but her mum's expression is bleak, and she daren't ask her.

'I don't think we need to keep hearing about it, do we?'

Lottie takes the sandwich that her mum offers her and bites into it. It is bland and dry. She closes her hand around the Piskies and feels their little pointy hats and shoes jab into her palms.

* * *

'And when are you expecting this Miller?' Annie shrugged.

They had been waiting in silence, watching the story of Tegen unfold across the media. Her mother walked to the window and peered out through the curtains.

'I can't stand sitting in the dark like this, not in broad daylight.' She turned back to Annie. 'Why don't we try and leave, Annie? They can't really stop us.'

Annie joined her. There were a couple of cars now, and it looked like quite a discussion going on among the people standing around. They'd have to rely on the group moving out of the way. Besides, Miller had told her to stay, and she didn't want to run this time.

'No, I need to stay. You go, I'll be fine.'

Her mother rolled her eyes and switched on the TV, sitting down decisively on the sofa.

'We're hearing that the police will be making an announcement later this afternoon in the case of missing school girl, Chloe Hills. Earlier today, police were called to an incident in Westhurst at the home of convicted sex offender, Malcolm Danvers. An angry crowd clashed with police at the scene but have now been largely dispersed.'

Annie recognised Kieran again in the earlier images, but he wasn't among the small group that remained.

'What's the matter, Annie? Did you recognise one of those guys?'

Annie called Miller again. This time he picked up. 'I need to talk to you. You shouldn't have arrested Berman,' Annie said.

'Annie, I can't speak to you right now, but I will call later. Are you safe?' It was an odd question for him to ask, but maybe he knew about the journalists outside.

'There are people gathering outside my house, because they know I'm the witness who saw Berman, and they think it wasn't him. And,' she paused to take a breath, 'I don't feel safe. Can I come to the station?'

'You need to stay there, Annie. There are press all around the station. I'll get a patrol car to pass by.'

Annie threw down the phone in frustration.

'Annie, I really think we should go.' Her mother grabbed her hand and pulled her upstairs so they could look down onto the road. More men and women had gathered around the journalist. As they watched, a car pulled up and three more got out. Annie recognised Kieran among them and felt fear twisting in her stomach.

'How will we get past them?'

They ran downstairs, and Annie grabbed the small bag she'd taken out the night before. She should have just kept going, walked all the way to the railway station. She turned to her mother and gave her a hug. 'I'm glad you're here.'

Her mother snorted and pulled the front door open a crack to look out. They could hear voices in the crowd shouting to each other, and the journalist from the silver Golf stood in Annie's driveway interviewing a woman with her back to them. 'Bloody cheek.' Annie's mother squeezed her hand. 'Ready?'

No one noticed as Annie pulled and locked the front door behind her, but, at the sound of the car doors opening, a cry went up, and the crowd turned towards them. Annie's mother turned the key, and the engine roared as she pressed the accelerator hard in warning. Annie hit the door locks, and they leapt forward, giving the couple standing on the drive only seconds to jump out of the way. But when they reached the top of the drive, a car pulled across it, and they were forced to stop or ram it.

'Shit.' Annie gestured at the driver to move, but he got out of the car and put his hands on his hips. An unpleasant smile curled his lips, and Annie grabbed her phone and dialled 999. Her mother hit the horn. A few of those nearest jumped in reflex, and she inched the car a little forward. All the while, Annie was conscious of flashes as photographs were taken of both of them through the windscreen. She could picture the headlines:

Mother and daughter attempt to flee after their part in another child abduction is revealed.

'Where's Chloe?' A hand slammed onto the window beside Annie, and a face appeared beside it. She shrieked.

'Sorry, Annie, we'll have to go back. Can you get the front door open before they reach us?'

Annie pulled out her keys and looked at her mother. 'I'm sorry.'

Her mother nodded. 'I know. Hold on.' She put the car in gear, and the car shot backwards. The man fell away from Annie's window, and she heard a scream. Her mother stopped at the front door, and they both leapt from the car. The crowd picked the man off the ground and then surged down the drive as Annie fumbled with the key. Eventually, the door gave way, and she pushed her mother inside and tried to slam the door behind her, but a hand reached through as she tried, and a head followed. Kieran stood in front of her.

'The police are on their way,' she shouted in his face. 'You should leave now!'

'Not until you take back whatever you said about Berman!' He pushed her back into the kitchen. Behind him, more bodies poured in. Through the crowd, she could see the journalist filming it all on his phone, and the woman taking photographs on her camera. Her mother started screaming, but, when Annie glanced through to the living room, she could see that she'd just been pushed down on to the sofa while cushions went flying and furniture was pulled around as they hunted for clues. She was just creating drama for the journalists. Boots pounded on the stairs, and Annie could hear shouting on the landing. She tried to push Kieran off.

'Look, I'll let you go when you tell us where Chloe is and stop fitting up Berman. Not much to ask.'

Annie opened her mouth, but no sound came out. Kieran stepped right into her face, and she reached back to steady herself, the skin on her hands stung as she leaned on the counter, but her fingers touched the blade of the knife she'd left out after making lunch. She couldn't see her mother now, but she could hear her yelling and felt her courage rising.

'I don't know anything. I've nothing to do with Chloe going missing or Berman being arrested.' She looked right back, eye to eye with Kieran, pulling the knife closer with her fingers until she felt the hilt. 'Ask them,' she nodded towards the stairs. 'You won't find her here.'

There was a shout of frustration from the landing above, and Annie sensed Kieran's stance change. He moved closer, his face in hers, and she pressed herself further back slipping the knife down behind her leg. Behind him, her mother appeared in the doorway, holding the car keys in her hand. Annie heard footsteps start back along the landing to the stairs, and Kieran reached and wrapped his hands around her neck. She tried to push him away, but he grabbed her arm, and she struck out in fear, the knife getting caught on something. His grip loosened, and she darted after her mother out the front door to the car.

Another roar behind them. 'She's stabbed him!'

And then they were in the car and accelerating up the drive. Annie watched people pouring from her house and running after them. Then her mother slammed the brakes hard, and Annie was thrown forward. Two police cars blocked their exit, and the crowd behind began to leap over the low front wall as they saw the police officers getting out of their cars. Annie looked down at her hand. It was red and sticky with blood.

34

TUESDAY EVENING

Annie hadn't stopped shaking. The lawyer she'd been assigned sat beside her, scrolling through her phone. She desperately wanted to drink the tea, but she knew she'd knock the flimsy plastic cup over. Besides, her hands still smarted, though she couldn't stop twisting them in her lap.

Eventually, DS Miller appeared with DC Singh and sat down.

'A man, Kieran Baker, was stabbed inside your house tonight.'

'Is he all right?' She thought of the blood on her hands. How would she possibly bear the responsibility of another lost life?

Miller frowned at her. 'Was it you, Annie? Did you stab Kieran Baker?'

The solicitor had turned slightly to watch her, and she now leant across and whispered 'no comment' in Annie's ear.

'They thought I'd taken Chloe. They thought I'd lied about Berman. The crowd. They were out of control.' Annie kept her hands beneath the table to stop them searching for something to pick at.

Miller sat back comfortably in his chair and waited. It was a pose that said, *You'll tell me in the end.*

'But I didn't take Chloe. I don't know where she is.'

'Just tell us what happened tonight, Annie.'

Her solicitor shifted in her chair.

'Okay, Annie, have you seen this knife before?' Singh pulled out a clear bag with Annie's knife inside it. The blood was still on the blade, and Annie put her hands to her mouth. She'd done that. Singh glanced at the burns on the back of Annie's hand and then looked away.

Annie nodded.

'For the tape, please.'

'It's mine, from the knife block in my kitchen.' Annie remembered the feel of the blade beneath her fingers. Sitting in that bright room with the tape machine recording her words and the three others there, it seemed like a dream. 'Is my mother here?'

'Tell us what happened next, Annie.'

Annie sighed and waved her solicitor away when she opened her mouth to speak again. She took a breath and described hearing the crowd arriving, trying to leave with her mother but the car blocking their way. The angry mob entering her house.

'There was a journalist filming,' she said. 'You can see all of this for yourself.' She felt tired. Why were they even asking her when they knew what had happened?

'Go on,' Miller replied. 'We want to hear it from you.' Annie closed her eyes and tried to picture exactly what she'd done. Her mother had just appeared in the doorway with the car keys when Kieran put his hand up to her throat. Annie remembered lifting her hands to shove him off.

'I thought he was going to kill me,' Annie looked DS Miller in the eye. 'I just wanted to push him out of the way. I'd forgotten the knife was in my hand.' She stiffened her jaw to stop it wobbling. She didn't deserve their pity.

A similar crowd had killed Gwen. The hysteria of the mob. People who usually were perfectly normal, held down jobs, had families and helped to look for lost children, could be killers in the right circumstances. Just like perfectly ordinary children could be too.

Annie couldn't look at DC Singh. The woman looked uncomfortable, as if she wanted to tell Annie something. Annie looked back to Miller, her fingers laced together to hold her hands where they were, despite the pain on her skin. Miller waited.

'But, yes, I did it. He let go of me, and I ran.'

Miller sat back, eyebrows raised. 'When we arrived, you and Mrs Marwood were in her car trying to leave the scene.'

Singh looked up from her notebook.

Annie licked her lips. 'We thought they would hurt us.' Annie felt hollowed out. 'I didn't mean to kill him. I never wanted to hurt anyone.' Singh looked pointedly at Miller, but he ignored her. 'I should never have let it go this far. I need to tell you what I was doing when Chloe went missing. Why you can't use anything I said about other people in the car park.'

Singh smiled at her, and Miller sat back in his chair. Annie took a deep breath. Her solicitor suggested they talk in private, but Annie declined.

'And I need to tell you that my name used to be Charlotte-Anne Marwood-Rowe. Marwood is my mother's name.'

'We're releasing you.' Miller came back into the room and sat down beside her. 'Your mother's already left.' Singh stood in the doorway behind him. 'There was enough footage to show that you acted in self-defence.'

'But I've killed someone.' There was no way Annie could risk the temptation to flee again. She had to take responsibility. Every sinew of her body was poised to run, prepared for it, and it took all her effort to stay where she was.

Miller laughed. 'No, he'll be fine. And it turns out we need to speak to him about an incident earlier in the day in Drayton Drive.'

Annie frowned. 'But do you believe me about Chloe? I didn't see her at all, and I didn't see Berman or anyone else.'

Miller and Singh exchanged glances. Miller shrugged. 'She'll find out soon enough.'

Singh turned to Annie. 'Chloe's been in touch. She's alive and well, that's all I can tell you.'

'Actually, Annie, we never thought you had seen her. The CCTV shows you getting into your car. The headlights turn on, but then you get out again before Chloe was seen and head towards the alley through to Mr Brand's apartment block.' Annie feels her cheeks burn. 'You didn't get back to your car until later, long after Chloe had gone. Hadn't you realised you left your lights on?'

Chloe was alive? Annie felt her limbs turn to jelly. The tiny gritty kernel of guilt and doubt that she'd been hiding inside her softened, and she felt relief flood her body. It wasn't her fault. She hadn't done anything to Chloe; she hadn't even forgotten seeing her. Annie couldn't remember Chloe in the car park because Annie hadn't been there after all. 'You knew all along that I hadn't seen anything? And you kept asking me for information?'

Singh sighed loudly.

Miller glanced at his colleague, and Annie noticed something awkward pass between them. 'I was curious as to why you would claim to have seen Chloe, when we knew that you hadn't. At first, we thought you had to be involved. Then we thought you were trying to give yourself an alibi, so we wouldn't consider you for the break-in at your boss's flat.'

Annie cringed, even though she'd asked Paul to tell the police it was her. 'At first?'

Miller waved his hand. 'Don't worry, we're not going to pursue that. Mr Brand has told us it was just a misunder-standing.'

'So, you did suspect me?'

Singh looked away.

'Oh, I see.' She had been right to fear that they would suspect her. 'But you knew from the CCTV that I wasn't with Chloe at the station, so why?' Then she understood. 'You already knew who I was?'

Of course, they had checked her background straight away. She felt the years of hiding collapsing on themselves like a concertina. It had all been a farce, her fear of being found out. They must have been laughing at her, both of them, with her attempts to be helpful. Suspicious, too.

'You knew who I was all along?' Shouldn't they have arrested her or something? Surely she had to answer for what had happened to Tegen.

'But if you knew I wasn't there, you must have known I didn't see Berman. Why did you arrest him?'

Annie's head swam as she tried to work it out. She hadn't been there, so there was no way she could have helped, and they'd let her believe she might have the answer. Miller was watching her intently. He was the one who'd pushed her to give the description that led to Berman's arrest.

'Is Berman involved somehow?'

Miller didn't respond, but Singh looked uncomfortable. Had they wanted her to describe Berman? She couldn't remember what Miller had asked. She'd described Berman by accident, hadn't she? Because she'd seen him earlier that evening. She frowned. There was nothing to hide now.

'I saw Berman on Saturday evening talking to Kieran Baker and another man before I saw you. He was just on my mind when you were asking those questions.'

Miller looked pointedly at Singh and then spread out his hands. 'Look, we've got enough now as far as Chloe is concerned. Singh will drive you home in case there's any, err, problems. You can tell her what you saw.'

'Aren't you going to arrest me for Tegen's death?'

'It's not my case, and there's no outstanding warrant for your arrest.' Miller stood up. 'The local police may need to speak to you, but, as far as we're concerned, you're free to go.'

Singh took the corner at speed, and Annie gripped the door handle.

'At first, he just wanted to keep an eye on you, see if you could be involved in Chloe's disappearance given your history. Then when the CCTV showed you weren't in the car at the time Chloe walked past, it made us wonder why you came forward.' Singh glanced over at Annie where she slouched in the passenger seat. 'I guessed it was because you needed an alibi for breaking into your boss's flat.'

Annie traced the line of the mouldings on the door. 'So, when he was pushing me to describe someone in the car park, he knew I hadn't seen anyone? He really did want me to describe Berman?'

Singh sighed. 'I wasn't happy about that, to be honest, but

it turned out to be a good call. Chloe got in touch when she heard he'd been arrested.'

Annie considered what that meant. 'The rumours about Berman are true?' Singh didn't respond. It wasn't Annie's business anyway. 'I overheard Berman and Kieran talking about confronting someone on Saturday night. It sounded like they knew who had her and were going to get her back, but I didn't hear everything. I wanted to tell you, but I was worried it would make you suspect me more. I'd already muddled things up enough.'

Singh glanced across at Annie. 'We might need to take a statement from you about that if we decide to make a case against Kieran.' Annie's head swam with all the strands that Singh and Miller needed to unpick.

She scrolled through the news. The Babes in the Cave case was making headlines again, and Annie recognised her own photo as a six-year-old alongside Gwen and Bronnen's. When she saw the photo of Tegen's mum, holding a tatty old Paddington, under the headline 'The Agony of Losing a Child', she stopped reading. Mrs Hancock stared at the camera as if she was looking at a ghost, the fine lines around her eyes etched in shadow in the flashlight. Annie could smell the marmalade-y scent of Paddington, feel the stickiness of his fur on her fingers when she held him for Tegen. A tear ran down her cheek and dropped onto the image, distorting it.

'I don't know what to do.'

Singh looked across at the image. 'You probably don't want to stay here.' There were a few cars parked in front of Annie's house. 'I'll come in with you while you pack and make sure you can get your car out. I gather your mum's gone to a local hotel. Will you join her? Until it's announced that Chloe is safe, at least?'

Annie wiped the tear from her screen and took a deep breath in. 'I think I'm going to stay.'

Singh swung the car off the road onto the drive and turned the engine off. 'Right, well you'd better put the kettle on then while I see if I can get rid of these guys. They'll make the announcement soon.'

Annie had made tea and started clearing up the mess when Singh came in. Something knocked against Annie's foot, and she reached down and picked up the sandstone figurine. It felt warm and solid and soft in her hand. She set it down on the table, so its face pointed away. 'Can I speak to Tegen's mum?'

Singh picked up the figurine and turned it over in her hand. 'First, you need to speak to Trehaven police, then we'll work out if it's safe for you to stay here.'

Annie nodded. She'd already spoken to her own mother, who was at this moment planning a driving holiday across the country. Annie didn't mind; she wanted to sort this out on her own, and her mother didn't need to be involved. In fact, her mother had taken it all surprisingly well. *I was thinking I should get out on the road again, love,'* she'd said. *'I'll drop you a postcard when I get settled.'*

'What about my mother? Is she in trouble for taking me away?'

Singh paused while she considered. 'You weren't under arrest. But I couldn't say.' She looked around at the books that had been pulled off the shelves, cushions thrown from the sofas. 'Do you have anybody who can help you with this?'

Annie shook her head. 'I'm fine.' She hadn't heard from Lauren or Paul, but that was okay. She'd call Paul later and ask if she could come into work the next day, if she still had a job. Right now, the most important thing she had to do was speak to Trehaven Sands police.

Singh checked her phone. 'They're announcing Chloe's

safe now. Hopefully, you'll be left alone on that score, but I can't guarantee they won't harass you about Trehaven.'

Annie considered where she could go. 'I guess I'm just going to face it.'

Singh stood up. 'Well, I can stay for a little while.' She tapped at her phone, and passed it to Annie, the other end already ringing. 'Best you get that call out of the way.'

35

POSTSCRIPT

Annie was at the railway station early to avoid the busiest part of the rush hour. She'd pulled her hood tight around her face and avoided making eye contact as much as possible. Even so, she felt anxious when a couple got into the same carriage and sat near her.

'I can't believe her parents had no idea,' the woman was saying to the man. 'If one of our children told me a friend of ours was harassing them, I'd be right round to sort it out and that would be the end of it.' The man tried to open his paper, but the woman continued. 'Don't you agree? That poor girl told her parents Berman was abusing her, and they didn't believe her.'

The man sighed. 'Look, Deidra, we don't really know the facts yet. We should wait until the trial's over.'

The woman crossed her legs and raised her voice so the man still couldn't open his paper. 'Listen, my darling, have you ever heard of a twelve-year-old girl being organised enough to hide away for nearly a fortnight for nothing?' She sat back as if that was proof enough and folded her arms. 'And I heard from

Shelley that she'd been in touch with Berman to ask him to tell her parents the truth and, all this time, he let the Hills believe she was truly missing, might be dead. Man's a pig.'

Chloe also let her parents believe she might be dead. Annie felt a burst of anger at the girl and her friends. She'd been right to suspect that they were involved after all. How many people around the country had been caught up in the search for Chloe? And she was safe. Safer, in fact, than she was at home, though, Annie reminded herself. Chloe had tried to tell her parents the truth, it seems, and if they'd listened to her properly, she would never have needed to run away. Annie took a deep breath and felt her chest judder as she released it. Her own life had been changed forever by Chloe's actions, too.

And it turned out she had known something about Chloe. The voice that she'd heard when she woke in Paul's flat was Chloe's. She'd taken the spare key to one of the empty apartments on Paul's floor from her father's office. She'd stayed there the whole time with Hannah and Megan bringing her food and company when they could sneak away. Annie grimaced at the irony of being right about the girls knowing where Chloe was. She should have focused on that. Maybe her subconscious would have made more of those memories.

She settled back into her seat. Most of the attention had been focused on the salacious details of the Chloe Hills case, though Annie had had offers from several newspapers to tell her story. The money was certainly attractive, but Annie decided it wasn't her story to tell; it was the Hancocks'.

'The thing is,' the woman was saying, 'I don't know how that family's going to be able to hold their heads up around here again. I mean, the cost of that search and all the time and effort people put in.'

And the released sex offender was going to be hounded,

too, now, Annie thought. He would bear the scars of Kieran's attack for the rest of his life.

Searching for Chloe had led to Annie's exposure, but, in many ways, it was a relief. She itched to check the news, to find out what people were saying about Chloe, what they were saying about her. But she left her phone turned off at the bottom of her bag.

Instead, she sunk back into the seat and closed her eyes. Paul had been remarkably understanding. It was as if knowing the truth about Annie had made it easier to understand her. The reactions of the others in the office had been mixed, but, after an initial period of sly looks and whispering, she'd come in one day and told them everything. That was after she'd spoken to the Trehaven Sands police and, through intermediaries, to Tegen's family. She had signed up for restorative justice, so that if Tegen's mother ever wanted to speak to her she could.

Most of the time now, though, it was in the background. She knew today would be difficult. The press would be around, so she'd worn her hair differently and practised keeping her face still.

The court was silent as the verdict was given. Then a few voices began, and, as more joined, the sound intensified with the clatter of feet standing up, the swing of coats, and the sweeping of paper and files from tables. Annie could feel the stares and sense the comments being made, so she straightened her back, stuck out her chin, and waited, but no one came up to her. The court was almost empty before she stood and pulled on her own coat, took up her bag, and walked back to the doors. As she paused to look around one last time, an official approached her and took her to the back of the court building where the offices were.

'If you walk through the car park, you'll see a gate out onto the road. You should be able to avoid the press out the front. It's a bit noisy.'

At home, she picked up a letter from the doormat and let her keys drop onto the table. The silence of her empty home rushed at her. She sat at the table and opened the envelope. It was a letter from the restorative justice service confirming that Mrs Hancock would meet with her. Lottie rested her head on her arms and allowed herself to cry for little Tegen.

ACKNOWLEDGEMENTS

That I actually managed to finish this book is largely due to the unfailing support and encouragement of Sam Brace at Agora Books. As my editor, Sam has been a patient and brilliant guide shining light onto those passages that needed it most. More than that, Sam has calmly let me rant about all the unrelated things that I needed to clear away before I could get down to work. So sorry, Sam, and thank you! Huge gratitude to Peyton Stableford at Agora who is a brilliant copyeditor, a marketing whizz and always full of encouragement and positivity. Thank you also to Alice Marwick for designing the stunning cover.

I quote some figures about missing children and am grateful to the charity, Missing People*, for answering my questions. I would also like to thank Paul Green at the UK Missing Persons Unit for pointing me in the direction of police search procedures and answering my rookie questions. Any errors are entirely my own.

Huge thanks to my writing buddies who've provided inspiration and feedback along the way, Eleni Kyriacou, Kate

Wheeler and especially to my Beta reader, Liz Ottosson. Thank you all.

I'm so lucky to have had the unfailing support of my mum, Gillie, and my brother Jeremy and his family, Amanda, Cameron, James and Robert. Big love to you all. To all those friends who've laughed, walked, swum, sympathised or raised a glass with me while I was procrastinating or handwringing, you're all amazing. So grateful to know you all.

Absolute love and respect to the special people who live with me every day. James, Ben and Louis. It's definitely my turn to make dinner.

*__Missing People__ is the only charity in the UK dedicated to supporting people affected by a disappearance and bringing missing people back to safety. The charity operates a free and confidential helpline that's open 24/7, thanks to support from players of People's Postcode Lottery. Call or text 116 000. For more information about Missing People, please go to www. missingpeople.org.uk

A LITTLE BIRD TOLD ME

PROLOGUE

They say I'll never find her.

Kit says it doesn't matter because we still have each other but not a day goes by when I don't long for the truth.

I feel her absence aching and flowing through the gaps in our story where the pieces don't mesh. I see her presence in the spatter of freckles on Kit's nose and the straight curtain of hair I can't keep out of my eyes.

They say no one knows where she is.

What they really mean is, they couldn't find her. I know that's true because I've read the news reports. But there is one person who knows where she is.

Family is blood and pain, he said, *'and, one day, I will hunt you down and teach you the meaning of that.'*

His breath was bitter with the smell of cigarettes, his eyes spilling sparks of fury and the scar on his cheek stretched and twisted as he spoke. Or it might have. I read about that too, long after Matthew took us far away from here.

'I will hunt you down,' he said, and I know he will.

If I'm ever going to find her, this is my last chance. But if I start looking, he'll come looking for us. I can't help that — there's something I need to put right.

Besides, if you were one half evil, wouldn't you want to know about the other half?

CHAPTER ONE

1976

Yuk! A curled plaster moves stodgily through the shafts of sunlight that bend in the water towards the blue tiles at the bottom of the pool. I pull my right hand out from under my hip and put it into the water, waggling my fingers through the beams in front of Mum's diving mask. They look like pink fish. My other hand is holding the strap bunched up at the back of my head because really and truly it is far too big, like Mum said it would be. I might get one the right size for my tenth birthday, but that's ages away. I just have to hold the snorkel against my ear with my shoulder. It works, but it's hard to remember to breathe through my mouth without gagging on the plastic flavour of the mouthpiece.

As I concentrate, I can still feel the dry grass scratchy under my hips where the tiled path around the pool ends. The little hairs on the back of my legs tickle as they dry out and spring upright again. Suddenly, all the breath is squeezed out of me as the soggy weight of Kit lands on my back.

'My turn, Squirt!' he shouts. I bring my feet up hard to try and kick him off, but he laughs and whips off the mask as he rolls me over.

'That's not fair!' I say, but he has already gone, running around to the far side of the pool before jumping, pulling up his legs as he goes, and bombing into the water so that he showers all his friends. I have bits of grass and mud all over me now, so I keep rolling around until I drop into the pool. I manage to keep one hand on the side and land in the water on my back, my face still dry. At home, Mum has a postcard with a lady in a long dress lying in a river. Her hands and face are out of the water, and I wonder how she can hold that position unless her elbows and bottom are actually resting on the mud of the riverbed. I give up trying to copy her and flip over when I see something round and shiny rolling towards the lip of the pool. As I go to catch it, a brown foot slaps down hard and its owner shouts,

'That's my money!'

When I have pulled myself out, I can see that the boy is smaller than me. I take a step forward to show him that I'm not scared anyway, because now that Kit is at the senior school I have to stand up for myself a bit more. I immediately feel guilty when the kid cringes straight backwards.

He jerks his thumb over his shoulder and says, 'That man gave it to me. He wants you to go over and talk to him.'

'What for?' I say, but the kid just shrugs and walks off. I look across to where there is a man alone in the shade of the trees that fringe the pool area. He stands out because he is fully dressed. I can't make out his face at all. It's hidden under the brim of his hat which is pulled right down like a cowboy's.

I look around for Kit. There is no point shouting to him because all that is visible is the yellow snorkel and the slick wet back of his head. I tug my swimming costume down over my behind where it clings too much and pull my hair over one shoulder to squeeze some of the water out so that I am respectable.

Instead of walking directly to the man, I first go past where we have set up camp with our towels. Kit's is in a heap, then mine pulled straight, and then Debbie's held in place with her gonks. Debbie is in my class, but sometimes, like now, she likes to hang around with some of her sister's friends. She waves as I look over, and I just have time to wave back before she turns away again. I make sure that my sketch pad is not sticking out too much from under my towel in case those girls, the WendyCarols, the ones who found it last time, are here.

When I get to the man, my hair is still dripping, and the shade feels chilly.

'My friends are watching,' I point back towards the pool. He laughs, and I can see into the soft bit at the back of his mouth as he drops down to my height. I wait until he stops laughing.

'I've brought you something,' he says, and holds out a closed fist, knuckles towards me, 'for both of you.' He looks towards the pool where Kit is still splashing. When I look down into my hand there are two small smooth pieces of wood. I flip them over with my thumb and see that they have been carved and polished into the shape of babies wrapped up tight, just like Jesus in the manger.

'What are they?' I ask.

'Magic,' he says. 'For protection.'

'My Mum says I shouldn't take gifts from strangers.' I say, still holding the babies out on my palm.

'Your mum?' He makes a snorting noise. 'Well, she's probably right.' He grins and stands up again. 'But matter of fact these are yours already.'

He must have started walking away while I looked back

down because when I lift my head again there is just the dun leather of his hat visible behind the kids queuing at the ice cream booth.

I hand one of the wooden babies to Kit while we are waiting to pick up our things from the locker room. Debbie is very excited. She loves mysteries and already thinks we're a little bit magic because we appeared from nowhere and our house is always full of people.

'Jinkies,' she says in her Velma voice. 'But who was he?'

'Maybe it's a secret message from our dad,' I whisper, and, in my chest, my heart does a little skip. Kit rolls his eyes.

'Just some loony,' he says, tossing his baby up and down into the air and frowning a little. He throws it back to me and I drop it into my bag where it nestles next to mine. We collect our baskets and carry them with difficulty. Even sitting the basket part on the floor, the hanger part of it is nearly as tall as I am. They remind me of the cages for the children in *Chitty Chitty Bang Bang*, and I am always glad to give them back.

Debbie walks home with us because she wants to know what Mum will say about the wooden babies, but, when we get there, we can see she's having one of her Friday night parties. There's no way we're going to be able to ask her anything.

'Stay and have some burgers, Debbie!' Mum says when she notices us, but she's gone again before she hears that Debbie has to go home. Debbie's mum doesn't like her being on the other side of town too late even though it's light well after bedtime now.

'Come straight round to mine in the morning,' Debbie says to me before she goes. 'I'm bursting to know what they are.'

LOVE AGORA BOOKS?
JOIN OUR BOOK CLUB

If you sign up today, you'll get:

1. A free novel from Agora Books
2. Exclusive insights into our books and authors, and the chance to get copies in advance of publication, and
3. The chance to win exclusive prizes in regular competitions

Interested? It takes less than a minute to sign up. You can get your novel and your first newsletter by signing up at
www.agorabooks.co

 facebook.com/AgoraBooksLDN
twitter.com/agorabooksldn
instagram.com/agorabooksldn